Read on Arrival

Also available by Nora Page

Better Off Read

Read on
Arrival

A BOOKMOBILE MYSTERY

Nora Page

NEW YORK

PUBLISHER'S NOTE: The recipes contained in this book are to be followed exactly as written. The publisher is not responsible for your specific health or allergy needs that may require medical supervision. The publisher is not responsible for any adverse reaction to the recipes contained in this book.

Published in the United States by Crooked Lane Books, an imprint of The Quick Brown Fox & Company LLC.

Crooked Lane Books and its logo are trademarks of The Quick Brown Fox & Company LLC.

Library of Congress Catalog-in-Publication data available upon request.

ISBN (hardcover): 978-1-64385-003-0
ISBN (ePub): 978-1-64385-004-7
ISBN (ePDF): 978-1-64385-005-4

Cover illustration by Jesse Reisch
Book design by Jennifer Canzone

Printed in the United States.

www.crookedlanebooks.com

Crooked Lane Books
34 West 27th St., 10th Floor
New York, NY 10001

First Edition: May 2019

10 9 8 7 6 5 4 3 2 1

To Gigi and a long and beautiful life,
always with a book

Chapter One

Cleo Watkins considered herself quite unflappable. After all, she had seventy-five and three-quarters years of living behind her. Most importantly, she was a librarian, the longest serving biblio-professional in Catalpa Springs, Georgia. Librarians saw a lot. They read even more. Librarians were a hard bunch to shock.

"Good gracious," Cleo said. She gripped her peach-colored cardigan tight and steadied herself against the doorframe of the vintage Airstream camper. Music boomed from outdoor speakers, blaring across the park and vibrating through Cleo's soles. Words written in morphing red, white, and pink light flashed across the tin-can ceiling.

Cleo's eyes caught a word: *"READ!"* Cleo was all for reading. *That's nice,* she reassured herself. She chased down more: *"INNOVATE! WORD! SPARK!"*

It was downright dizzying, as close as Cleo had ever come to a disco and near enough by far. Except this wasn't a dance club. It was *supposed* to be a bookmobile. The vehicle's name pulsated across the ceiling: "BOOK IT!" Cleo tore her eyes downward and resumed her search. The shiny interior included laptops, a TV screen, and gaming consoles Cleo recognized from her grandkids' visits.

Where were the books?

Cleo drove a bookmobile, an entire school bus, fitted with shelves, named "Words on Wheels." Here, she saw no spines, smelled no scents of paper and ink. Cleo released the doorframe and stepped farther inside. *Ah, there was a book.* A beleaguered copy of *Gone with the Wind* propped up a window. Cleo turned away.

"Isn't this delightful!" exclaimed the man beside her. Mercer Whitty clasped bony hands, sounding as giddy as the children running around outside. The kids had the excuse of sugar overload. BOOK IT! had arrived with accompaniments more suited for a carnival than a mobile library: a cotton candy machine, buckets of suds and giant bubble wands, and—most astounding—a miniature pony named Lilliput. As if on cue, the little horse neighed. Kids squealed, and words that made Cleo shudder sliced through the din: *Lilliput, no! Don't eat the book!*

"Delightful?" Cleo repeated.

"Thrilling," Mercer declared. He unlocked his thin fingers only to clap and clasp them once again. He beamed at the woman to his left.

Fresh shock shook Cleo. Mercer Whitty, president of the Catalpa Springs Library Board, was not a man given to thrills. Although only in his early sixties, Mercer seemed ages older, as stiff and serious as an antique portrait. Small and slight, he wore his usual outfit of fastidious pinstripes and a polka-dot bow tie. Something scaled—snake, alligator, or armadillo—had perished to produce his shoes. Cleo eyed him, thinking he resembled an amphibian. A snapping turtle with a beak of a nose, a chin tucked tight to his chest, and a tongue twitching to lash out.

"Simply stunning," Mercer continued, head shaking in apparent awe. "Don't you agree, Cleo?"

The question challenged Cleo's manners. She could hear her dear, departed mother, and generations of southern ladies before her, issuing that most trite but true adage: *If you don't have anything nice to say, shush your mouth.*

"Well . . ." Cleo patted her fluffy white hair, buying some time.

Two pairs of eyes watched her. Mercer's narrowed toward his beak. The other set sparkled with pearly eye shadow and belonged to Mercer's invited guest, Belle Beauchamp, driver and self-proclaimed innovator of the book-lacking BOOK IT! Belle and the Airstream hailed from Claymore, a neighboring town to the west. Their reputations preceded them through the local librarian grapevine.

Belle had recently retired from corporate branding—at the young age of fifty-something—and moved back down from Atlanta to be near her aging parents. Retirement hadn't suited her, so she'd rebranded herself, creating the title of "outreach innovator" and convincing the Claymore library to hire her. Her first big act was starting up a bookmobile.

Cleo fully understood Belle's issues with retirement. Cleo had tried retirement too. Twice. It hadn't suited her either. She also understood the joy of bookmobiles. Cleo planned to keep driving Words on Wheels for as long as her eyesight and the DMV allowed. She adored the open road and the wind in her hair. Most of all, she loved delivering books to all those who depended on the mobile library.

Belle leaned in expectantly. Her platinum hair shimmered in a sleek, asymmetrical bob. Her perfume smelled of musky lilacs. "Well, what do you think? Isn't BOOK IT! the cutest?"

"It's very . . . uh . . . very bright," Cleo said. "Bright and uncluttered." There. She'd said something nice and hadn't fibbed.

"Aren't you a doll!" Belle slapped Cleo's shoulder. "That's exactly what I'm going for! Streamlined. Fresh. Like you say, I didn't want to clutter it all up with too many books."

"I didn't say—" Cleo protested.

Mercer cut her off. "Yes, take note, Cleo. New. Fresh. *Exciting!* We in Catalpa Springs could learn a thing or two from this marvelous bookmobile. You're an amazing woman, Ms. Beauchamp."

Belle rewarded him with an affectionate arm squeeze and deemed him a honey doll.

Cleo awaited his snap. Mercer loved to mock phrases lacking literal sense. He preyed on common, benign idioms and endearments. *Honey doll* would surely make a sweet target. Cleo waited. Mercer wasn't snapping. *"GLOW!"* in pink light flashed across his gaunt cheeks. Underneath, Cleo could swear that Mercer Whitty really was glowing. The man was blushing!

"Oh, no, no," Mercer stammered. "I'm honored. *We're*

4

honored. Honored you accepted my invitation to join us today, Ms. Beauchamp, and bring such verve to our dull little bookmobile event."

The music covered Cleo's huff. Mercer wouldn't have noticed anyway. Cleo marveled. Could it be? Could cold-blooded Mercer Whitty be smitten? He was laughing—giggling—at something Belle said.

Cleo had seen enough. "This is lovely, but I shouldn't keep you. I need to get back to Words on Wheels."

"Why?" Mercer's grin twisted into a mean smirk. "You don't seem to have many patrons. All the more reason to stay and learn. Look at the crowd Ms. Beauchamp has attracted."

Cleo bit her tongue.

Belle waved a flirty hand. "Y'all are so sweet!" she said. "I'm blushing!"

It was Mercer who was aflame. "You know, Ms. Beauchamp," he said, fingers twining. "The Catalpa Springs Library has a job opening. We're looking for a woman with just your exciting skills."

Cleo had been backing toward the exit. She stopped. "Just a part-time position, nothing *exciting*," Cleo said quickly, although she considered all library work a thrill. "We need someone to fill in hours. Our library is reopening soon. I'll still be head librarian, but I'll be on the road a lot with Words on Wheels. We have another part-time librarian returning, and we recently promoted my assistant, Leanna. She'll become full time when she graduates from college in a few years. She's studying library sciences and technology, and taking extra classes to get done early."

Cleo could gush on. She was proud enough to burst, picturing young Leanna taking over the library helm, the perfect protégé to carry on Cleo's legacy. Leanna had overcome a tough childhood. She'd bounced about in foster care, with only one place she'd always called home: the Catalpa Springs Public Library. In the disco din, Cleo smiled, remembering Leanna as a shy kindergartener, craning her chin up to the circulation desk to request more books. Or the many times she discovered little Leanna rehoming misshelved volumes or stepping in to help patrons. Leanna was a natural librarian, the best kind: she cared about people and books.

Mercer made a *pah* sound. Cleo had heard the same noise emitted from vultures. "She's inexperienced, a girl," Mercer said.

"She might only be twenty-two, but she has loads of library experience and passion, and she's acing all her classes," Cleo countered. She held in further protests, knowing Mercer fed off getting under people's skin. "I'm sure Belle wouldn't be interested in our job," Cleo said. She prayed this was true. She didn't need a librarian who considered books clutter.

Belle, however, did look interested. "I *am* in the market for new opportunities. A place I can stretch my leadership and innovation skills."

"You've come to the right place," Mercer said.

No, you haven't, Cleo thought. Then, however, she reconsidered. If Belle wanted to butter someone up, she'd definitely come to the right man. As board president, Mercer had sway over the other members and the library's budget. He also had buckets of old money and a family foundation through which he dribbled small grants to causes that appealed to him and people he liked. He definitely liked Belle.

"We already have new directions at the library," Cleo said, both to remind Mercer and to dissuade Belle. Cleo embraced new technology and trends. But she also held certain traditions sacred. The reading room was quiet. Books filled the shelves and were handled with respect. "Our plans are well on their way. We'll be brand new and freshly reopened soon."

Cleo's stomach fluttered, thinking of all there was to do. Last spring, a toppled tree had shuttered the library. A shifty mayor had then almost shelved the institution permanently. However, thanks to a new mayor, an unexpected inheritance, and loads of work, the main library was about to be back in business. The grand reopening was just over three weeks away. Cleo and Leanna planned to throw a big party. The whole town was invited, and Cleo wanted everything just so, from the restored shelves to the technology station Leanna had designed. Cleo took a deep breath. They had it all arranged, a fine, sensible plan.

Cleo continued on. "Our part-time position entails shelving, checking books in and out, and helping patrons. I'll still be in charge of the day-to-day operations of the library and the bookmobile. Leanna will be managing some library-science interns from the college."

Mercer snorted. "How dull."

Belle shrugged slender shoulders covered by a red suede jacket. "That's a pity. I always say, going with the flow doesn't break the mold. I like to break the mold." She winked at Mercer and added, "But then I can be a little naughty."

If Mercer were a puppy, he'd be a puddle of wags and wiggles. "I'll see what I can do," he said breathlessly. "Cleo, with you out of the way driving that bus, it's a perfect time to break the mold. We can change up the old ways in the main building. Yes, yes . . ."

Old ways? Out of the way! Cleo had heard enough. In tight yet sugary tones, she thanked Belle for the tour and bolted.

*　*　*

The bouncy dance tune grated on Cleo's ears but made her feet tap. She stood on the top metal step of BOOK IT! The chilly breeze helped clear her head. The familiar view grounded her. Fontaine Park, the leafy heart of her hometown, looked lovely. Early camellias bloomed in ruby and cream petals around pollen-gold prongs. The air smelled of wood smoke and the cinnamon scents of autumn. It was the first week of November, Cleo's favorite time of year, a season to stock up on cookbooks for holiday meals and novels for chilly nights.

Feeling braced by the fresh air and view, Cleo made her way down the steps. BOOK IT! stood on the park's lawn, ruts marking its track and that of the cherry-red pickup that pulled it. Mercer was right about one thing. Belle's bookmobile had attracted a crowd. Kids ran in giddy circles. Adults clustered in chatty groups. The little horse wore a velvet cape and hooved a periodical.

Among the throngs, Cleo saw a familiar figure. Leanna. She spotted another welcome sight too. Books! A side panel of the camper was rolled up, accordion style, revealing two bookshelves.

"What do you think?" Cleo asked when she reached her young protégé. She valued Leanna's take. Leanna was up on the current library tech and trends, if not fashion, which she preferred retro. Today Leanna wore head-to-toe cable knit, from thick mustard tights to a pumpkin sweater dress. A knit band decorated with a crocheted cat face held back her honey-colored hair.

Leanna turned to Cleo, eyes wide behind sparkly cat-eye glasses, her tone set to scandalized. "Do you see this? These books—they're arranged by color! Spine color! And look! Look at this cover! Oh, I can't even . . ."

Cleo selected a book and quickly grasped what Leanna wasn't able to utter. "Someone put on new covers." Inside, the title page revealed a recent bestseller. The teal canvas reminded Cleo of a craft project she'd undertaken with her grand-daughter. They'd decorated a kitchen stool with decoupage, using magazine images and pretty bits of cloth. She'd never dismember a perfectly good book.

Leanna tapped her shoe, a shiny Mary Jane with a silver buckle. "This novel is brand new. So are the others. It's like someone tore off the original covers and glued on canvas, for no good reason. Is this legal? Ethical? I bet not. I should ask my professor. And look at the organization. There is none! Mystery, romance, fiction, nonfiction—they're all jumbled together. Not a Dewey decimal in sight! It's not right!"

"The person who designed this bookmobile is new to libraries," Cleo said charitably. "Belle Beauchamp. She's inno-vating, she says."

Leanna huffed. "*Innovating.* More like endangering. Did

you see the giant bubbles the kids are making? All that sticky cotton candy? And the little horse . . . He's as cute as a speckled puppy, isn't he? But he's eating a magazine! We don't even allow gum onboard our bookmobile."

They both glanced toward Words on Wheels. The refurbished school bus stood up on the street, quiet and legally parked. *Lonely*, Cleo thought.

Cleo patted Leanna's arm. "We should get back to work," she said. "Let's make sure our displays are in order."

Leanna's shoe tapping ended in a stomp. "That's the worst of it. Why's everyone over here? We have our new fall reading list and actual books. Shelf after shelf of *books*! Plus, our bookmobile is just as pretty. Prettier!"

"Absolutely," Cleo said. She thought Words on Wheels was the most beautiful bookmobile in the South, if not beyond, but then she was admittedly biased. A grandson and some of his Boy Scout pals had repurposed the decommissioned school bus. The clever boys had replaced most of the bench seats with handmade bookshelves. They'd lined the floors with squishy, colorful tiles and designed a backseat reading nook and kids' section. The exterior was just as fun, with *"READ!"* painted across the brow, flanked in airbrushed flames. Along each side, cursive script in opalescent emerald paint spelled out "Words on Wheels."

"Our mascot is better too," Leanna said.

Cleo agreed with that as well. Her pretty Persian cat, Rhett Butler, lounged on the bookmobile's hood, his fluffy orange belly aimed at the November sun.

"You know how folks are," Cleo soothed. "They're attracted to the bright, new, and flashy. Books will always endure."

Leanna exhaled heavily. "You're right, Miss Cleo. I wasn't just fussing about the shelving and covers. It was ugly jealousy, plain and simple. Like my kindergarten teacher used to say, blowing out another's candles will *not* make yours burn any brighter."

"Swamping another's boat won't help yours float," Cleo said.

Leanna grinned. "Be nice if it kills you!"

A shiver shook Cleo. "Let's not go that far."

Last spring had seen more than the library wounded. A patron had been murdered, and Cleo and Leanna had almost joined him in the grave beyond.

When they reached Words on Wheels, Leanna leaned over the hood, tapping her fingernails. Rhett yawned, stretched, and deigned to saunter over for a chin scratch.

"Who would hire a librarian with no experience?" Leanna muttered to Rhett, who purred in response.

"Not us," Cleo said. She wouldn't upset Leanna by revealing Mercer's smitten enthusiasm for Belle. There was no need. Cleo and the full board ultimately made the hiring decisions, and they'd already agreed on the skills they wanted for the extra part-time position.

Leanna rubbed Rhett's ears and gave him a quick kiss on his furry noggin. "Can you two hold down our patron rush?" she joked. "I have a computer delivery coming at the main library soon. Then the painter's stopping by to test more paint colors. It's going to be gorgeous! I can't wait!" She glanced toward the party atmosphere. "I just hope people will come."

"They will," Cleo said firmly. "Our patrons are loyal. They're readers and library lovers. We have absolutely nothing to worry about."

A horn blared over her final words, rumbling low and long, like a foghorn across a watery deep. Rhett's fur bristled. Cleo's scalp prickled. She didn't have to look. She knew the vehicle. She knew who'd be driving it too.

Leanna groaned. "Nothing to worry about? I'm not so sure."

Neither was Cleo.

Chapter Two

Captain Ahab had his whale. His quarry. His quest. His obsession.

Cleo had Dixie Huddleston. She liked to think she stopped short of obsession.

"Dixie," Cleo muttered, squinting out the windshield of Words on Wheels. A white whale of Buick swung toward the curb, horn still blasting.

Rhett hopped to the dash and swished his tail. Leanna had run along to the main library. Other than Rhett, Cleo was alone in Words on Wheels, and now she was glad of it. Her encounters with Dixie tended to end in embarrassing defeat. At least she knew what to expect. She'd had decades of dealing with Dixie.

Dixie was the kid who'd driven teenage Cleo out of the babysitting business. Twice young Dixie swilled perfume under Cleo's watch, pricey concoctions from Bourbon French Parfums of New Orleans, requiring pricier trips to the emergency room. On other occasions, Dixie ran off, all to tell her blessed mother she'd told her so: *No one can babysit me!*

Adult Dixie had turned her get-her-way nature to profits. At sixty-five, Dixie was a well-off divorcée and savvy business-woman, ranking as Catalpa Springs' number-one real-estate professional. All around town, her face beamed down from billboards, underlined with her logo: "Come Home with Lady Luck." Her hobby continued her competitive streak. Dixie entered contests, from dahlia-bloom competitions to high-stakes bingo. She often won, and Cleo had heard the grumbles around town. Dixie was said to cheat, to be strong-armed, manipula-tive, and outright greedy.

Cleo knew what Dixie would say to such charges. She'd attribute her success to good fortune, which she didn't sit back and wait for. Dixie grabbed, snagged, and gathered luck at any opportunity. Cleo knew all about that too.

Her gripe with Dixie wasn't about the babysitting or lost raffles.

It was much more important. It was about a book.

Dixie Huddleston held the most overdue book in Catalpa Springs. And not just by weeks or months. Not even a few years. Cleo frowned, recalling the day Dixie checked out *Luck and Lore: Good luck, death lore, and deadly omens of the Deep South.* It was as memorable as another milestone, Cleo's thir-tieth birthday, celebrated at her favorite place, the Catalpa Springs Public Library. A colleague had made cake, straw-berry with fluffy icing and a blaze of candles. Patrons and staff had gathered around the circulation desk to sing "Happy Birthday."

Cleo could practically feel the moment. She'd filled her lungs, closed her eyes, made a most lovely wish, and—poof!

There'd been a gust, a collective gasp, and a waft of smoke. Dixie Huddleston had blown out all Cleo's candles.

"Ha! Made my wish first! Got your luck!" Dixie crowed.

Forty-five years, seven months, and four days had come and gone since that birthday. Cleo could calculate so precisely because she'd recently consulted her roster of lost and overdue books. She craved a clean slate before the grand library reopening. She had little hope of getting it with Dixie in the picture.

Dixie considered *Luck and Lore* to be one of her luckiest charms. Her fortunes had turned, she said, on the day she checked it out and grabbed Cleo's birthday wishes.

"That afternoon I got my first house listing!" she'd told Cleo more than once. "I wished on your birthday candles that I'd become the best and most successful realtor in Catalpa County, and look—it came true!"

In rare moods of generosity, Dixie would thank Cleo, calling Cleo *almost* as lucky as her lucky-charm library book. Cleo suggested that the best thanks would be to return *Luck and Lore*. Dixie always got a good laugh about that. In fact, all Cleo's attempts brought Dixie a trickster's glee, as if Cleo's chase and Dixie's evasions were their own favorite game.

It wasn't a game to Cleo.

She wanted *Luck and Lore* back and had tried every trick in the book to get it. She'd sent polite notes to Dixie. She'd called and faxed and parked her bookmobile outside Dixie's door. She'd tallied the towering late fee, now teetering toward $800. Once, Cleo had even issued the worst threat she could imagine: banishment from the library.

Cleo hadn't carried out the library exile. She couldn't be

that cruel. However, she did suspend Dixie's borrowing privileges until e-books and their automatic return procedures came along. Perhaps most frustratingly, Dixie made no attempt to hide the overdue book. She read it in public, at the Spoonbread Bakery, in Fontaine Park, even *in the library*! She'd bring it back when she was good and ready, she always said.

When might that be? Cleo occasionally asked, hoping against all logic that the answer might change.

Dixie never said never. *"A cold day in Georgia, Cleo! A cold day!"*

A leaf blew by the window. It was a chilly day for the southern edge of the Peach State. Cleo tamped down absurd hope. She could guess what would happen. Dixie would lower her window. She'd wave. She'd blast the horn, attracting everyone's attention. Right before she peeled out, laughing, flaunting the book.

Cleo gripped the keys to Words on Wheels, picturing herself revving her own engine and chasing Dixie down.

The key bit into her palm. The fantasy fizzled. Cleo had raced after Dixie before, an infamous defeat when Dixie said Cleo could have *Luck and Lore* if she could catch her. Not only had Cleo failed to keep up, she'd gotten a whopper of a speeding ticket. Cleo released the key. She wouldn't give Dixie the satisfaction. She certainly couldn't afford *another* speeding ticket. Rhett's fluffy tail brushed Cleo's nose. She took it as a warning.

"You're right, Rhett," she whispered. "We can't let Dixie get to us." Turning from the window, Cleo made a show—to no one but her cat—of straightening up the New Reads shelf.

Her mind, however, kept stirring the same old pot of grievances. It wasn't about the book, per se. It was the *principle*! Dixie was violating the trust and honor that allowed public libraries to exist. Why, if everyone acted like Dixie Huddleston, there would be no more libraries!

Cleo's eyes slid back across the dash. Dixie's taillights had gone dark. The driver's door opened, and Dixie stepped out. Her hair rose in spiky maple-leaf red. Her outfit resembled an autumn landscape reflected in rippling water, silky layers pinned down by cascades of crystals on glittery chains. Her pants shimmered like copper, each leg as wide as a gown. The cuffs skimmed the ground. Like a hovering ghost, Cleo thought, and she was suddenly gripped with the oddest urge: not to chase after Dixie, but to flee.

The spell broke as the Buick's passenger door opened, and Dixie's friend Pat Holmes shuffled after Dixie to muffled calls of "Wait up!"

Cleo steeled herself. *Oh, dear . . .* Dixie looked to be in a warpath mood, and Cleo could guess why. The newspaper. The *Catalpa Springs Gazette*, published once weekly, had done a feature on the library reopening. They'd interviewed Cleo, who'd happened to mention the overdue book and her desire to clear her roster. The young reporter had leapt on it. Forty years was a hunk of a fine, a good story. The issue had just come out, adorned with the blaring headline *Most Wanted: Local Librarian Hunts Bold Book Thief, Demands Payment of Forty-Year Late Fee.*

Cleo felt some remorse for her loose lips and the sensational headline. On the other hand, it was true, and Cleo hadn't broken her librarian's vow of secrecy. Cleo never revealed or judged her patrons' reading choices. Dixie would recognize herself, though. Others might too.

Dixie thumped up the steps. "There you are! I've been looking all over for you, Cleo Watkins. How is anyone supposed to find your library if you're moving around all the time?"

"I knew." Pat puffed up behind her. "The schedule is online."

Pat ran a cleaning company, Holmes Homes, a tough business that often left her looking as weary and washed out as her mops. Her hair was beige and chopped in thick bangs that mimicked the blunt cut falling just above her shoulders. Her too-large T-shirt bore her company logo: "Holmes Homes: We clean your grime when you don't have time."

"Hi, Pat. Hello, Dixie," Cleo said, dropping her pitch for the latter greeting. "Here for a book, Pat?" Cleo placed her hand on the door lever. She'd wrench it shut if Dixie tried to swipe anything.

"I'm good," Pat said, still catching her breath. "I have to finish up our mystery for book group tomorrow."

"I'm not good!" Dixie snapped.

Cleo stood firm, not about to apologize for the newspaper article.

Dixie stomped down the aisle and back again, her hand slapping bookshelves as she went. Several books propped up for display fell.

Pat followed, murmuring comforts and righting the books. "It's okay, Dix. It's going to be fine."

Dixie ignored her, turning sharp eyes to Cleo. "You're wondering why I'm here."

Cleo suspected she already knew. Dixie, however, surprised her.

"I'm ready. That's right. Ready." Dixie rested a shaky hand on a shelf displaying autumn-themed reads.

A cold gust swept up the steps. "Ready?" Cleo repeated.

"That's what I said, isn't it?" Dixie clawed at her spiky locks. "You don't have to rub it in. You win, Cleo. I'm done with that book. Done with everything!"

Pat murmured, "No, no." She reached for her friend, who swatted her off.

Cleo backed into the dashboard. Glee and skepticism wrestled. That more realistic emotion won out. This was surely a trick, a punishment for the newspaper article. On several April Fools days, Dixie had called the library, telling Cleo she could come pick up *Luck and Lore*. The first two times, Cleo had arrived to find a note on Dixie's door: *Got you! You're the April Fool!* The third time, when Cleo resisted Dixie's tease, the infuriating woman called to say she'd been waiting, book in hand.

"Well?" Dixie demanded. "Aren't you going to beg for your precious book?"

Cleo wouldn't be fooled again. "Oh? When shall I stop by, then?" Cleo said, stretching her syllables into an icy drawl. "On a cold day in Georgia?"

Splotches rose across Dixie's cheeks. "What? You? *You're* mocking me? My former babysitter? The town librarian? I suppose I should have expected this after you taunted me in the newspaper. So rude, Cleo. Rude, rude, rude!"

19

There it was. Confirmation. Dixie had read the paper. Cleo straightened her cardigan, pleased she'd sidestepped a trick.

Dixie's shoulders twitched, rippling the silky layers. "Fine. What does it matter to me?"

Outside, Lilliput neighed, and a gust sent leathery magnolia leaves scraping along the sidewalk. Dixie lurched toward the nearest window, eyes wide and scanning. She gasped and drew back.

"Dixie?" Cleo said, concern overcoming her stern stance. Something wasn't right. Dixie seemed truly upset. Scared, even. "What's wrong?" Cleo asked. She sharpened the point. "Why are you offering to give back that book?"

A tear slipped over Dixie's high cheekbone. She swiped angrily. "That book of yours! It's turned on me! I've used up all my luck. I'm a dead woman walking. I'm dying, Cleo!"

Pat protested and was again rebuffed.

Cleo slapped a palm to her heart. "Oh no, Dixie, surely no—" Her mind reeled with potential afflictions. Dixie was only in her sixties. So young. But age wasn't the only decider, Cleo well knew.

"You've been to a doctor," Cleo said, as close as manners would allow to asking the cause.

Dixie scoffed. "I don't need a doctor to tell me what I know. I've seen the signs, Cleo. I'm a goner."

"There has to be a mistake," Pat said. She turned wide doe eyes on Cleo. "It's a misreading of signs and omens, surely."

Cleo breathed out in relief. Here was another trait of Dixie's. She was . . . Cleo searched for the right word. *Superstitious* was most apt but seemed a tad judgmental. Cleo tried to respect other people's beliefs, however outlandish they might seem to her. Dixie's death signs did sound downright ridiculous. She was listing them, rambling on about crows and doves.

"Birds!" Dixie shouted, hands waving. "Birds in my house, Cleo! In my kitchen! A live bird! A dead one too! You know what that means, don't you?" Dixie scowled outside, eyes narrowing on the bookless bookmobile party.

Cleo glanced again too, but this time her spirits lifted even more. Henry Lafayette made his way through the crowd, accompanied by his aged pug, Mr. Chaucer. Cleo didn't call Henry her "boyfriend." That sounded too young and frivolous. Henry was her "gentleman friend," a kindred spirit, a lover of books, and an awfully nice person to snuggle up with beside by a fireplace. Henry and his dog paused to gape at a giant soap bubble sailing across their path. Mr. Chaucer sneezed, breaking the low-floating bubble. When he'd recovered his balance, they continued their trek toward Words on Wheels.

Cleo turned back to Dixie. "Birds do fly inside sometimes, and it is migratory season. Snowbirds of all sorts are coming down in droves. People, hummingbirds, ducks, cranes . . ."

"This isn't about *weather*, Cleo, or wildlife. There's more." Dixie listed cows, baying at midnight. A hound, bellowing her impending death to the moon. Clouds of ominous shapes. Black cats, ladders, cracked mirrors, a wasp the size of a hummingbird in her bathroom.

Pat raised her shoulders in a helpless shrug to Cleo.

Henry and Mr. Chaucer reached the door. The elderly

dog—gray-snouted with wrinkly fawn fur—launched himself up the steps, as if using all available momentum. At the top, he promptly plopped on the floor next to Rhett, who was glowering under Cleo's seat.

"Morning, ladies. Cold weather we're having, isn't it?" Henry said, following more leisurely. Henry, an antiquarian bookseller, had grown his white beard Santa Claus fluffy for the season. His hair waved in tufts over prominent ears and around the felt cap he was now politely removing. His wire-rim glasses were slightly fogged. Like Cleo, Henry was on the short side of average height and pleasantly padded around the middle.

Dixie's eyes widened. "It *is*. It is a *cold* day! Just like I always said. You'd get your book on a cold day in Georgia, Cleo."

"Dixie, really," Cleo soothed. "I don't think—"

"You don't *think*?" Dixie said. "Well, how about the Reaper outside my window? I *saw* him. I saw the coffins too, with my name right on them. I don't care what you or anyone says—I *know* I'm a goner."

Henry moved close to Cleo's side. Mr. Chaucer whimpered.

"What's happening?" Henry asked, looking anxiously from Cleo to Dixie and on to Pat, her forehead as furrowed as Mr. Chaucer's.

"Oh, we're just chatting about my upcoming death," Dixie said with panicked levity. She eyed Cleo. "I'm setting my affairs in order. Atoning. If there's an afterlife, I'll rebuild my luck there."

Cleo thought Dixie was overreacting. Selfishly, however,

she saw an opportunity. "You want to return *Luck and Lore*, then," she said. "I can take it back right now, and you'll surely feel much better."

Dixie scowled, a more familiar and reassuring look. "Not now. I had it yesterday but couldn't *find* you. It's at home. Besides, your library book isn't the only account I need to settle. Come to my house tomorrow. Ten. Or noon. I *should* still be around then."

"I have a book group at nine thirty." Cleo nodded to Pat, who was a member of the Who-Done-It mystery readers. "I can stop by afterward." Cleo was the group's moderator and couldn't back out. Besides, part of her didn't trust Dixie. A big part. They settled on just before noon.

"Hopefully I'll be there," Dixie said, and she was down the steps in a wave of silk and chiming charms.

"She will!" Pat agreed, hurrying after her friend.

When they were gone, Cleo tried to explain to Henry what had happened. She wasn't sure she understood it herself.

"Signs?" Henry asked. "Death signs? Do you think they're for real?"

The white-whale Buick peeled out, kicking up gravel and dust that hung in the sunlight after Dixie was gone. A dread lingered over Cleo. She almost said yes. "No," she said instead. "No, of course not. Birds and noisy cows? Clouds shaped like skulls and caskets? The Grim Reaper? Dixie seems truly afraid and might actually believe it, though. I'll know she does if I get that book back."

Henry stroked his beard, his signal of an idea taking form.

Cleo asked before he did. "Do you want to come along? I have to stop at the Pancake Mill for a book group beforehand, and I can't guarantee that Dixie will give up *Luck and Lore*. I suspect she's punishing me for mentioning her overdue fine in the paper."

"Pancakes? Books? Possible treachery? Sounds delightful," Henry said. "Except for the treachery. You'll need a guard dog in case any real reapers or death hounds show up."

Mr. Chaucer, guard pug, lay on his back, wrinkles puddling, a paw twitching in a dreamtime romp. Henry smiled, clearly dismissing the potential for danger.

Cleo wasn't one to see signs and omens, but she feared this morning's encounters with Dixie Huddleston and Belle Beauchamp didn't bode well.

Chapter Three

"She deserves to die!"

The words wafted over Cleo, as ethereal as the fine mist rising from Pancake Spring just outside the wide, paned windows. Inside, pancakes sizzled on tabletop griddles, the signature feature of the Pancake Mill, a historic sugar mill turned to pie and do-it-yourself flapjacks. Butter and blueberries snapped and spit. The discussion by the Who-Done-It mystery readers club was equally heated.

Mutters of indignation arose, peppered with nervous giggles and clinking cutlery. For the past hour, the seven women and sole man had been analyzing every victim in a long and bloody mystery, issuing judgments on why each had death coming. Cleo sat at the head of the table. Although officially the moderator, she hadn't contributed much. Her thoughts kept drifting. She wasn't bored. She was distracted.

By pie, for one. A waitress sailed by with a golden slice of honey chess pie, the November special. Cleo craved a piece, but her cruel yet well-meaning doctor had her on a low-sugar diet. The view distracted too. Pancake Spring peeped in and out from under its fog cap. Ripples crisscrossed the deep waters, tracing the trails of hardy lap swimmers. On the banks, the trio of resident peacocks fanned and fluffed, and two walkers slowly strolled. Henry and Mr. Chaucer were both bundled up for the chilly morning. Henry wore a thick wool coat and scarf. Mr. Chaucer sported a puffy pug jacket that seemed to tip him further off balance.

"Death would be her ultimate atonement," a female voice proclaimed, and Cleo hazily decided they'd reached the book's final murder. Points and counterpoints volleyed around the long table. Cleo tried to focus, but her mind kept swinging to Dixie, her main distraction. Dixie wanted atonement. Cleo wanted her book.

She allowed herself to fantasize again while it was still possible. Cleo pictured herself victorious, *Luck and Lore* in her hands. She'd speed straight to the library and put it back in its rightful place on the shelf. *No,* she thought, taking a sip of tepid coffee. *That wouldn't do.* Dixie might grab it again if her luck turned. Cleo would have a display case made, from shatterproof glass and secured by lock and key.

She glanced at her watch. The Who-Done-Its should be wrapping up soon. Then they'd all go out to Words on Wheels, rouse a snoozing Rhett, and pick a new mystery. After that, Cleo, Henry, and the pets would head over to Dixie's. Excitement mixed with dread shot up Cleo's middle.

"You're awful! That's terrible and off-topic!" Another voice—female, loud, and angry—jolted Cleo from her fantasies. She blinked and refocused. Pat Holmes sat a few seats down, red-faced and sputtering like a boiling berry.

Across the table from Pat, Iris Hays grinned wide and toothy, an unusual expression on the artist, whose mood usually mirrored her murky landscape paintings. "I *am* on topic, Pat, darling," Iris said, touching choppy ink-jet hair, teased on top like a windblown bird's nest. "It's just like in the book—a treacherous, greedy villain goes looking for atonement and redemption, but it's too late for her. She gets what she deserves. Tragic? I think not." Iris cut a thick wedge of pancakes and chewed with puffed, pleased cheeks.

Pat sputtered. "Stop it! You're wrong and awful!"

With a sinking feeling, Cleo realized she'd let the book discussion derail. She clinked her spoon to her mug. When that failed to cut through the arguing, she rose and waved the book.

Eight sets of eyes turned her way. "Good," Cleo said brightly, as if they'd all just engaged in spirited literary debate. "So we've reached the end? We're all done?"

"Not until Dixie Huddleston croaks like she promises!" Iris said, aiming a pitcher of batter at a smoking skillet. She recklessly poured a pancake the size of a deflated basketball.

Pat gasped and burst up so abruptly her chair tipped backward, banging another diner. Chaos ensued. A pitcher crashed to the floor, shattering and splattering. Someone yelped in pain from a palm touching a griddle. Voices rose and a pancake flew, whether accidentally flipped or hurled intentionally, Cleo couldn't tell.

"I'm done with this drama. I'm done with Dixie Huddleston," Iris declared. She abandoned her oversized pancake, threw down her napkin, and stomped toward the door.

Pat stood, slumped and sobbing. A waitress came running.

Cleo sunk low in her seat. She'd lost control of more than the book discussion. She'd lost control of the Who-Done-Its. *Again*.

* * *

"I swear, I'm going to restrict all y'all to outdoor meetings for easier cleanup." Mary-Rose Garland shook her head in exaggerated weariness. Mary-Rose, Cleo's best friend since infancy, was also the owner of the Pancake Mill and the gracious hostess of several local book clubs, among which she claimed the Who-Done-Its were the most prone to high emotions and food fights.

"Reading arouses passions," Cleo said, rehashing an old but truthful line.

Mary-Rose sniffed. "Word Warriors and Dante's Devotees manage to maintain their table manners. Babes and Books are lovely guests. They'd never hurl pancakes or tip over the buckwheat batter, which is the most difficult batter to clean up, mind you. Even the infants in Babes and Books are well behaved. Little angels, every single one of them."

Cleo loved babies as much as the next devoted grandmother, but she suspected Mary-Rose of exaggerating. What little one didn't love throwing flapjacks?

Waitress Desiree swept in with a mop for the floor and tissues for Pat, who was beet-faced and apologizing and offering to do the mopping herself. Three members comforted her. The other three members had hurried after Iris.

"Pat's probably never raised her voice or tipped pancake batter in anger in her entire life, bless her heart," Cleo said.

"I'm sure she feels awful about that spill. She's a professional cleaner."

Saying this reminded Cleo that she needed to reschedule Pat's cleaning company for periodic library visits. Before the toppled tree took the library out of commission, Pat's "ladies" had come by monthly to make the place sparkle. Pat often tagged along. To help and supervise, Pat said, although she usually spent the time chatting with Cleo and relaying her woes.

Pat had troubles on top of troubles, so much so that folks—Cleo included—often stuck "Poor" onto her name as if it were part of it. Poor Pat had recently celebrated her sixty-fifth birthday with a kidney stone the size of a kumquat. Her knees acted up in the heat and the cold. She had unexplainable aches and a husband who took off on long golfing excursions. And now she hunched in pained shame.

"Pat and Dixie are childhood friends, like you and me," Cleo said to a still sputtering Mary-Rose. "You know how Dixie Huddleston can evoke strong emotions."

Cleo had told Mary-Rose about Dixie's promise regarding the overdue book. As a good and blunt friend, Mary-Rose informed Cleo she was heading for a duping.

Mary-Rose chuckled and patted her loose but elegant bun, silver with highlights of natural ginger red. A rosy knit dress billowed from under her spotless white apron. "Oh, I do know about Dixie and riling up emotions. I know about defending a friend too. In fact, Cleo Jane Watkins, I should step in right now and forbid you from running off to make a fool of yourself. You know Dixie's out to trick you. *I* saw that newspaper interview. *'Librarian on the Warpath.'* What a headline. Dixie's not going to let that stand."

"That was a highlighted section heading," Cleo mumbled, as if that made it better. The paper's new reporter was young and seemed to have tabloid aspirations.

Mary-Rose rolled her eyes. "Tell you what, after these rowdy mystery readers leave, you and Henry stay and have some nice pie and coffee. The special's honey chess pie . . . your favorite."

Most pies were Cleo's favorites. She did love chess pie, especially the honey variety, with its sweet custard thickened by a touch of cornmeal. She was tempted. Very tempted. However, silly, absurd hope still burned within her. Getting back *Luck and Lore* would be the icing on her cake for the grand reopening. With her rosters clear and old business tidied up, she'd truly feel free to step aside from her circulation-desk duties and continue captaining Words on Wheels.

"Dixie *is* going around saying she's dying," Cleo rationalized yet again. "That's what has Pat upset. Of course, I hope Dixie's wrong, but she wants to settle accounts. One of those is her library account. I may even forgive part of her fine, if she hands over the book nicely without any trouble."

Mary-Rose shot Cleo a loving yet pitying look. "Dixie needs to settle something with Iris Hays if Iris's wishing her dead over breakfast and books. What's going on? You didn't hear what sparked that talk, did you?"

Cleo said she must have drifted off. "Thinking about this month's book," she fibbed.

"Sure you were." Mary-Rose grinned. "Thinking about *getting* a certain book, more likely. You are *obsessed*, Cleo. I'll be reading all about it in next week's paper. *'Local librarian's obsession leads to extreme embarrassment. Best friend says she told her so.'*"

Cleo raised her chin in an attempt at dignity. Except for absent Iris, the mystery readers were returning to collect their coats, books, and notes. They left hefty tips on the table for Desiree.

"I *like* this bunch," Desiree whispered as she trundled by with cash and cleanup items in hand.

Mary-Rose sighed. "Well, Desiree likes y'all. Guess I can't ban the Who-Done-Its yet."

"Next time we'll behave," Cleo said. "Speaking of next time, I have to go help with the December book selection." She gave Mary-Rose a hug and hurried to catch up with the members gathered by the door.

"I have interesting choices for next month," Cleo said brightly. She'd brought along some classics, a new bestseller, and several mysteries set in small towns with enterprising amateur sleuths. She hoped they'd pick the sleuth with a feline sidekick.

Pat blushed afresh. Others looked down or away, scuffing their shoes and furtively glancing out to the parking area, a gravel lot mostly masked by leafy palms. After a minute, their de facto leader spoke, a steel-haired school principal who, even among friends, went by the moniker Mrs. K.—preferable to the "Mrs. Kranky" nickname her surname Krankovitz inspired among students.

"Well . . . ," Mrs. K. said with uncharacteristic hesi-tancy, "we thought we might shake things up a little next month."

"Shake things up?" In the awkward silence that followed, Cleo heard music. She cocked her head. The tune grew louder, closer. Cleo recognized the melody: "The Devil Went Down to Georgia." Fiddles sawed and wailed. A cherry-red pickup bounced in, hauling a silver Airstream. Cleo's stomach clenched. So did her fists.

"Ooh! I hope Belle has that little horse with her!" a voice cried amidst similar excited statements. "He's the best!"

The Who-Done-Its streamed out, leaving Pat behind to admit what Cleo already guessed. The mystery readers would get their next book from Belle Beauchamp and BOOK IT!

* * *

"She seems nice," Henry said as Cleo navigated Words on Wheels toward Dixie Huddleston's.

Cleo stomped the gas. She took a deep breath and deceler-ated. She was being petty. The Who-Done-Its could choose any book they wanted, from wherever and whomever they wanted. Belle Beauchamp could be friendly and flirty to whomever she wanted too. So what if she called Henry a "cutie pie" and chatted him up and made Mr. Chaucer topple in roly-poly pug joy when she showered him with tummy tickles?

"She said she might apply for the job at your library?" Henry continued.

The bookmobile surged. Cleo eased up and took another

calming breath. "Yes, Mercer Whitty, our board president, is smitten with her. However, she has, uh . . . *questionable* ideas regarding libraries."

They'd come to a four-way stop, so Cleo could turn to face Henry. He sat on the front bench seat, a pug snuggled on one side, a Persian purring on the other. He was buckled up and had a hand protectively looped over each pet.

"She thinks books clutter up a place," Cleo said.

Cleo's mood improved when Henry visibly shuddered. Her gentleman friend owned and lived above The Gilded Page, an antiquarian bookstore packed floor to ceiling with books. In the back, Henry had a book surgery, where he repaired and tended to old and wounded texts.

"She rips off perfectly good covers and replaces them so they'll match a color scheme," Cleo added, surging on toward Dixie's.

Henry groaned. "She asked me to give a talk on book-binding at the Claymore Library," he said. "A workshop."

"Maybe you can change her ways," Cleo said. She doubted it. People didn't easily change their ways. Maybe they couldn't even if they tried. Her stomach gave a little flip. Like Dixie. Once a trickster, always a trickster. They were nearing Dixie's street. Cleo could still turn the bus around and head back to the Pancake Mill. Except Mary-Rose was right, Cleo admitted to herself: she was a teensy bit obsessed.

She turned up Mulberry Lane, a street known for its wide lots and pretty homes, each vying to outdo the neighbors. None could compete with Dixie's place, the last stop on the dead-end lane. Peach orchards and graceful live oaks framed manicured gardens and a Victorian home even more stunning than the setting.

"My, this is where we're going?" Henry said. "When I first moved to Catalpa Springs, I saw this house in a tourism brochure and went looking for it. It's magnificent, isn't it? Look at all that gingerbread trim and those turrets."

Cleo murmured agreement. She was concentrating on turning the long bus around in a many-point turn. No matter what the outcome of their visit, Cleo anticipated wanting a speedy departure.

They left the pets snuggling in Rhett's peach crate. "You're better off here, Rhett," Cleo told her cat, who frowned but purred as he kneaded his canine friend's back. Mr. Chaucer's eyes drooped in contentment.

At the gate, Cleo and Henry paused to take in the view. The house sat atop a pedestal foundation of pale stone. Wide steps led to a rounded porch dripping in ornate scrollwork. Three turrets in varying sizes gave a fairytale air, as did the Mardi Gras paint colors: gold, deep green, and rich purple in an array of hues. Spiky iron banisters ringed the balconies and upper decks. A top-heavy roof crowned it all, capped with a widow's walk.

"A family called Peacock lived here when I was young," Cleo said.

"A fitting name." Henry ran his hand along a twined-vine metal gate. It creaked open.

Cleo told him how she and Mary-Rose used to sneak into the gardens and orchards as kids, imagining the turreted house was their castle.

Henry, who'd meticulously renovated the former pharmacy that became his bookstore, agreed that this was a fine fantasy home. "Unless you're the painter having to touch up all that trim," he said. "Or the gardener or cleaner. This place would be a lot of work."

They climbed the front steps, to a cast-iron bell hanging by the door. Cleo took a few more deep breaths before grasping the ringer and striking hard. The ring echoed in her ears, but only a talkative jay responded. Cleo's anxiety and excitement—along with her silly optimism—dimmed.

"Mary-Rose told me so," she said glumly.

"Now, now," said Henry, ever an optimist. "Let's not give up. Her car's over there by the carriage garage. Maybe she's in the back and can't hear the bell. This porch winds around. Let's take a peek. If nothing else, we can check out this amazing house."

Cleo half-listened as Henry gushed about architectural features: flat-sawn balusters, spindle work, and decorative brackets. She paused at windows, peering in, frustrated by pretty lace curtains blocking her view.

"Ah!" Henry exclaimed as they rounded the curve. "Look, the back door is open. She's likely waiting for us. Waiting for *you*, that is."

"Waiting to play her joke," Cleo muttered. She looked around for a mocking note calling her a fool. She saw none. To their left, steps led down to a brick footpath winding toward a squatty cottage. To their right, a scroll-trimmed screen door hung wide. The glass-paned door behind it was open a crack.

"I'll knock," Henry offered.

But Cleo stepped up. This was her folly. If Dixie was waiting to laugh in anyone's face, it should be hers. Cleo balled her fist and took aim at the doorframe. The chatty jay landed nearby. His song had changed to a sharp chirp. Cleo thought of Dixie's fear of bird-induced bad luck.

"If that jay flies inside, Dixie's likely to keel over in fright," Cleo said, trying for levity she didn't feel. She sniffed. "Do you smell smoke?" Cleo knocked and pushed the door open, calling out Dixie's name.

She was momentarily dazzled. Glittery crystals and light-catchers hung from the windows and ceilings. Shamrocks, horseshoes, and ladybug charms filled the walls. Dixie had decorated in a dizzying array of luck.

Henry, behind her, exclaimed, "The stove! Fire!"

Cleo gasped. Smoke seeped from a pot and slithered from the oven. A flame licked the bottom of the pot. They yelled Dixie's name as they burst inside. Cleo rushed to shut off the burner. She opened the oven door. When smoke billowed out, she slammed it shut again and hurried to the nearest window. She was leaning over the sink, trying to heft up the heavy old glass, when a bee buzzed her head, wings touching her nose. With a yelp, Cleo let the window fall back. She swatted wildly, sending the bee and smoke swirling. She turned to Henry to tell him. He stood strangely still, a hand on the long, marble-topped kitchen island, an ear tilted toward the front of the house.

"Listen," he said. "Hear that?"

"There's an angry bee by the sink." But when Cleo tuned

in, she realized a single bee couldn't create such a sound, a white noise of angry vibrations. Cleo and Henry stared at each other, and she saw her rising fear reflected in his eyes.

On tiptoeing feet they slowly walked the room, ears perked.

"It's coming from here," Cleo whispered, stopping by a narrow door with a cut-glass knob and a skeleton key dangling from it. Cleo reached for the knob. Henry put out his hand to stop her. "Let me."

He tugged and turned the knob. When the door wouldn't budge, he tried the key. Cleo mentally chanted, *Hurry, hurry,* until the lock turned with a metallic click and the door creaked open. They peered warily inside.

The pantry had neatly arranged shelves and a diamond-paned window at the end. It would have been pretty, except for the creeping mass of bees swarming the window and Dixie Huddleston lying twisted on the floor.

Chapter Four

Henry jerked the door shut. Just as quickly, he flung it back open. "Stay here," he said, but Cleo wasn't about to let him go in alone. She pushed in behind him, her eyes fixed on Dixie.

"She doesn't look good," Cleo said. Dixie looked worse than not good. Her face was frozen in a grimace of pure fear. Her hands clenched in fists. Her eyes stared, unblinking, toward the high ceiling. Cleo stomach turned. She looked up to catch her breath. A crack ran across the plaster. A bee walked along it, upside down and waggling its stinger in a dance.

Cleo closed her eyes. She murmured a prayer, for Dixie's sake and to calm her quaking knees. When she opened her lids, she saw Henry kneeling by Dixie.

"She's gone," Cleo whispered, confirming what his expression said. She reached out to help him up.

He took her hand and squeezed, but remained squatting. "Look," he said, pointing toward Dixie's far hand. Beyond her fist lay a piece of paper, black matte with jagged white writing. It was the size of a bookmark and shaped like a coffin.

"Death signs . . ." Cleo gripped Henry's hand tighter. "Dixie said death was coming for her."

He heaved himself to standing. The bees sounded louder, mingling with the whooshing through Cleo's head. Cleo pushed back her bifocals and leaned over Dixie, keeping her eyes on the note beyond. She read the note aloud: *Good luck saving yourself now, Dixie Huddleston. Welcome to your new home.*

Cleo stepped back. "How awful!" A bee zoomed by her ear. Another bumped her nose. She felt wings and sticky insect feet but thankfully no stinger. The blob on the window was coming apart, taking flight. Coming their way.

Henry took her arm and tugged her out, slamming the door behind them. They hurried across the smoky kitchen, Cleo's heart racing. When they reached the door, Cleo was ready to hurl herself outside. She needed air. She needed to get away from that terrible scene.

Henry, always chivalrous, reached the door first and held it open. Cleo burst outside, thinking, *Thank goodness*—right before she screamed.

* * *

Henry caught Cleo as she lurched backwards. Her ears rang, and her knees went jiggly again from the fresh fright. She faced two startling faces. They were white and chalky with eyes lined in jagged black circles and full red lips painted in smiles. One was a woman, the other a man.

"Clowns!" Cleo blurted, thumping a hand to her heart, aware of her rudeness as soon as the word left her mouth.

"Mimes," the female of the pair corrected, her eye-roll and head-shake suggesting Cleo had made a fool's mistake. "Mimes in the classical French theatrical tradition."

Cleo patted her thumping heart. "Of course." She felt Henry squeezing out the door behind her. Cleo moved aside and gathered a breath along with her manners. "Pardon us," she said. "You gave us a startle. There's been a most upsetting—."

"*You* startled us!" the woman interrupted. "Who are you anyway? What is that smell? Is she-of-the-manor burning lunch again?" Her large nose wrinkled and twitched. She turned to her companion. "I *told* you we should have just gotten something to eat in Claymore. Why do we even try?"

The male mime was busy with an exaggerated performance. He peeked shyly over his sputtering companion's shoulder and wiggled his fingers in greeting. They were dressed alike in all white, from their puffy-sleeved tops to ivory leggings, billowing pantaloons, and lace-up slippers.

The getups looked old-fashioned, as in Shakespearean old. Cleo's thumping heart slowed in a grim realization. She could hear Dixie's voice, as clear as the sky above: *That clown of a son of mine and his drama queen wife!* Cleo had overheard Dixie at the supermarket a few months ago, complaining about Jefferson, her only son. He'd moved back to town. His wife, a professor of drama, had gotten a job at Claymore College. They were living—freeloading, as Dixie put it—in her backyard cottage. Cleo hadn't intended to eavesdrop. Dixie was a loud talker.

"Jefferson," Cleo said aloud.

He mimed a querulous look and surprised *Who, me?* gestures.

Cleo knew it was him. She recognized his soft baby face now, oddly tiny atop a big man's body. She tried the more talkative, although certainly less friendly, woman. "Are you Mrs. Huddleston?"

"No! I am his spouse, but I have my own name. I am *Doctor* Jacquelyn Ames."

"Of course," Cleo said again. She took Henry's coat sleeve and gently moved him and herself through the door, closing it and forcing frowning Jacquelyn to step back too.

Jacquelyn made more huffy sounds. "Let me guess, the royal *she* won't be accepting any more visitors today, even though she insisted we come for lunch, at no notice? Jefferson, let's just go. She only ever invites us if she wants something. Like kicking us out. She was probably planning to serve up an eviction notice."

Jefferson's sad makeup looked more appropriate now that Cleo realized who he was. He mimed confusion and weeping. Cleo wished she weren't about to make him truly sad. She didn't know Jefferson well as an adult. He'd been away at college, grad school, and jobs elsewhere before returning to Catalpa Springs.

However, Cleo had watched him grow up, and she suspected he'd changed little. Jefferson was the sort of child who attracted bullies like lemonade draws wasps. He was clumsy and pear-shaped, with thick glasses and hobbies that included reenactment and elaborate costumes and role-playing. His disapproving mother hadn't been much kinder than a common bully, yet he'd always sought Dixie's affection. Cleo knew he'd be crushed.

"Jefferson, dear," Cleo said, ignoring his bristly wife. "Do you remember me? Cleo Watkins? The librarian? You used to come in and help me read to the littler kids during story hour. Remember? You'd act out stories for them?"

He nodded slowly, lines of concentration creasing his makeup. Cleo wondered if he remembered the time Dixie—his own mother!—had sent him inside with *Luck and Lore*, telling the anxious kindergartener to wave it at Cleo and run off. Cleo hadn't held that against him. She'd always had a soft spot for Jefferson. He liked reading and followed his passions, even if they got him mocked.

His older sister used to come into the library too. She'd been more like Dixie, prone to walking off without checking out books and racking up late fees. Cleo's mind fixated absurdly on trying to recall the girl's name. She hadn't been around town in years.

Jefferson was miming out the joy of reading.

Henry groaned and stepped up. "Sir. Ma'am—" Henry said.

"Doctor," Jacquelyn snapped. "Almost doctor," she said, nodding back toward her husband.

Henry forged on. "There's been a . . . uh . . . problem. A medical issue . . ."

"Jefferson," Cleo said, reaching for his hand, which eluded her grasp, raised to his lips in a bashful act. "We're so awfully sorry. We came to see your mother. We had an appointment, but we smelled smoke and went inside and found her . . . deceased. She's gone. Passed on." Nerves made Cleo ramble.

"Deceased? Mother?" Jefferson's voice, finally used, came out adenoidal and cracking. "No," he said, head shaking so vigorously his white beret slipped down, revealing pale hair thinning over a paler crown. "Nope. Sorry. Don't believe it. Mother's been going on about dying, but it's all show. If you know her, you know how she is. Tricky. I mean, a jokester. You *do* know Mother. I know you do. She has a funny sense of humor." His laugh caught in his throat and ended in a coughing fit. His wife slapped him hard on the back.

Cleo did know how Dixie was. For a second, she wavered. Could it be a trick? If so, she'd certainly been fooled this time. Oh, wouldn't Dixie be beyond delighted. So would Cleo.

She pictured Dixie rising from the floor, laughing and waving the overdue book. Cleo almost turned back and checked again. Then she glanced at Henry, his expression grim. They'd both seen her, that awful note, and the death's grip that could never be faked.

"I wish that were so," Cleo said. "I'm awfully sorry."

"Dead?" Jacquelyn said. "You're serious?" She put a hand to her mouth, but not fast enough to hide a grin. She reached behind Cleo for the doorknob. "This I have to see to believe. Maybe you're wrong. You said you're a librarian? Librarians aren't qualified to judge medical issues or death."

Unfortunately, Cleo did have experience with death, both natural and not. She wedged herself firmly in front of the door. "Mr. Lafayette and I are about to call 911," Cleo said.

"You really shouldn't go inside, dear. No one should until the police get here."

Jacquelyn began to grumble about Cleo's use of "dear." She stopped mid-fuss and frowned. "Police? Why do you say police?"

"The circumstances are unusual," Henry said carefully. "It's dangerous inside too. There's a natural hazard."

"A swarm of bees," Cleo specified, watching the two closely.

Jefferson yelped. He grasped for his wife. "Bees! Let's go! Come on, come on, we have to get out of here!" He swung around and ran, stumbling down the back steps and lumbering down the brick path, dutifully following its twists and curves to the squatty cottage.

"Oh for goodness sake," Jacquelyn said through a sigh. "Fine. You two call the police. We'll be hiding inside from bees."

Cleo and Henry watched her cross the yard. Her step was springy, and she whistled as she cut a straight path across the grass.

"Odd," Cleo said as she pawed through her purse in search of her cell phone. "That woman had a strange reaction to her mother-in-law's death."

"Perhaps it's the shock," Henry said, grimly charitable. "Some folks can't process a death unless they see firm evidence. Even if they do take it in, they might cover their grief with inappropriate reactions."

This was true. Cleo had seen it happen before. *But what if it wasn't grief or even surprise?* She located her phone, which she'd turned off for book club. It leisurely awoke in a series of lights, chipper icons, and a screensaver of Rhett's furry face. Cleo's mind brought up less pleasant images: threats over pancakes, the swarming bees, Dixie's terrified expression, and a note written on a coffin.

When Cleo finally reached the 911 operator, she didn't use a euphemism or mince words. "A woman is dead," she said. "We believe she's been murdered."

Chapter Five

Chief Silas Culpepper smiled at Cleo, a real-life rendition of the smiley faces dotting his red suspenders. The chief had broad shoulders, a mountainous middle, and twiggy legs under waif-worthy hips. He wedged thick thumbs under the already strained suspenders and pushed out, sending the happy faces into contorted screams. Cleo inched back a smidge. She wanted to be clear of the snap zone should the elastic fail.

In truth, she wanted to be anywhere else. Home with Rhett, reading on her front porch. In her bookmobile, surging down the highway. Back at the Pancake Mill. If only she'd taken Mary-Rose up on her offer of pie and coffee and a stroll around the peaceful spring.

She, Henry, and the chief stood on Dixie's pretty back porch with a view of the peach orchards and a crime scene. Clouds had smudged out the sun. It was quiet, but not peaceful. The sirens and shouts and stomps of the first responders had turned to tense waiting.

Through the open door, Cleo could see the two EMTs

leaning on Dixie's kitchen island, chatting with a fireman in full gear. Sergeant Earl Tookey, bless his heart, stood at the sink nursing a bee sting and sullenly munching a candy bar. Cleo's favorite deputy—and favorite neighbor—Gabby Honeywell slowly paced the kitchen, hands behind her back, head swiveling.

Following Tookey's sting, the chief had ordered the pantry closed off. A beekeeper and pest professional had been summoned to corral and capture the swarm.

"I *do* understand," the chief repeated for what must have been the third time. "I *empathize*." He released his suspenders. They smacked his puffed chest with a thunk. He laid a hot mitt of a palm over Cleo's elbow.

Cleo only half-listened. Her eyes kept fixing on Gabby. She tried to imagine what the clever young deputy might be seeing in the kitchen. Cleo wished she'd taken in more details herself. At first she'd been so dazzled by all the luck charms. Then there was the rush to turn off the burner and check the oven. She sniffed. The smoke was escaping, creeping out the open door and fleeing with the breeze.

Cleo willed her mind to stop its mental walk at the stove, but the pantry kept flashing back. Cleo clutched her sweater closer. Poor Dixie. The stubborn woman might have vexed Cleo for decades, but she didn't deserve death. Henry shifted closer, touching shoulder and hip to Cleo's.

"I completely understand why you did it," the chief said. "I might have done the same myself. Nope, correction, I *definitely* would have done the same. You have no reason to feel bad."

"What?" Cleo blinked, forcing herself to focus. "You mean, feel bad about calling nine-one-one and requesting you all? Well, yes, I was sure we needed the police, and then there were those bees. It's all suspicious. When you get back inside, be sure to preserve that note. It's the size of a bookmark but shaped like a coffin."

"So you said." The chief nodded, lips pursed. "I hear you. A bookmark. You'll want it back."

Cleo frowned. *Want it back?* The man was acting awfully odd. Usually Chief Culpepper was too busy expounding and explaining to hear anyone but himself. She freed her elbow from his grip by pretending to clean her bifocals. They did have a smudge, but when she put them back on, the situation was no less foggy.

"The pantry door was locked with a key from the outside," she said. "Dixie was trapped in there with those bees. She looked terribly afraid. Well, anyone would. I wonder, could that have killed her? Fear? Or was it the bees? We didn't see blood . . ." Cleo leaned closer to Henry. "It's awful," she summed up, shaking her head.

"And understandable," the chief repeated. "We see this all the time. The bullied, taunted party snaps and lashes out and then, being a good person, realizes what they've done. It doesn't mean you're a bad person—just the opposite. You care. A little too much, obviously, but—"

"What? Taunted party? Lashing out?" Cleo felt the conversation had taken a wrong turn.

Henry looped his arm through hers. "Perhaps we should wait in the bookmobile, unless we can give our statements later at the station. I need to rest my legs. We should check on the pets." He tugged Cleo gently in the direction of away from Culpepper.

With a flash of clarity, Cleo realized what was happening. "Wait, you think *I* hurt Dixie? Me?" She might have been more offended if she hadn't been so shocked.

Chief Culpepper shrugged. "You did 'find' her," he said, adding irritating air quotes. "You had a beef with her. It's well documented. I read all about it in the paper."

Heat rose in Cleo's cheeks, primarily from embarrassment. "I never named Dixie Huddleston as the holder of that overdue book. The article was *supposed* to be about the grand reopening party at the library. The reporter exaggerated."

The chief beamed. "Ah, so you admit you sought to hunt her down and make her pay."

Cleo turned her gaze to the peach orchard, where she set about counting calming trees. She reached twenty-two and a stump before she felt fit to respond. "Mr. Lafayette and I came to visit Dixie because she wanted to *return* that book. I had no reason to be upset."

The chief raised an eyebrow, pale like the close-cropped hair receding from his brow. "Oh? Where is the book?"

Henry answered, saying they hadn't had time to look for any book, nor had they cared to.

But I was looking for the book, Cleo thought. It seemed so petty in retrospect. After turning off the oven, she'd scanned the room, searching the kitchen island and counters, the shelves overflowing with lucky knick-knacks. She hadn't seen *Luck and Lore.* She'd felt vexed that Dixie hadn't been there, holding it out, begging Cleo to accept her apologies and the late fee.

Cleo shifted in her loafers, feeling guilty. But not guilty of murder! Straightening to her full height of five foot three, she said, "I'm sure the book will be there, probably sitting by the front door." She wasn't sure at all. Dixie might have been planning a trick, until someone got the best of her first.

* * *

"Chief?" Gabby interrupted the chief's smiling suspicions. The young deputy lugged a duffle bag and wore a grim expression. "The pest guy called, saying he's delayed. The beekeeper will be here soon. The doc says he'll take that syringe we found to the coroner's to be sent out for testing. The fireman wants to talk to you about burned bread. I can take statements while we wait."

Chief Culpepper slipped back to his natural bluster. "I better get in there and handle all this, then," he said, as if Cleo and Henry had been stopping him. "Deputy, search the perimeter. Collect and record anything odd or out of place. Leave it to me to decide what's relevant. And get statements from these two. Get their fingerprints too."

He marched to the kitchen.

"Elimination prints, I'm sure he means," Gabby said politely.

Cleo released a held-in huff. "No, the chief suggested I was a cold-hearted but relatable killer."

Gabby let the duffle bag drop with a thump and retied her ponytail. The youngest member of the police department,

Gabby was also the only female, African American, and former beauty queen on the force. Cleo's twenty-five-year-old grandson, Ollie, had a serious crush on Gabby. The dear boy dissolved into stammering and blushes whenever he saw her, which was usually often since Gabby lived next door and Ollie lived in the little mother-in-law cottage in Cleo's back garden. For the past month and a half, however, the back cottage had sat lonely. Ollie was down in Louisiana, helping an environmental group clean up an oil slick. Cleo knew he was doing good work, but she couldn't wait to have him back home for the holidays.

Gabby fluffed her curls. "Relatable, you say? I can guess what's happening. The chief went to a workshop last weekend and learned all about 'offering a theme.' It's an interrogation technique. The detective offers a suspect a theory that justifies or minimizes the crime, making it seem like something the detective empathizes with. Like, *'Oh, your roommate ate your yogurt? I get it. I'd have killed him too.'*"

Cleo sniffed indignantly. "He suggested I killed a woman over an overdue book."

A grin flickered through Gabby's serious expression. She swung her ponytail and hefted the duffle. "No offense, but I *can* see you getting worked up about a book, Miss Cleo. It wouldn't be that forty-year overdue book I read about in the news, would it? That's more than a book. That's like a thorn in your foot."

"The newspaper reporter embellished my emotions," Cleo repeated. "What really matters is why Dixie was volunteering to give the book back. She was acting strangely yesterday.

Frightened. She claimed she was about to die. She'd seen signs that death was coming for her, and she wanted forgiveness. That's why she offered to return the book."

They all looked back toward the kitchen. After a beat, Gabby said quietly. "She was right about death coming for her." She shifted the duffle to her other shoulder. "So . . . I should look around the perimeter. Since you're a suspect, I *should* forbid you from coming along."

"What if Henry and I kept a few steps back and volunteered helpful information?" Cleo asked.

Gabby headed down the porch, not answering directly. "This one's creepy. I suspect we'll need all the help we can get."

The young deputy produced a camera from the duffle and looped it around her neck. She began another methodical march, this time around the perimeter of Dixie's fairytale home.

Cleo and Henry followed the promised few steps behind. "You said you found a syringe?" Cleo prompted, hoping Gabby would share.

Gabby photographed a rip in a window screen. "The chief won't want me sharing info with suspects. On the other hand . . ." Gabby glanced over her shoulder and then at Cleo and Henry with a wry twist of her lip. "I could ask y'all, as suspects, if you dropped a generic brand Epi-pen into the floor vent near Mrs. Huddleston's body?"

Cleo played along with the grim game. "No," she breathed. "How terrible." She hadn't been looking in vents. She'd been focused on the note. "Dixie had medicine but dropped it? Oh, she'd be frantic."

Gabby nodded, grim-faced. "Yeah, she would. But the syringe appeared to have been used. Something went wrong."

Cleo and Henry shared a solemn look.

"Tell me about this morning," Gabby said encouragingly. "I need a time line."

Cleo liked details, any good librarian did. She settled into providing an account of the morning. After some internal debate, she decided to tell Gabby about the argument during the Who-Done-It meeting. "I don't want to get anyone in trouble," she said as disclaimer. "It sparked from a heated book discussion."

Gabby was squatting, head tilted, eyes practically on the ground. She snapped a photo of a bent flower stem and another of the dirt below it. Cleo stepped closer and spotted an indentation, possibly a footprint.

"Dixie said she saw the Grim Reaper outside her window," Cleo said.

Gabby rose with an easy fluidity Cleo's knees hadn't allowed for in years. "Okay, we'll add the angel of death to the suspect list. Tell me about this book-club argument. We need a better suspect than you, Miss Cleo, and all information is helpful." She craned her chin up. On a diamond-paned window a few inches above Gabby's head, a dark blob moved against the pane. Cleo realized they were under the pantry. Dixie was just inside. Cleo stepped back and told Gabby about Iris Hays and her outburst over pancakes.

"I don't know why Iris was being so rude, yelling about wanting Dixie dead," Cleo said. "It upset Dixie's friend Pat Holmes," Cleo said. "The whole book group got involved. Some pancake batter got spilled."

"We'll need to talk to Dixie's friends," Gabby said. "This Pat, do you know where I can find her?"

Cleo started to tell Gabby about Pat's cleaning business. "It's at the same property as her home, over on the southwest side of town. Or she could be out running errands after book group or—"

"Or right here," Henry cut in. He pointed across the lawn. Chugging toward them, head dipped and arms churning, came Pat. She stumbled across a bed of bright impatiens, not bothering with the winding path of mowed grass. "Cleo!" she called, waving and nearly tripping.

Gabby stepped out to meet Pat, who stopped just short of the deputy, hands on her knees, gulping like a flounder out of water. Cleo reached Pat and put an arm around her shuddering shoulders.

"Oh, Pat," Cleo said to the sobbing woman. "You must have heard. I am so very sorry."

"I was downtown," Pat said through gasping breaths. "Someone said Dixie Huddleston's dead. Dead! I didn't believe it. I *don't* believe it!"

She turned to Cleo. "There's an ambulance—that means she's okay, right? I told her just yesterday that she was fine, that the signs didn't mean anything."

"I'm sorry, ma'am," Gabby said, her slow headshake and grim expression saying the rest.

Pat sank to the ground. Her fingers clutched at the grass.

Cleo lowered herself too, ignoring the ache in her knees and the chill under the damp grass. She held Pat's limp palm in both of hers. "Henry and I found Dixie. I'm afraid the EMTs couldn't help her. She was too far . . . gone."

"Gone," Pat sniffled, tears making rivers down her cheeks. "Why? How? I didn't believe her! I didn't listen to her. If anyone should have, it was me."

Henry proffered a neatly folded cotton handkerchief. Pat blew and wiped and sniffled some more. Then her eye caught the moving blob on the window. She pointed. 'What's that?" Her eyes widened, as if just now taking in Gabby and the implications of her uniformed presence. "Why are *you* here? The police, I mean. What's going on?"

Cleo looked to Gabby for direction, unsure of how much she should say.

Gabby had regained her composure. "We have some questions regarding the circumstances of Mrs. Huddleston's death," she said briskly.

Pat hefted herself up. With a hearty heave, she helped Cleo to her feet too. Gabby held out an arm to keep Pat from getting too close to the flowerbed with the footprint, but the window was clearly visible and in it, the beekeeper. He wore a mask and protective coveralls and aimed a net at the swarm.

"Did your friend have any trouble with bees getting inside her home?" Gabby asked. "An infestation?"

"Bees?" Pat gasped. "No! Dixie would never let bees get inside. She was allergic. Terribly, deadly allergic!"

Gabby drew out a small notebook, pen poised over it.

"Who else knew about her allergies, ma'am? I'm sorry to keep asking you questions, but we have to know, and time is critical."

Pat stood rooted, mouth open, staring up at the window. The beekeeper came in and out of focus, net waving wildly. Cleo imagined she could hear the swarm fighting back, loud and angry, stingers zinging.

But it was a sharper, clearer sound she heard. A whistle, soft at first but coming closer.

Pat heard it too. She pointed toward the sound, although there was nothing to see in that direction but dense holly hedges. Beyond would be the edge of the back porch and the pathway leading to the cottage.

"Them!" Pat cried, pointing toward the holly. "They knew! Dixie's son and daughter-in-law. They were upset with Dixie. She told them she wanted her cottage back. She was going to kick them out."

Pat's voice had risen to just below a bellow. The whistling went silent for a few moments. When it resumed, it was fading farther away, yet lighter and jollier than before.

Chapter Six

S ome mornings demanded hot biscuits. This was one. Cleo
awoke the next day to church bells announcing the early-
bird Sunday service. She squeezed her eyes shut and burrowed
under her grandmother's quilt. When the next hour chimed,
she squirmed and pried open a heavy eyelid. The quilt was perfectly cozy, but there was a problem. She had biscuits on her
mind, and while Cleo could make biscuits in her sleep, dream
biscuits wouldn't appear in her oven or buttered on her plate.

Cleo resigned herself to rising, both for baking and to
appease Rhett Butler. The Persian stood on her chest. Four cat
paws pressed down. She closed her eyes, yet could feel his
intense stare. He wanted breakfast. Whiskers tickled her face.
A cool kitty nose rubbed her forehead.

"Oh, all right," Cleo said, extricating herself from her cat
and covers. "It *is* Sunday. When will you learn to sleep in?"
Rhett hopped to the floor, mewing in victory, tail pluming
high. Cleo tugged on a long, fluffy bathrobe and stepped into
her winter-fleece slippers. In the bathroom, she threw cold
water on her face, Rhett twining around her legs impatiently.

Last night she'd gone to bed early and exhausted by yesterday's shocks. Rest, however, had eluded her. Nightmares woke her in paralyzing chills. Vaporous images roamed her mind, disturbing flashes of mimes whistling and a silver Airstream speeding toward her to a roaring buzz of bees. It didn't help that Rhett decided to make his version of biscuits on Cleo's head around five thirty, claws kneading, purr like a sump pump in a storm. Cleo didn't chastise him. She was too glad for his furry company.

Rhett bounded downstairs. Cleo plodded. At the foyer, the cat came to a claw-skidding halt. He rubbed his whiskers against the doorframe and stared at the threshold, tail twitching, suggesting someone—or something—was outside. The Persian could be as keen as a bloodhound. Or he could be making things up. Rhett was big on spotting imaginary prey.

Cleo pressed her bifocal to the peephole. In fisheye perspective, her porch looked fine and ordinary. The floorboards were a glossy midnight blue, freshly painted just this fall. The ceiling was a lighter blue. Lots of southern porches sported similar sky-blue ceilings. Haint blue, her grandmother called it, for the belief that it scared off ghosts. It was supposed to fend off bees and wasps as well. Cleo searched her memory. She thought Dixie's porch had a blue ceiling. It certainly hadn't worked.

Cleo was about to turn away, when she heard a squeak, metallic and repetitive. Rhett meowed to be let out.

"Let me check first," she told her cat, who was as prone to leaping into trouble as she was. With Rhett, trouble came in tangles with skunks or aggressive jays.

Narrow windows flanked Cleo's door. She edged back the filmy curtain. A pair of scarlet boots sailed upward, attached to rosy stockings, a flowery dress, a red-wool jacket, and a face she'd known and loved since they were babies.

Cleo swung the door open. "Mary-Rose!" she exclaimed. "You must be freezing." Rhett shot out, heading straight to the screen door, where he meowed more demands.

Cleo continued her faux chastisement of her best friend. "Why didn't you knock?" It was so chilly Cleo thought she might almost see her breath.

"Nonsense." Mary-Rose hopped off the swing and patted Rhett before doing his bidding and holding open the door for him. "Cold air is invigorating. I didn't knock because I thought you might be resting." She nodded at Cleo's fluffy robe and slippers. "I was right."

Cleo tugged her robe tighter. "Come get inside. I'm about to make biscuits."

Mary-Rose slipped off her boots and led the way to the kitchen, where she drew a jar from the inner pocket of her jacket, like a spy turning over state secrets. Her cheeks glowed, as rosy as her name, and her long hair was twisted up in a braided bun. "It's forbidden," she warned. "We won't tell your doctor."

Cleo read the label. "Pecan jam? That sounds delightful."

"It's like pie in a jar," Mary-Rose said. "I had a sample, and I said to myself, 'It's Sunday and Cleo's had a shock finding another body.' Plus being accused of murder is unsettling. I should know."

She did know. Cleo had helped her friend out of that

trouble last spring too. She'd offered friendship and clues, but hadn't thought to bring by pie in a jar. Cleo felt new urgency to get her biscuits going. She set out the ingredients, rationalizing as she tied an apron over her bathrobe. "It looks like it has a lot of nuts. Nuts are healthy. It's spreadable. That means it hardly counts."

"Exactly," Mary-Rose said, leaning back in her chair. "It's a condiment. Like ketchup or hot sauce or pickle relish. No doctor should deny you flavoring."

Cleo's doctor denied her sugar, and Mary-Rose often took the good doctor's side, disregarding Cleo's orders at the Pancake Mill and serving her bitter unsweetened tea and whole-wheat pancakes with plain berries on top. It was kind of Mary-Rose to bring her a restorative treat. Cleo felt better already.

"Why are you out so early?" Cleo asked as she measured out the not-at-all-secret ingredient in her towering biscuits: White Lily flour.

"Early church," Mary-Rose said.

Cleo felt a twinge of guilt. When her dear husband, Richard, was alive, they'd gone to the early service every week, seven thirty on the dot. Everything Richard did was on the dot. Since his passing—heavens, some ten years ago, now—Cleo had shaken up her Sunday routine and a bunch of other routines too. She reassured herself that she'd been right to sleep in today.

Mary-Rose gave a bashful grin. "I shouldn't lie on a Sunday. I went for uncharitable purposes as much as worshipping. Remember how William's childhood pal came for vacation and has since lodged himself in our guest room? I swear, Cleo, my husband has regressed. William has turned into a gossipy, giggly teenager who snickers at bathroom humor. I needed a respite, so I took myself to church. Afterward, there was a lady outside, selling this jam out of the trunk of her car. Sweet temptation. I thought of you."

Cleo told her she was honored.

"I can help more too," Mary-Rose said. "I have a clue, something that'll point to another suspect than you."

"There are other suspects much better than me already," Cleo said. "The chief was just being silly. He'd been to a workshop." She hoped that was all it was. He couldn't *really* suspect her, could he? She cut the butter into her biscuit dough with a strength enhanced by a healthy helping of irritation and a dash of worry.

Mary-Rose popped her jam jar open, unsealed the lid, and breathed in. "This smells like a Thanksgiving dessert table," she said. "I agree. It's silly of the chief to suspect you. But there is a whole newspaper headline about you being on the warpath to get that book back. Some ladies at church were talking about that. Don't worry—I walked by and dropped a loud 'Judge not lest ye be judged' on them." Mary-Rose nodded, looking pleased.

"Very kind," Cleo said, thinking the quote, while good and church-appropriate, didn't actually specify her innocence. *How irritating that people are gossiping about me. How absurd!* She took care not to let her frustration affect her biscuit dough, which she rolled out gently and cut into quick squares. Her mother would have pinched off equally sized rounds or employed the biscuit cutter. Cleo was going for speed. She set the oven timer for a long fifteen minutes.

Thankfully, hot coffee already awaited them. Cleo warmed cream and poured two cups. She was about to ask Mary-Rose about her new suspect when the doorbell rang. This time, the peephole revealed two friendly faces, one glistening, the other furry.

Gabby wore Spandex tights, a pink windbreaker, and flashy running shoes. She was still catching her breath from what must have been a vigorous run. Rhett snuggled in her arms, purring yet frowning.

"I'm delivering a wet Persian," Gabby said, holding Rhett up to reveal damp belly fur, messy with bits of grass clippings and a stray leaf. "He was standing in my yard, holding up his paw. I thought he might be hurt, but he seems fine."

Cleo tsked. "He's silly is what he is. He gets stuck if he runs out into wet grass. He doesn't want to put his paw down on it and thus can't move." She plucked the leaf from his belly and said, "You're just in time. I have biscuits in the oven and a possible clue."

"A fresh suspect!" Mary-Rose called from the kitchen. "And pie in a jar."

Gabby let Rhett down and wiped her brow. "Those all sound like things I need, if you don't mind my appearance."

"You're lovely and dewy, dear," Cleo said. To Rhett's displeasure, Cleo toweled off his feet and belly before getting him his breakfast. While waiting for the biscuits, they made polite chitchat about topics other than murder, like pie and the weather. The timer chimed, but Cleo wouldn't have needed it. She could tell biscuit perfection by the buttery aroma filling her kitchen.

Cleo took out the tray and asked, "Should we wait a decent moment for them to cool?"

"I don't need decent," Mary-Rose said, already unfolding her napkin.

"I don't either," Gabby agreed.

Cleo snagged three biscuits straight from the baking sheet and put them on plates, pleased with the towering layers. She'd learned her biscuit technique from her mother and grandmother and honed it in college, working her way through library school by baking in the dining hall. The layers gave way with a gentle tug, releasing buttery steam. Cleo slathered on more butter and a hefty spoonful of jam. She closed her eyes for the first bite and assumed her guests would be doing the same.

"My," Cleo said after some savoring. "It *is* just like pie."

"Divine," Mary-Rose said. "Fortifying for the unjustly accused." She waved a half-eaten biscuit at Gabby. "*You* don't believe that Cleo here killed a patron over an overdue book, do you? You know our Cleo has all sorts of librarian codes. I assume not murdering the readers is one of them, right, Cleo?"

Cleo was busy helping herself to more pecan jam. Besides, she took that as a rhetorical question.

Gabby made a noncommittal sound. "The chief says we have to 'cast a wide net.' He learned that in a seminar too. Anyone we can suspect, we should. He claims it's only fair."

"True," Mary-Rose said. "Cleo *could* have murdered Dixie."

Cleo nearly choked on her biscuit. "Mary-Rose Garland!"

Her friend looked wickedly pleased. "You're always saying, Cleo Jane: we senior ladies should *not* be discounted because of our age or our gender. We can do anything we set our minds to. Well, except for perhaps that *American Ninja Warrior* reality show. Your knees and my hip would not permit the mega-warped-wall challenge."

Her best friend considered her capable of murder. Cleo decided that, overall, the sentiment was complimentary. "For the record, I did not murder Dixie Huddleston," she said. She added more cream to her coffee before asking, "Do you know the cause of death? Can you say?"

Gabby hesitated. She stirred her coffee, although she hadn't added any cream or sugar. She sipped and stirred some more, gazing over Cleo's shoulder toward Cleo's back garden and the cute little mother-in-law cottage. Cleo knew without looking that she needed to fix up the flower boxes. It looked so lonely without Ollie there.

"What if you guessed and I gave a signal about whether you're on the right track?" Gabby said.

"Allergic reaction," Cleo said.

Gabby gave an obvious signal. She nodded grimly. "The coroner will have to confirm it, but, yes. Beestings."

"You can't charge bees with murder," Mary-Rose said.

"We can charge whoever put them in Dixie's pantry and locked her inside," Gabby countered. "Prosecutors have won murder cases against less. Bullies who forced allergic classmates to eat peanuts, say, or tampered with their lunch, even as a joke. Trapping and terrifying Dixie along with basically poisoning her with allergens? That's no joke. It's a crime. Dixie had her medicine, but it clearly didn't work. We're waiting for tests."

Rhett hopped up on the empty seat by Gabby. She rubbed his ears, and he collapsed in a purring puddle.

"A swarm of bees isn't as easy as a peanut to sneak in," Mary-Rose pointed out. "You don't just hide a hive in your purse."

Cleo looked around her kitchen, with its warm cozy scents and morning light and, blessedly, no bees. "That might narrow down your suspect pool," Cleo said. "I wouldn't know how or where to find bees."

"Oh, I'm sure you could read up on it," Mary-Rose said. "I bet the library has books on beekeeping and bee-thieving too."

Cleo waggled a finger at her friend. "You're determined to make me into a murderer, aren't you?"

Mary-Rose shrugged. "I'm just saying, books provide a world of knowledge. I thought *you'd* appreciate that."

Gabby watched them, head swinging from Mary-Rose to Cleo and back. "Y'all sound like my sister and me," she said with a grin. "My sister claims I could commit the perfect crime because I'm a cop."

"Probably true," Mary-Rose said agreeably.

"I'll be sure to add myself to the suspect list, then," Gabby said. "Along with an angry artist, the son and daughter-in-law, a librarian on a warpath, bees . . ."

Cleo hoped the angry artist didn't know who mentioned her to the police. "Have you spoken with Iris?" she asked.

Gabby got up and gathered more biscuits. "Never better than when they're hot." She placed them on a plate she delivered to the middle of the table. Three hands reached for biscuits.

Gabby concentrated on buttering hers before answering. "I guess I'm not revealing any big police secrets," she said. "Tookey and I tried to talk to Iris, but she wasn't in. She lives with her mom, and mom claims her delicate daughter got up late yesterday, went straight to the book club, and then on to an art fair. It's somewhat of an alibi, since Dixie seems to have died early yesterday morning."

"*Somewhat* of an alibi?" Cleo said.

Gabby shrugged. "It's better than your pre-dawn alibi of being in bed with Rhett Butler, Miss Cleo. But it's not iron-clad. You probably know the Hays place? That big sprawling farmhouse out off Old Coopers Highway? Iris lives in a separate wing in the back. Her studio's back there too. She could hold a dance party, and I don't know if her mother would know."

An absurd image popped into Cleo's head: BOOK IT! throwing a bookless disco bash in the rambling back half of the old Hays farm. She rubbed her head, thinking she was slipping back into last night's nightmares.

"Then there are the most obvious suspects," Gabby said, breaking into Cleo's thoughts. "Do either of you know anything about Dixie's relationship with her son and his wife?"

"I don't think it was that good," Cleo said. "I overheard Dixie calling them 'freeloaders,' and Jacquelyn had an odd reaction to her mother-in-law's death. She looked pleased."

"Those two are odd in general," Gabby said. "They wouldn't let us in their cottage, which seemed strange. You're right—Dixie didn't want them there, but Jacquelyn claimed they were happy to go. Jefferson said up and down that he loved his mother and can't think of anyone who'd even disliked her. He also confirmed Dixie's bee allergy and went on and on about his bee phobia. Now, I get that one! Even after the beekeeper left, stray bees were flying around that kitchen. Tookey got stung again."

Mary-Rose rapped the table repeatedly with coral-colored nails. She cleared her throat pointedly.

Cleo got the hint. "Sorry, Mary-Rose! You have a new suspect. Who is it?"

"I thought you'd never ask!" Mary-Rose leaned over the table. "I heard a *death threat* against Dixie Huddleston. I didn't remember it until this morning, when church gave me time to think. Let me tell you how it happened . . ."

Mary-Rose was a natural at what Cleo's granny called porch lies, tales stretched as long as a lazy summer afternoon. Mary-Rose got comfy, wiggling into her seat like she was warming up for a lengthy elaboration.

"Only the facts," Gabby said.

Mary-Rose lowered her voice. "It was the farmers' market at the elementary school, the day ice fell from the sky."

"That thunderstorm with hail last Wednesday," Gabby murmured.

"Exactly. Well, I'd had too much sweet tea and felt the need to use the ladies' room, which, you know, the school forbids. Safety, my . . ." Mary-Rose stopped short of uttering any rudeness herself. "In any case, I visited the HoneyBucket portable they park over by the gymnasium door. That's when I overheard it. A woman I couldn't recognize, yelling to the tune of 'You'll get what's coming to you! You'll be sorry!' Then there was a slap. Whap! Skin on skin. I didn't recognize the yeller, but when I stepped out of the HoneyBucket a discreet moment or two later, there was Dixie Huddleston, and wasn't she just holding a big red splotch on her cheek?"

"Another threat," Cleo said, feeling bad for Dixie. Dixie used to brag about her good luck and fortune. She hadn't been fortunate at all if so many people disliked her.

"It dilutes suspicion from Cleo, doesn't it?" Mary-Rose said eagerly.

Gabby nodded. "But you didn't recognize the speaker? Anything distinguishing? Pitch? Old, young, definitely female?"

Mary-Rose shut her eyes and squinched her face in concentration, repeating the threatening words. "No," she said, hazel eyes popping open. "I didn't recognize her. Definitely female. Angry. A Southern accent with a little bit of a trill? That's all I have. I think I'd recognize the voice if I heard it again."

"It's something," Gabby said. "Come down to the station later, and I'll make an official report."

Mary-Rose looked rosy-cheeked pleased. "I'm delighted to help. I have other good news too. Well, not *good*, exactly. There's going to be a wake tomorrow."

Cleo had just bitten into another biscuit, so Gabby beat her to the question she wanted to ask.

"A wake?" Gabby said, sounding incredulous. "But we haven't released the body, and I'm not at all sure when we will. It could be days or even weeks." Rhett hopped on Gabby's lap and head-butted her hand, demanding rubs. Gabby obliged, scratching under his chin, a move that sent his back leg kicking. "Goofy guy," she murmured.

"It's not a wake where you actually have to watch over the body," Mary-Rose clarified. "My minister shared the news. Jefferson Huddleston has been calling all around town, saying he and his wife are holding a remembrance ceremony and 'special event' at Dixie's house. Tomorrow evening, five till seven. BYOB and a dish to pass."

"But," Gabby said, frowning in incomprehension, "they're holding it at the main house? That pantry is still roped off as a crime scene. A murder scene!"

Mary-Rose held up her palms in a don't-ask-me gesture. "I know, but relatives do need to mourn, and everyone loves a wake. It'll give folks something to look forward to on a Monday." She winked at Cleo. "It's a good opportunity to look around for clues." She turned an innocent smile to Gabby. "For you professionals, I mean. The police should be there. What if the suspect returns to the scene of the crime?"

What if the suspects were hosting the party? Cleo helped herself to a big spoonful of pecan jam and forced her mind to the important decision of what to bring. Something sweet, she decided. Her Pecan Everything Heavenly Blondies would do. Even better would be the company of Henry Lafayette.

Chapter Seven

"Is this a receiving line or the security checkpoint at Atlanta International Airport?" Mary-Rose stretched her neck, peering over Cleo's and Henry's shoulders. The sun had slipped behind the trees an hour ago. Dim solar lights lit the pathway to Dixie's home. Lights glowed in every window, reminding Cleo even more of a fairytale castle, the turrets outlined against the blue-black sky. In fairytales, bad things happened in such pretty places. That happened in real life too.

Gabby and Leanna stood in front of them, Gabby in her "undercover" outfit of black jeans and a sweater, Leanna hard to miss in her black-and-white polka-dot swing dress with a black cat appliquéd on the front. Only Mary-Rose had stuck to her signature rosy hues and her contention that a wake was for celebrating life as much as mourning death.

No one was doing much of either yet. After ages waiting, Cleo's little group still stood a good two dozen visitors back from the door. Behind them, the reception line stretched down the street and into the darkness.

Mary-Rose gave another impatient huff. "We'll wither out

here. We should have brought snacks." A double-decker pie holder rested between her feet. Cleo had her Heavenly Blondies tucked in a picnic basket along with Henry's funeral potatoes. The dessert bars included chocolate chips, coconut, and pecans—everything heavenly. Henry's potatoes lived up to their name too, containing enough cheese, butter, and artery-clogging potential to prod diners toward their own last rites.

"I'm sure we'll get in soon," Henry said. "It's a lovely night. Not too warm, not too cold. Just right."

Cleo thought again of grim fairytales. She smiled affectionately at her gentleman friend. His beard was freshly trimmed, and Cleo thought he looked adorable in his charcoal wool suit with a red tie and matching silk handkerchief peeking out the front pocket.

The line inched ahead. Feet and baskets scooted forward until they reached the bottom step to Dixie's front porch. The house was certainly done up, Cleo noted with approval. Swaths of magnolia leaves looped along the banister and up and around the door. Icy-white string lights twinkled. A floral wreath spelled out "DIXIE" in white carnations.

Murmurs came down the steps.

"Pass it on," said the lady in front of Gabby. "The clown at the door wants everyone to provide a word that describes Dixie Huddleston. You can't get in until you do." Cleo recognized the woman as another realtor. *How nice,* she thought. Dixie's competitors had come to pay their respects. She quickly corrected that impression.

The woman's companion, a clean-cut young man in khakis and a logo-embossed jacket, shared his word for Dixie.

"Scheming," he said in a stage whisper that carried down the line. "Underhanded." He giggled. His friend raised a shushing finger but tittered.

"One word? Oh, that's difficult," Leanna said. "Lucky? I suppose that's taken already."

"Unlucky?" Mary-Rose countered. "Dead . . ." she murmured darkly.

That clown at the door. Tipping on her tiptoes, Cleo saw Jefferson, framed by light and funeral flowers. Dixie's only son wore black leggings and a flouncy-sleeved blouse, also black. His face was literally painted in grief, from the teardrop drawn on his cheek to his upside-down smile. "Oh dear," Cleo said. "Jefferson's in his mime getup. I hope folks come up with nice words, for his sake."

"Maybe that's what's taking so long," Mary-Rose said.

* * *

"Resolute," Cleo said when it finally came her turn.

Leanna and Gabby had gotten in with *reader* and *realtor*, respectively.

"Fine." Jefferson sighed at Cleo's word, gloomily scribbling it in a lined notebook. Pencil lead and waxy white paint smudged his hand. "This is going to be harder than I thought."

Cleo launched into her go-to statement for grief. "Your sadness and loss will never go away, but with time, the happy memories of your mother will shove aside the sorrow." Her nose twitched from the pollen-sweet scent of lilies. Behind Jefferson, blooms filled the foyer. White lilies, chrysanthemums, carnations, and purple-black roses. Cleo rubbed her nose to keep from sneezing on the bereaving.

"No, not that." Jefferson tapped the pencil with irritation. "It's these words. I'm making a performance poem from them. How am I supposed to work with *indefatigable*? Nothing rhymes with that. Tall is fine but boring, and I have it three times already. *Fierce.* That could be good. I could do spoken word. Slam poetry. Yeah . . ."

Cleo settled on silence as the most polite response. She stepped aside and let Henry give the word she'd provided him: *shrewd*. It wasn't cheating. Henry had only met Dixie the other day, and then, under odd circumstances.

Jefferson took note, mumbling in cadence under his breath. "*Tall* and *fierce, shrewd* and *malicious . . . realtor . . .*" He frowned. "Kitchen is in the back. Oh, but you know that."

Cleo and Henry paused in the foyer. Amidst the floral explosion, good-luck charms covered the walls and sideboards, reminding Cleo of a kids' picture puzzle, so crowded with objects they were hard to pick out. She counted a dozen shamrocks, half as many horseshoes, assorted ladybugs, two white elephants, and a ceramic cat with a bobbing paw. She didn't see a lucky book, at least not out in the open, waiting for her in the foyer. Gabby had searched the whole house looking for *Luck and Lore*, with no luck.

Mary-Rose joined them. "Finally!" she said. "I cheated. I gave two words: *pancake fan*. I don't know if that's true. The few times Dixie visited the Pancake Mill, she informed me her pancakes were better than mine."

"Fighting words," Cleo said. "I won't tell the chief, or he'll put you on his suspect list too."

They made their way toward the kitchen, down a photo-lined hallway.

"Dixie sure liked photos of herself," Mary-Rose observed, as they passed frame after gilt frame of Dixie receiving prizes, Dixie with dignitaries, Dixie posing with "SOLD" signs outside expensive properties. "Is that Jefferson?" Mary-Rose pointed, squinting at a small, framed snapshot. "I think he's in the background in this one. Wasn't there a daughter too? Surely she'll be here?"

Cleo again racked her brain for the daughter's name, sorry she hadn't remembered to look it up. How could she not recall? Amelia? Anna? The puzzled distracted her until they reached the kitchen and lightheadedness caught her by surprise. Cleo caught the doorframe.

Henry placed a hand on her elbow. "Are you okay?"

The kitchen looked nothing like the terrifying scene they'd encountered the other day. The only smoke rose from a skillet of fajitas sizzling on the buffet table. The buzz came from animated chatter. Dixie wouldn't be here—Cleo knew that for sure. Still, she drew a breath and held it as she looked toward the pantry. Police tape crossed the closed door, like terrible gift wrap.

"You're looking pale, Cleo," Mary-Rose observed, frowning at her. "You need food. Let's get to that buffet table."

"I'm okay, honestly," Cleo said. "I just need a moment." She took in the room, recognizing many familiar faces of friends and patrons and folks she saw about town. Gabby had gone to

speak with the chief and Sergeant Tookey, who were both bel-
lied up to the dessert table. Pat stood in a corner, handkerchief
to her nose. Several Who-Done-It mystery readers stood sup-
portively around her. Cleo saw another well-known group and
frowned.

Mercer Whitty stood on the far side of the room, his chin
tucked coyly to his bow tie. Three library board members and
Belle Beauchamp hovered close to him. Belle's blonde bob
shimmered. She laughed at something he said, touching his
arm.

"Why's she here?" Cleo murmured.

"She?" Henry asked. He followed her gaze and said, "Oh,
your bookmobile rival. Did she know Dixie?"

Cleo searched her mental map of Catalpa Springs connec-
tions, but came up blank. "Mercer's looking awfully merry,"
Cleo said. Her mind turned to how Mercer knew Dixie. They
likely crossed in well-to-do circles. Perhaps she'd sold some
property for him? Yes, Cleo thought, sifting through her memories. Dixie had listed a lovely piece of riverfront property Mercer owned. Her billboard and smiling face had hovered over the
parcel for years. Mercer had demanded an exorbitant price.

Cleo blinked. With a jolt, she realized she'd been staring
and spacing out. Worse, she'd been caught. Belle waggled
sparkly fingers at Cleo, smiling brightly and mouthing something Cleo couldn't make out. Cleo managed a weak wave in
return. She knew she should go say hello, but the thought
of Mercer gushing about Belle and bookless BOOK IT!
seemed too much to stomach on top of the already unsettling
occasion.

Mary-Rose touched her elbow. "Cleo Jane, you're looking downright weak. It's not like you to resist a potluck. Are you sure you're okay?"

Cleo let herself be led to the buffet. She dutifully assembled a plate of her favorite foods: three varieties of cheese straws, Henry's potatoes, stuffed mushrooms, cocktail shrimp, and little quiches as pretty as dollhouse pies. Mary-Rose got caught up chatting with a friend. Leanna, who disliked crowds, found a fellow introvert to sit quietly with on the unpopulated back porch.

Henry suggested they find a quieter spot too. Cleo felt a claustrophobic closing-in of warm bodies, hot dishes, and disturbing memories. She was all for finding someplace serene and for doing a little looking around too. When they'd piled their plates, Henry led the way to a sitting room they'd spotted on the way in. Wood trim gleamed, framing the tall doors and windows and magnificent floor-to-ceiling bookshelves. As if tugged by literary magnetism, Henry and Cleo headed straight for the shelves.

"It's odd the police haven't located *Luck and Lore*," Cleo said. She searched all the spines. No luck. Where would Dixie keep a treasured lucky book? By her bed? Under the mattress? A grand staircase wound up from the foyer. Perhaps they could sneak up after Jefferson got through greeting guests and collecting words.

Henry had been tipping his head to read titles. Still sideways, he grinned at Cleo, smile lines fanning.

"I am not *obsessed*," Cleo said, lest he suggest so. "The book's absence is a clue, isn't it? Even if Dixie were about to play a trick on me, she always kept *Luck and Lore* close. She liked to dangle it in front of me and then snatch it away." Cleo checked the shelves again. "It *should* be somewhere in the house, but Gabby looked and couldn't find it. It doesn't make sense."

"So, say Dixie had the book, ready for your arrival," Henry said, picking up the speculation. "But the killer arrived first." He straightened and rubbed his beard in such deep thought that his plate tipped. A cheese straw rolled toward the edge. He righted the plate just in time. "Perhaps we should sit."

Cleo saw the perfect place nestled in the curve of a turret. The half-moon space included two padded armchairs, a little coffee table between them, and low built-in bookshelves under the window. *A perfect reading nook.* Cleo imagined the view in daylight, across the gingerbread-trimmed porch to the pretty gardens and peach orchards.

They settled in. "So the killer comes by," Cleo continued, waving a cheese straw. "He—or she—somehow gets Dixie into that pantry and locks her inside with the bees."

"With that note too, and apparently her medicine," Henry said, shaking his head. "Was it a prank that went too far?"

Cleo had considered that. "But why take the book? Unless Dixie had it somewhere else. Her car? Oh, but Gabby said they searched there too."

"The returns slot at the library?" Henry suggested, chuckling.

Cleo smiled. "That would be just like Dixie. I'll check." She made an effort to enjoy her food, tasting a little bit of everything, from cheesy quiche to a marvelous cheese-straw hybrid filled with pimento cheese. She'd be cheese-logged if she finished every crumb. She put her plate down, dropping her plastic fork in the process.

"I'll get it," she and Henry said, simultaneously ducking under the coffee table. They bumped foreheads, blocking each other's reach, hands sweeping blindly. They lingered a moment, heads together, until Cleo cleared her throat and Henry found the fork.

"Got it," he said, reaching and then straightening. But Cleo had noticed something else. She leaned down farther to investigate. It was a bit of paper, nearly shoved under the bookshelf. A bookmark? One of those pesky magazine inserts? No one—certainly not the homeowner—would care, but now that Cleo had seen it, she wanted to retrieve it.

When she did, she dropped it like a hot potato on fire. It landed between their plates.

Henry drew back with a sharp intake of breath. "It's just like the coffin note left with Dixie, except it's blank."

"Unless . . ." Cleo used a clean napkin to gently turn it over. White text in jagged capital letters filled the space. Cleo read the words aloud: *"Dixie Huddleston, Lady Unlucky, this will soon be your new home."*

Henry said what Cleo was thinking. "That sounds like Dixie's real estate billboards: 'Welcome to your future home.' 'Come home with Lady Luck.'"

They stared at the ominous note, Henry anxiously tugging at his beard, Cleo's heart thumping. "No wonder Dixie was afraid. We have to show this to Gabby," she said. She folded the napkin around the piece of paper. She found a glossy real estate booklet in the bookshelf and tucked the napkin inside for further protection.

"A clue appeared when we weren't even looking," Henry said. "That's some kind of luck."

Cleo prayed it would turn out to be the fortunate kind, and Dixie's killer would soon have a new home: a prison cell.

Chapter Eight

Neither Cleo nor Henry had height on their side. They stood in the kitchen doorway, facing a sea of people. Cleo took a deep breath, as if readying for a dive into the deep end.

Henry suggested they split up. "I'll go right. You go left?"

Right passed by the pantry crime scene. Cleo squeezed his hand and made a plan to meet back up at the dessert table if they lost track of each other. She watched the crowd swallow Henry up. Then she headed in too, gripping the real estate booklet tightly, spine down, so the coffin wouldn't slip out. She didn't get far. Iris Hays spotted Cleo approaching and waved a plastic cup filled with pink bubbly liquid. "A toast to you, Cleo! Woohoo! To Cleo, our finder of bodies!"

The artist wore a red mini-dress over black leggings, a departure from her watery grays. She lurched into Cleo's airspace, her breath vaporous and suggesting that at least one of the punch bowls—or Iris's personal cup—was seriously spiked. Iris looped her other arm around Cleo's shoulder, where it lodged hot and heavy. Cleo fought the urge to step back and free herself. It would be impolite. Besides, she couldn't. A group of realtors, talking loudly and clinking beer bottles, filled in the space behind her.

Cleo reminded herself that she wanted to speak with Iris, and the artist seemed more than happy to talk.

"You're amazing, Cleo," Iris slurred. "At your age . . . still working, driving, managing us Who-Done-Its, finding bodies . . . I heard you might have done *more* . . . Did you? Did you kill her? You can tell me. I won't tell anyone."

"Iris!" Mrs. K., stern principal of the Who-Done-Its, stepped up and informed Cleo of the obvious. "Our Iris has had a touch too much to drink."

Iris laughed and leaned heavily on Cleo's shoulder, her teased bird's-nest hair brushed Cleo's cheek. "I have. I'm celebrating."

"Why are you celebrating, dear?" Cleo asked, leaning her head away.

Mrs. K. sighed and rolled her eyes. "Please, don't get her started again," she muttered.

"Why, you ask?" Iris said. "I'll tell you why!"

Mrs. K. groaned. Cleo smiled encouragingly.

"Because she ruined my life—that's why—and now she's dead, and that's why I'm celebrating!" Iris's voice had risen to a sharp pitch that cut across the white-noise chatter. Cleo could feel the group of realtors shifting behind her. She glanced back and saw that they were all tuned in to Iris.

"Perhaps we should go outside," Cleo said. "For some quiet and privacy." If Mrs. K. cleared a path, Cleo could guide the artist out the back door. Cleo took a step that way.

Iris wobbled but didn't budge. "I want everyone to hear," she boomed. "Dixie Huddleston sold me a house that ruined me. I'm glad she suffered. She got what she deserved!"

Jefferson had been setting up a microphone by the back door. He stopped and gawped open-mouthed at Iris. At the buffet table, Chief Culpepper put down a serving spoon. The realtors made sounds of *ooh* and *mm-hmm*.

"Iris, we're at a wake," Mrs. K. chastised in a tone that surely made her students tremble. It had no effect on Iris.

"Mold," Iris breathed into Cleo's face. "She sold me a house and studio with toxic mold. Ruined my health and my career. Ruined me!"

Mrs. K. was briskly saying that this was a long time ago. "No one knew about the mold then. Your health is better now, living at your folks' house. Your painting is going well. We *love* having you teaching at the school."

Iris shot the principal a thunderous look, and for a second Cleo worried Iris might take a swing at Mrs. K. Instead, she took a swig of her potent punch.

"You know the words I used at the door?" Iris said. "I doubled up. *Good* and *riddance*. Ha!"

Chief Culpepper was coming their way. Mrs. K. was apologizing on Iris's behalf.

"*I'm* not sorry," Iris slurred. "Do you know, when Dixie Huddleston showed up, begging for my forgiveness, she ended up blaming me? She said I was 'too sensitive' and that if I'd had a tougher composition like her and spritzed some bleach around, then the toxic mold wouldn't have bothered me."

Cleo murmured appropriate sympathy, thinking that sounded like Dixie through and through.

Iris raised her voice to booming. "I'm not the only one either, am I? I bet half of all y'all here had troubles with Dixie Huddleston. She was a cheater and greedy and a bully. Am I right?" She pointed in the direction of the realtors, who quickly turned away. "You . . ." she said, her hand wavering toward half the room. "I know *you* did!"

"I'm taking *you* home," Mrs. K. said. With firm efficiency, she swiped Iris's drink, took the drunken artist by the elbow, and tugged. The heavy arm slipped from Cleo's shoulder, leaving her lighter and cooler and more than a little suspicious. Iris certainly had a grudge, a big one if she thought Dixie ruined her life.

"Woooo," Iris cheered as she was being half-led, half-dragged away.

The chief switched direction to follow the departing pair. Cleo was glad. She wanted to show the paper coffin to Gabby first. Gabby would take both it and Cleo more seriously, and she hadn't rudely accused Cleo of murder. Cleo resumed her search for her favorite deputy, but before she could move far, a bell chimed. A sharp ding-ding-ding, like an oven timer gone angry. Cleo covered an ear with her free hand, looking toward the stove before realizing the noise was coming from Dr. Jacquelyn Ames's cell phone.

Dixie's drama-professor daughter-in-law stepped up onto a spindle-backed chair, holding the phone high. Jefferson clambered up on another chair beside her. He gripped a crumpled page in both hands. His face was wax-makeup white, but his ears flamed in a natural blush. His wife had foregone any mime makeup, which Cleo considered wise for any occasion. A white carnation corsage decorated the front of her black dress.

Jacquelyn stopped the chime and tugged down her dress. Cleo's thoughts on her softened. Perhaps Henry had been right about shock and grief causing her previous snippiness. Jacquelyn and Jefferson had certainly done up the house. They'd reached out to the community and welcomed a crowd.

"Attention!" Jacquelyn clapped her hands. "We are here today to remember a woman of unusual character, Dixie Oakley Huddleston. In her memory, my husband and I will be announcing a new venture here at her—*our*—treasured family home.

Cleo's head tilted in curiosity. *A new venture?*

Jacquelyn waved her arms expansively. "But first, Jefferson, Dixie's first and only son, will give a dramatic reading composed of the many fine words you provided today. Jefferson is an award-winning poet and mime trained in the French classical tradition and specializing in slam poetical performance. Considering the solemn occasion, we did not bring an applause meter—the traditional judge of slam poetry contests—but I know you will join me in clapping the house down when he is finished. Let's practice now."

A smattering of tentative claps ensued.

"You can do better than that!" Jacquelyn chided.

Mary-Rose slipped through the crowd, reaching Cleo's side with a relieved "Whew." She leaned close and whispered.

"This is how much I care about you, Cleo. I spotted you having trouble with those Who-Done-Its, so I came to check on you. I abandoned the *dessert* table, which heaven knows is prime territory now that there's homemade poetry on the menu." She glanced at Cleo with concerned affection. "*Are* you okay? You have your color back, but you're looking a tad twitchy."

Cleo felt ready to burst. Of course, she enjoyed poetry. What lover of words did not? However, she needed to find Gabby, and she suspected Jefferson's poems might not be her favorite variety. He was alternately yelling, whispering, and singing out words. Jacquelyn had turned on background music, an acoustic-guitar version of the "Ride of the Valkyries."

"Tall. Realtor!" Jefferson proclaimed. "A woman! A winner. Mid-sixties. Determined. Blonde. Ambition." He lowered his voice. "Blonde ambition."

Mary-Rose groaned. She wasn't the only one. The room rumbled with whispers and movement. People shifted, some inching for the door, others edging toward the food. Still others stood frozen, as if stunned.

"I'm looking for Gabby," Cleo said. "Have you seen her?"

Her friend's eyes narrowed. "*Deputy* Gabby? That's another reason I left the dessert table for you, Cleo. You had that look in your eye. You're onto something, aren't you?"

Henry was making his way through the crowd, pointing behind him. "I found her," he said when he reached them. "Gabby's in the pantry. She was on the phone, but I indicated that we needed to talk to her."

Up on the kitchen chair, dear Jefferson waved solemnly

toward the heavens. "Competitor," he pronounced darkly. "Worthy opponent." The sniping male realtor from the reception line gave a whoop.

Henry led the way, with Cleo and Mary-Rose following single file behind. Crime tape hung loose at the pantry door. Cleo hesitated, remembering the bees and Dixie, telling herself neither would be here anymore.

"I'll keep guard," Mary-Rose announced. "I don't like small spaces or crime scenes."

Cleo didn't either, but Gabby was waving them in, her phone still pressed to her ear. She flashed a quick, tight smile at Cleo and Henry, raised an index finger, and mouthed, *Just a moment.*

"Yes, I see," Gabby repeated several times. "Okay, I'm looking for that right now. Yes. I know . . . like a plunger. Like the other one we found." A male voice that Cleo couldn't make out droned on the other end. Cleo might have guessed Chief Culpepper, but she knew he was nearby and probably wouldn't call.

Cleo looked around the little room, noting that Dixie had kept a nice pantry. The shelves were glossy white and neatly covered in contact paper in a four-leaf-clover print. Dixie had baking goods on one shelf, divided into dry goods, sugars, and canned fruits and extracts. Pickles—cucumber, green bean, okra, and watermelon rind—formed a pyramid in a corner.

Once again, one of Cleo's firmest beliefs was confirmed. Everyone, even opposites and nemeses, had something in common. She and Dixie kept tidy, well-stocked pantries. They shared a passion for books too. Especially *Luck and Lore*. Cleo vowed that after she handed over the clue to Gabby, she'd sneak upstairs and look around. It wouldn't hurt to search again.

Gabby was making signs of trying to wrap up her phone conversation. "Okay," she repeated. "Yes, okay."

Cleo busied herself. There was a bit of grime on an upper, opposite shelf. She tugged down her sweater cuff and reached up, prepared to wipe it away. The sweater stuck. So did her hand when the cuff slipped. A sticky substance coated her sleeve and hand. She sniffed.

"Honey," she whispered to Henry. The shelf held cereal boxes, neatly arranged in a row. As she reached for a box of granola nearest the honey smudge, a hand touched her shoulder. Gabby gently pulled Cleo back, her head shaking "no."

After more hurried "okays" and "thank-yous," Gabby slipped her phone into her back pocket.

"That was the coroner," Gabby said, her eyes stuck on the sticky substance. "Well, look at that. The crime techs said they checked the pantry. They must not have checked every item. You have an eye for detail, Miss Cleo."

Cleo tried not to preen. "Any decent librarian does," she said modestly.

Gabby extracted latex gloves from a slender cross-body purse that didn't look big enough to hold a crime-scene kit. She stood on tiptoes, her nose to the shelf.

"Yep, definitely honey," Gabby said, moving cereal boxes slightly. Two resisted with a sticky squish. Gabby carefully took them down. One box advertised a healthy honey-pecan granola. Its top was open, the box filled to the brim, but not with anything healthy. "A honeycomb," Gabby said, tipping the box to reveal a sticky frame. "This must be where the bees were." She laid out an evidence bag and put the box on top. "I'll need a bigger bag and a thorough search," she said. Her gaze turned downward. "I came in to look for another epinephrine injector. They're big, kind of tubular, you know what I mean?"

"Didn't you already find that?" Cleo asked.

Gabby confirmed they had. "The coroner found several puncture marks. He wondered if there was another syringe. The one we found was, uh . . . defective."

"Defective?" Cleo prompted.

Gabby, a yoga enthusiast, was putting her hobby to good use. She crouched low, chin to the floor, aiming her eyes and a mini flashlight under the narrow space between the bottom shelf and the floor planks.

"Dust bunnies," she murmured. "A clothespin. Ick . . . is that a mummified mouse?" She swiveled and began searching the other row of shelves. "Aha! Miss Cleo, can you reach in my purse and get me an evidence bag?"

Cleo found a packet of evidence bags tucked in beside some lip gloss, an eyeglass case, and a Taser. She handed a bag to Gabby, who dropped in her evidence with a satisfied look that dimmed as she inspected her find. The stubby syringe was encased in a plastic plunger, wrapped with a prominent prescription sticker.

"Looks used," Gabby mumbled. "Now I just need to find one more of these. Dixie's most recent prescription was for three injectors. Seems like a lot." She reinspected all the dusty spaces and the vent too.

"It seems like she didn't have *enough* medicine," Cleo ventured. "It couldn't save her. Were there too many bees? Was it faulty? Out of date?" Cleo wasn't ill often, thank heavens, but that meant she sometimes let her medicines expire. She promised herself she'd do better.

Gabby's lip twisted. "This isn't for spreading around," Gabby said. "I'm telling you because I want you to be extra careful, Miss Cleo. The perp is beyond cruel. The syringe we found before—it didn't actually have medicine in it. It was pure liquid disaccharide." She sealed the bag. "Sugar syrup. We'll need to get this one tested."

Cleo's mind stuck on the word "sugar." For a moment, she wildly misinterpreted. She corrected herself aloud. "The sugar didn't kill her."

Gabby shook her head. "Nope, but it sure didn't help save her from anaphylactic shock."

"Good luck saving yourself," Cleo murmured, reciting the note left in Dixie's clutched hand.

Enterprising Gabby was tucking the baggy and syringe into the hard-covered eyeglass case and then safely into her purse. "Why were you looking for me?" Gabby eyed the real estate guide. "Something with houses?"

Outside, Jefferson's voice rose, followed by some obliging clapping.

"In a way," Cleo said. She briefly outlined Iris's ire about her moldy house and studio. "But most of all, we wanted to show you this," Cleo said. She unwrapped the paper coffin.

Gabby was already readying another evidence bag. Once the paper coffin was inside, she held it up to read. *Dixie Huddleston, Lady Unlucky, this will soon be your new home.* 'Soon,' it says. I wonder when Dixie got this?" She turned the bag, as if to tip out an answer.

Raised voices came through the door, along with the loudest clapping of the evening.

"What is going on out there?" Gabby asked. She put her hand to her purse, and Cleo remembered the Taser inside.

"Just some slam poetry," Cleo said. It sounded like a group slam fest of angry words now. Even so, Cleo was anxious to leave the pantry. She turned the doorknob. It twisted, but the door didn't budge. Her heart skipped. She turned again and pushed hard. The door opened to an apologetic Mary-Rose.

"Sorry!" Mary-Rose said, inching the door open and peaking around. "I was leaning. You might not want to come out here. There's a brawl brewing!"

Gabby didn't hesitate. Neither did Cleo. They stepped out to slamming that wasn't the poetic kind. Jefferson teetered on his chair as two women shoved at each other beneath him. Cleo gasped, not just at the fight, but at who was involved.

She backed up until she hit the doorframe and could go no further. *She'd seen a ghost!* The image of Dixie, thirty years younger. Red hair, fiery eyes, a face pinched in combative determination. The woman sounded like Dixie too, her voice strident and demanding with a hint of grit, like she was chewing on rocks. Dixie's look-alike waved what seemed like a torn poster, rustling it in Jacquelyn's face before tossing it to the ground and tugging at a stunned Jefferson.

"This is my house!" she yelled, dislodging Jefferson from his chair. He fell, flailing, into his wife's arms.

The redheaded woman took his place on the chair. "I am Amy-Ray Huddleston. I am Dixie's eldest child, and this is my house. I won it. Everybody out!" She put her lips to the microphone and chanted, "Out! Out! Out!"

Chapter Nine

"Well, that was interesting," Mary-Rose said, poking bobby pins into her off-kilter bun. "Nice when the whole family gets involved in a wake, isn't it?" She grinned, eyes twinkling in the dim light of Cleo's keychain flashlight.

"You're wicked," Cleo said to her friend.

"Just trying to lighten the situation." Mary-Rose jabbed in another pin. Her hair had come undone in the crush to get out.

"I think you have some lemon pudding cake on your ear," Cleo said. She reached out with her sweater sleeve to brush it off, before realizing the sleeve was still sticky with honey. She let the dessert stay where it was.

They stood on Dixie's lawn, the sounds of night creatures and chattering people all around them. Overhead, no stars poked through the clouds. Henry had gone to look for Leanna. Cleo hoped he would find his way back to them. She was keeping her keychain flashlight on as a beacon.

"You shouldn't have waded into that melee," Cleo further chided her mussed friend. "It's like they tell you on airplanes:

In case of an emergency, don't grab your carry-on luggage. Exit as fast as you can."

Mary-Rose was unrepentant. "You'd be down one picnic basket and some casserole dishes if I hadn't waded in," she said. "Who knows when any of us will get invited back to this place? I don't think Amy-Ray Huddleston will be sending out thank-you notes and handing back potluck dishes."

One by one, the lights in Dixie's windows were going dark. Cleo regretted that she hadn't had time to sneak upstairs, but now she could imagine the layout, and Dixie's likeness, roving from room to room, flicking the switches.

Jefferson and Jacquelyn were on the porch, illuminated by an outdoor chandelier and twinkling fairy lights. Jefferson slumped in a rocker. Jacquelyn waved in broad, angry gestures at Gabby. Cleo didn't have to be a trained mime to guess the conversation. Jacquelyn wanted Amy-Ray out of *her* house. She wanted Dixie's daughter arrested for assaulting Jefferson. Jacquelyn had been yelling such things—along with charges of police harassment—as Gabby and Tookey struggled to herd the unhappy family trio outside. They'd just gotten them out when Amy-Ray bolted back in, locking the doors behind her.

"Exactly what Dixie would have done," Cleo said, watching a silhouette take form in an upper turret window. The shadow waved, tauntingly, before fading back and disappearing.

"Her spitting image too," Mary-Rose agreed. "Dixie would be so proud."

Would she? As far as Cleo knew, Dixie and her daughter hadn't spoken in years. "Amy-Ray hasn't shown her face in town for so long, I forgot her name," Cleo confessed. "It's a shock to see her. I thought I was seeing a ghost, she looks so much like her mother."

"Maybe she is a ghost," Mary-Rose said. "It would be just like Dixie to come back to haunt us. I notice you haven't found your overdue book yet. That's what ghost Dixie would do too. She'd hide it from you. Run off straight through walls, waving it at you. It gives me the shivers."

"You don't believe in ghosts," Cleo pointed out. "You've told me."

Mary-Rose shrugged. "I *wish* I did."

Three figures emerged through the darkness. Henry had a little flashlight on his keychain too, having bought a matching set for himself and Cleo. He lit the way for Leanna and Pat.

"Thank goodness Mr. Henry found us!" Leanna said. "It's chaos."

"It's a disgrace," Pat sputtered. "Dixie would be so upset. Her wake was ruined!" She sniffled and Henry produced another clean handkerchief.

Cleo tried to console Pat. "It was a fine event before the fight. Such lovely flowers. Nice of Jefferson to read his poetry too."

Poor Pat remained stubbornly inconsolable. "Dixie thought chrysanthemums and lilies were bad luck. She called them death flowers. She didn't like poetry either. Jefferson should know that."

"The food was fabulous," Mary-Rose said. "Even if some of it got in my hair. I should get home and take a shower. This has been *something.*" She gave Cleo a sticky hug. Leanna headed home too, saying she needed to study.

"I suppose we should go as well," Cleo said. She felt ghoulish, watching the family drama. Ghoulish didn't seem to bother the bulk of the guests. As they made their way carefully across the dark grass, Cleo overheard bits of excited conversation. Folks played back the fight and theorized about the murderer. Cleo was guiltily heartened *not* to hear her name. That is, until they passed the real estate agents.

"I saw that librarian sneaking into the *death pantry,*" the snarky male agent said in a scandalized stage whisper. "The white-haired one. I read about her in the paper. She's on some warpath, like she's vowed never to rest or retire until she gets back an overdue book. They say she might have killed Dixie."

"Oh!" Cleo huffed.

Pat took her arm. "Come on," she said, sounding less shaky. "Don't listen to them. Some people enjoy being mean. *I* believe in you, Cleo."

"Me too," Henry said, his hand resting on her back. "You ladies take your time. I'm going to go along ahead and get the car turned around. The lane is apt to be a parking lot."

Pat and Cleo made their way slowly down the dim walkway. At the gates, they stopped and looked back. Chief Culpepper pounded at the closed door. Jacquelyn continued to gesticulate, now to both Sergeant Tookey and Gabby. The house had gone completely dark except for the blinking string lights.

They were turning to leave when Pat gasped. "What is *that?*" She pointed upward. A torn banner fluttered above them. Another, higher up, was still intact.

Cleo squinted to catch the text. The banner was white, with glow-in-the-dark green text. "'Huddleston House—Future Home of Mime over Matter School of Productions'? Is this what Jacquelyn meant when she said a 'new venture?'"

"Dixie would die again if she saw this!" Pat cried, throwing a hand to her heart. "A mime school would be her worst nightmare for her home. This is why they invited us, isn't it? To promote their awful school." She gasped, turning wide-eyed to Clco. "Is this why they killed her? Or was it Amy-Ray? What's she doing back here, claiming her mother's house? Or Iris—she was being awful too!"

Pat was as quivery as the tomato aspic passing by in the hands of the minister's wife. Cleo reached out a comforting hand. "The police are working hard," she said. "There are new leads and—"

"But Cleo," Pat cut in breathlessly. "*You* remember what happened last time. The police got off on the wrong track. You solved the case. You could do that for Dixie." Pat clutched at Cleo's sleeve. "We could do it together. I *have* to do something, Cleo. She was my best friend."

Cleo was glad Henry had gone ahead. The parking situation looked truly atrocious. Besides, the dear man would have fretted to see her seriously considering the idea. Cleo felt bad for Pat and wanted to help her. She might just help herself too. Nabbing the real killer would clear Cleo's good name.

* * *

Henry likely would have come inside. Barring that, he might have given Cleo a gentlemanly kiss. As it was, they stood on

Cleo's front steps under the dark sky, Pat a solid block between them.

"See you soon," Henry said, leaning around Pat. Pat had accepted Cleo's offer of beverages. Henry had politely begged off. He had a pug to walk and he was tired. "It's been an . . . interesting . . . outing," he said.

Cleo's mother had two uses of the word *interesting*. One came straight from the dictionary: "intriguing, riveting, arousing of curiosity." The other was a polite slap-down, issued in a syrupy drawl and used in such phrases as, "My, isn't ham an *interesting* addition to this orange Jell-O."

Henry's *interesting* was clearly the meat-in-gelatin usage.

Cleo watched her gentleman friend go, thinking things had been going so well, with her relationships, her work . . . with *not* coming across dead bodies. That was the thing with good fortune. One often didn't notice it until the pendulum swung the other way, crashing everything in its path.

"I'm intruding, aren't I?" Pat said, wringing her hands. "My mother always said, I'm an an overstayer. I should go. I have work schedules to figure out for tomorrow. Half my cleaning staff wants off for the holidays, and Albert is out of town, *of course*, of all the times."

Albert was Pat's husband, a jolly man who treated himself to lengthy golfing excursions. He was in Arizona, Pat was saying, adding why *she'd* never go there: too hot, too dry, too many things that bite. She swatted away a November-slowed mosquito and declared that she also couldn't tolerate spicy Southwest foods.

"You're not intruding at all," Cleo said, as good manners

sometimes required polite fibbing. Truth be told, Cleo yearned to kick off her shoes and settle in on the sofa with Rhett and a good book. But Pat was clearly anxious and upset, and understandably so. It had been an *interesting* evening.

Cleo unlocked her front door and nearly got bowled over by a galloping Persian. Rhett yelled a meow, turned tail, and trotted back to his food bowl. In the kitchen, Cleo fed Rhett an evening snack and made hot herbal tea for herself and Pat. She hadn't had a chance to hit the dessert buffet, so she also brought out the "extra" Heavenly Blondies she'd kept behind. She offered the plate to Pat first.

Pat held up a palm and turned her head, as if Cleo were serving up sin. "My doctor says I'm on the verge of obese. High blood pressure, bad cholesterol, arthritis, weak knees, low vitamin D, brittle bones, jaw and spine troubles. It's all in my mother's family, in our genes. My mother and grandmother and aunts and all the women before them too, every one of them were gone before they hit seventy. No, that's not quite true. My eldest sister made it to seventy and a day."

"Surely not," Cleo said. "Everyone's different."

"That's what Dixie used to say," Pat said with a weak smile. "She said I dwelled on health problems too much and that dwelling would make them become real, and it'd be my own fault if I got sick. She never liked to talk about her own health. That's why I feel so bad too. She tried to tell everyone about the omens, and we all blew her off. Even me! Those omens sounded so . . ." Pat looked down at the table. "So silly. So unreal."

"You had no way of knowing the threats were *real*," Cleo said. She made a decision. If she was going to investigate—and if Pat wanted to help—they both had to acknowledge what they were dealing with. A terrible person, someone who'd taunted and terrified Dixie right up until her death. Cleo selected an indulgently massive blondie and told Pat about the coffin notes, the threats she and Henry had found tonight and earlier by Dixie's body.

Pat leaned back in her chair, mouth and eyes widening in horror.

"She didn't tell me," Pat said in a small voice. "Why wouldn't she tell me?"

Cleo wished she knew. More than that, she wished she had a clue as to who'd sent the notes. She took a fortifying bite of blondie, thinking her slightly raised glucose levels were minor compared to Pat's family history. She let Pat think about the situation and then asked, "Are you sure you want to look into this? It could be dangerous."

Pat bobbed her head, her bangs flapping. "Yes! More than ever! Does this mean you'll do it? You'll investigate?"

"I'll do my best to help the police," Cleo said, slightly concerned by Pat's enthusiasm.

"Where do we start?" Pat asked. "What did you do last time you caught a killer?"

Luck popped to Cleo's mind. But it wasn't only chance. Cleo had done research and interviewed people. She'd chased down details and engaged in a little deception too. "Librarians gather information," she said, glossing over the rest. "That's all I did."

Warm peppermint wafted from their teacups. Cleo sipped, breathing in the herbal mist.

"You're being too modest," Pat said. "Who should we start with?" She put down her teacup hard. Tea sloshed and she jumped to mop it up with a napkin. "Oh, but maybe you don't really want me tagging along. I might be a burden to you. I don't know anything about detecting."

Cleo hurried to assuage her worries. "I'm no professional either, but I do know you're one of the most valuable people in this investigation, Pat. You knew Dixie best. You'd know who she might have had troubles with too. Her enemies . . ."

Pat stared into her tea. "I hate to think about that, but you're right. I suppose I do know some things."

"Like her children," Cleo prompted. "Who do you think her estate will go to? Jefferson and his wife? Amy-Ray? What do you know about Amy-Ray? Do you know where she's been living? What she's been doing?" She realized she was bombarding the poor woman. She halted her questions and smiled encouragingly across the table. "Sorry. I have a lot of questions."

"So do I," Pat said. She took a moment before answering. "If I had to guess, I'd say Jefferson would inherit," Pat said. "Or neither of the children. Dixie didn't like to talk about Amy-Ray, but I'd heard rumors she was living over in Claymore, working as a natural healer. Or was it a manicurist? A hairdresser? I can't recall. It's sad, though, her being so close, yet the two of them so far apart. What I wouldn't give for a daughter . . ."

Cleo knew that Pat had a son who was named after, took after, and favored his father. He'd moved away to a hot, dry place with many golf courses.

"Maybe Dixie reached out to her daughter?" Cleo asked. "She was making amends."

"I can't imagine Dixie going *that* far," Pat said. She raised her shoulders in a helpless shrug. "It's hard to explain. Giving back your library book would be one thing, but admitting she was sorry to her own daughter? That's personal. She'd have to have been desperate."

The wall clock ticked loudly in the silence that fell over them. Rhett hopped on Cleo's lap and purred. Cleo ruffled his fur. Rhett always knew when she needed some feline comfort. "Why did Dixie and Amy-Ray fall out?" she asked. Rhett stretched his head up to knock against her chin. His fur smelled of fresh grass. His breath had a whiff of Tuna Delight.

Pat smiled at him. "He's a cutie. I wish Albert wasn't allergic, or I'd get a kitty. Anyway, Amy-Ray . . . She and her mother butted heads like two billy goats. I think the last fight was about some boy Amy-Ray liked and Dixie didn't. Amy-Ray left the day of high-school graduation and said she wasn't coming back until Dixie showed her some respect. Those two should have been like peas in a pod. I know Dixie felt bad, not so deep down. But she'd never admit she was wrong or that she'd hurt someone. Dixie always thought folks would forgive her." Pat sniffled afresh.

Cleo refreshed their teacups, balancing a snuggly Persian in the crook of her elbow.

Pat stared out the window, to where Ollie's little cottage sat dark. "Dixie and I were friends since kindergarten. She said she never remembered how we met, but I always will. She stole the cookie out of my lunchbox."

Cleo chuckled. She relayed the tale of Dixie blowing out her birthday candles. They both had a much-needed laugh.

"That's Dixie, through and through." Pat chuckled. "I can see her doing it. Not everyone understood her. She was the way she was."

"What about Iris Hays?" Cleo asked gently, sorry to break the cheerier mood. "Iris told me tonight that Dixie ruined her life. Mold? Do you know what happened there? Mrs. K. seemed to know."

Pat didn't answer right away. "Yes," she said slowly. "That awful mold. Dixie sold Iris a house and studio years back. Turned out, both were riddled with mold, the worst kind, in the walls and under the floors, pretty much anywhere it couldn't be seen until too late. The mold got into Iris's paintings. The way Iris tells it, those paintings were going to be her big break—her ticket out of town. She went to show them at an exhibit in Atlanta. The mold spread to every painting in the place. She got kicked out and banned from future shows. She got sick too. Bad lungs. Headaches. She blamed the mold. To make ends meet, she had to take up substitute art teaching, which she detests. Dixie knew about that mold from the start, but always claimed she didn't. Last week, she finally admitted it to Iris, part of her making amends. It didn't help. Iris was madder than ever. I felt so bad for Dixie . . ."

Cleo felt bad for Iris. How terrible to have her dreams and health shattered. "I'll share this information with my neighbor Gabby, the deputy," Cleo said. "This will give the police the upper hand when they talk to Iris. See? You're already helping."

Pat twisted her teacup. "I wish I had a police officer next door. I don't feel good about this, Cleo. After what happened to Dixie? For all we know, the killer was right there among us at the wake! I don't feel safe!"

In what Cleo took as evidence of her shaken state, Poor Pat lifted the tea towel and grabbed the biggest blondie on the plate.

Chapter Ten

Work came first for Cleo the next morning, a frosty day cloaked in wispy clouds and breezy hints of winter. Cleo bundled up and added a woolier blanket to the peach crate Rhett snuggled in when they drove. Words on Wheels had several scheduled stops: a nursing home, a handful of home visits, and a drop by the preschool.

Cleo enjoyed every stop. Most importantly, so did her patrons. Cleo felt affirmed in her plan to keep up her bookmobile schedule, even after the library reopened. Kids loved visits by the mobile library. So did those folks who couldn't get out as much. For them, Words on Wheels was a window to the world. Cleo did a brisk book-lending business, as always. However, few patrons other than the preschoolers wanted to talk about books.

Gossip spun faster than Cleo's wheels on the open road. Most folks wanted to hash out the gory details of Dixie's disturbing death and the brawl at her wake. Others thought Cleo—Catalpa Springs' own Miss Marple—might have insights. She used her sleuthing reputation to turn the tables, asking folks for their theories and suspects.

She discovered what she already knew: residents of her tiny hometown had vast imaginations. It was a lovely trait for promoting reading. Not so useful for narrowing down murder suspects. Still, Cleo believed in the power of data and writing things down. By the last stop of the morning, she'd compiled a list that included various serial killers (real and fictional), the postman, a beekeeper, a hairdresser, a ghost said to haunt Dixie's home, another ghost, an honest-to-goodness extra-terrestrial spotted hovering over a local dairy barn, an entire real estate office, the Baptist Ladies' Raffle Club, and—most absurdly—Cleo herself. More realistic names included those she already knew: son Jefferson, daughter-in-law Jacquelyn, prodigal-daughter Amy-Ray, and angry Iris, as well as a handful of disgruntled real estate clients and colleagues and rafflers who'd lost out to Dixie's good luck and/or cheating.

After her final stop of the morning, Cleo treated herself to lunch at the Pancake Mill. She craved restorative pancakes and the company of her best friend. She then headed back to town, where she dropped Rhett at home and proceeded on to Fontaine Park. She had one more scheduled stop before meeting up with Pat.

While the bookmobile sat at the center of town, Cleo enjoyed visits by Henry, who was out walking Mr. Chaucer, and her cousin Dot, who ran a little general store downtown. She was even happier that Dot had brought some fortifying oatmeal cookies, which they savored while sitting on a park bench. What Cleo didn't enjoy was a visit from the pesky reporter from the local paper. The persistent young man had snapped unwanted photos of her and Words on Wheels, crouching low and angling his zoom lens up.

"Ignore him," Dot advised.

Cleo tried. However, she feared he'd captured all the worst angles of her chin and her frown, and would twist her polite refusals to speak of Dixie's death and her missing book. The experience left her edgy. When Dot returned to the store, Cleo retreated to her bus and the comforting presence of books.

At five minutes to two, Cleo was tidying her shelves, readying the bookmobile to close for business as soon as Pat arrived. Three minutes later, Pat thumped up the steps, apologizing and breathing hard.

"Sorry I'm late!" Pat scraped back her bangs, which promptly flopped back over her flushed brow. She wore a tan windbreaker, faded jeans, and a T-shirt advertising "Holmes Homes Cleaners." She looked bedraggled, in outfit and spirit.

"You're not late at all," Cleo said. "You're a couple minutes early, in fact."

Pat breathlessly explained that she'd had to cover for one of her cleaners. Then she'd had troubles with her van's engine and a tractor that held her up on the highway. She exhaled loudly and sank onto the back bench seat flanking the kids' corner of the bus. She rolled her neck and stretched her ankles, wiggling her sneakered feet up and down.

"If you're tired or don't have time, we can do this another day," Cleo said. Or she could go herself, which might be for the best. Last spring, Cleo's sleuthing had almost gotten a loved one hurt. She didn't want to put anyone else at risk.

Pat planted her feet firmly on the floor tiles. "No, I asked you to let me help and I meant it." She stood, smoothing down her windbreaker, which rustled right back to wrinkly. "Do you want me to drive? My van is working. It's just rattling in the engine when it starts."

Cleo had spent many misguided decades letting other folks take the wheel. "I'll drive," she said. "A visit from the bookmobile tends to put folks in a happy mood." She winked at Pat. "And off guard."

Pat twined her fingers. "I was worrying all night. Jefferson or Jacquelyn or *both* could be responsible. What if they come after us? I have bad ankles. I can't run or fight."

Cleo held up her cell phone and made a show of slipping it in her pants pocket. "I have my deputy neighbor on speed dial, and nine-one-one preprogrammed too. But I don't intend for Jefferson and Jacquelyn to know we're suspicious. We'll say we're stopping by to see how they're doing. They're hardly likely to attack two virtual strangers who've come visiting."

Cleo suspected that Gabby and Henry might see the situation otherwise. However, Cleo had known Jefferson as a child. He'd been gentle and sensitive, almost too passive even when bullied. Logically, he was a suspect, but Dixie's death had been planned, awfully and elaborately, for optimal terror. The killer was fueled by high emotion: greed, anger, hatred, revenge, or some mix of all of the above. Cleo simply couldn't see that person being Jefferson.

Pat continued fretting. "What if Jacquelyn is the only one there? She'll shut the door on us for sure!"

"I have a secret weapon." Cleo headed up the aisle, past the tidy shelves of books. She sat down in her captain's seat, buckled up, and nodded to the picnic basket tucked beside Rhett's crate. "I stopped by the Pancake Mill earlier. I have a fresh-baked blueberry pie." No Southerner would be so rude as to reject bereavement food. Especially pie.

* * *

The peach orchards surrounding Dixie's home looked lonely, the limbs darkened and stark in the rain. Drizzle spit from the clouds, and the Mime over Matter banner flapped in the wind. Dixie's house stood quiet and dark too. Cleo wondered if Amy-Ray was still inside, lording over the house she claimed she'd won. Cleo and Pat hurried up Dixie's walkway to the porch, both for cover from the rain and to peek inside.

Pat hung close to Cleo, glancing in each window nervously. "I keep expecting Amy-Ray to appear and throw us out," she said.

"It doesn't seem like anyone's inside," Cleo said. The house had an empty feel. She'd seen it happen before. A home took on the spirit and soul of its owner. When that person departed, so did the homey atmosphere. "Henry was saying, he's always thought this was the loveliest house in town," Cleo said.

Pat murmured agreement. "It is pretty. Albert and I thought about buying this place once. I had a connection with the owner. Thank goodness we didn't. Think of the cleaning!"

Cleo could see that if you cleaned for a business, you

wouldn't want to do it at home, especially in a massive Victorian mansion. They made their way around the porch and down the path to the cottage. The cottage windows were dark too, dimming Cleo's hopes of visiting/interrogating the occupants. She consoled herself. If no one was home, she'd just have to share the pie with Henry. Cleo was smiling, thinking of that enjoyment, as she knocked on the door, aiming for one of the few spots without peeling paint.

She jumped when it opened before the third knock.

Jefferson wore a frilly periwinkle apron splotched with damp spots and suds. Sweatpants flopped out at the knees.

"Oh!" Cleo said. "Jefferson, dear, we're so glad you're home." She held up the pie, as gorgeous as a jewel in its clear plastic carrier.

He eyed it suspiciously.

"Pie," Cleo said firmly. "Miss Pat and I were worried about you, so we brought you a pie. You remember Pat? Pat Holmes, your mother's dear friend?"

Pat nodded vigorously. Cleo stepped forward, putting a loafer over his threshold, smiling brightly. "We'll come in and visit a spell. Is that okay?"

He shrugged. "Sure. Okay. It's just me. Jacquelyn's at a conference in North Carolina. Lucky her to get out of town, right? I'm trying to clean up. I'm sorry it's a mess."

Cleo took this as the usual disclaimer against a little clutter. She was wrong. Jefferson was being modest in the opposite way. It wasn't a *bit* of a mess. It was a mess of massive proportions. Stacks of cardboard boxes brushed the ceiling and dominated most of the limited floor space.

"You're moving?" Cleo asked, feeling Pat hovering anxiously at her side.

"We never unpacked." Jefferson navigated around the box mountain. Somewhere under mounds of paper and bubble wrap, a coffee table likely stood. A sofa and two armchairs huddled against a wall, dressed in more clutter and rusty plaid upholstery that Cleo suspected would be scratchy.

"I was making coffee," Jefferson said. "Can I get you some?" He cleared papers from the armchairs, waving for them to sit. Pat perched on the edge of her seat, looking ready to jump up and flee. Cleo confirmed that the armchair upholstery was scratchy. As she waited, she read the labels on the nearest pile of boxes. "J. Office. Important." "J. Research files. Important." "Drama. J.'s Important."

Jefferson returned with a tray of mugs, a carton of creamer, and a box of cookies. "Do you need sugar?" he asked, looking worried.

Yes, Cleo thought. "No, thank you," she said aloud. "None for me. This is lovely."

"Lovely," Pat parroted. "No sugar."

The cookie box boasted its contents as sugar free, dairy free, wheat free, nut free, peanut free, gluten free, GMO free, and—most disturbingly—raw. Pat took two. Cleo, for once, found herself able to resist a cookie.

"Are these all your boxes?" Cleo asked, pointing to the "J. important" cartons.

Jefferson flushed. "Those are Jac's. All the important stuff. Her permanent office at the college isn't available yet, so she's keeping them here. Mine are over there." He nodded toward a stack labeled "Clown," "Mime," and "Jeff stuff." The handwriting matched the important labels. Cleo guessed it was Jacquelyn's.

"I remember you always liked theater and costumes," Cleo said. "I'm glad you found a calling you love. You're starting a school, we see?"

"Yes, we saw that," Pat said, her tone verging on accusatory.

"You'd be the only ones who noticed," he said petulantly. "It was supposed to be the grand reveal last night, until Amy-Ray ruined it."

"A reveal at a wake?" Pat said.

Pat wasn't the most subtle interrogator, Cleo thought, but she got to the point. Pat could be the bad, blurting cop to Cleo's pie-bearing good cop.

Jefferson shrugged and fumbled with untying his flouncy apron, muttering that he'd been doing dishes. "Why not at a wake? It's like a new rebirth for the house, a new beginning."

"Your sister," Cleo said over Pat's mutters. "That was quite a surprise. Did you know she was coming?"

Jefferson's face flared red. He tugged the apron off and tossed it on the coffee table. "No. We didn't know. We didn't invite her. No one's seen Amy-Ray for ages. The police had to go inside and drag her out of Mother's house. Now no one is allowed back in until after probate, and that won't be fun either. Amy-Ray says she has a written something or other from Mother, saying she gets the house."

Cleo glanced to the main house, which looked even more massive from Jefferson's cluttered little living room. The property would be worth a lot by Catalpa Springs' standards too.

Whether for sentiment or greed, it was a house she could see family members fighting over, maybe even killing over.

Jefferson took a raw cookie and chewed glumly. "Amy-Ray's always been a bully. I might never have been Mother's favorite, but she let me live here. At least she and I still *talked* to each other. That's more than Amy-Ray did." Tears welled, and he turned away.

Cleo felt bad. She hadn't intended to make him cry. "Pie," she said brightly. "Let's have some pie. I'll help you get some plates."

"None for me, thanks," Pat said. "I'm good with these wonderful cookies." She took a healthy bite and chewed as if gnawing on tree bark.

Cleo cut herself and Jefferson big slices, figuring they might as well divvy up Pat's portion. Settling back in the scratchy chair, she tried to lighten the mood. She smiled encouragingly at Pat and repeated, "We just wanted to stop by and see how y'all are doing, didn't we, Pat? It must feel lonely around here with the big main house empty."

Jefferson was tucking into his pie. "Yeah," he said between bites. "The police keep coming by, but Jacquelyn says we shouldn't talk to them without lawyers. The chief seems really nice. He understands me. He gets my art and poetry and miming."

"Oh, he's very understanding," Cleo said, thinking Jefferson would be a good target for Chief Culpepper's empathy-based confession technique. If Jefferson hadn't crumbled already, maybe he was innocent. She ate some pie, blueberries bursting under the buttery crust. It was so good, she almost forgot where she was and why.

"Did you do it?" Pat blurted out. "Did you taunt your mother with her fears? Kill her?" She slapped the coffee table, and they all jumped, Pat included. She flung a fist to her mouth and shot Cleo an apologetic look. "Sorry!" she said aloud. "Oh no, Cleo, you have pie on your . . . down your . . . It's my fault for startling everyone."

A blueberry balanced on Cleo's cream-colored blouse, prominently over her heart. She caught it with a napkin. A large purple stain remained.

"What?" Jefferson sputtered. "No! You're Mother's friend, how could you think that? I couldn't hurt Mother. All those death signs she saw? I never could have done any of that. The police say someone must have planted them—the dead bird and the Grim Reaper and stuff she said she saw and those bees! I couldn't do that, especially the birds and bees. I'm phobic about winged things. Ask my wife. She'll be happy to tell you what a big old baby I am when it comes to insects. Swear to the heavens, I get sweaty around butterflies. I couldn't even help Mother with those birds in her kitchen. I'm useless. Mother said so."

Pat squirmed in her seat. She caught Cleo's eye. "We should go?" she said, the statement rising in a question.

Cleo might have stayed longer. However, Pat was uncomfortable, and now Jefferson was too, and Cleo had pie on her chest. "Before we go, may I use your restroom to put some soap on this stain?" Cleo asked. "I don't want it to set." The stain did bother her. She also wanted to see more of the little cottage.

Jefferson gave directions to the only way to go, down the hall. The passage was dark and narrow with floorboards that cried out at each step. Cleo glimpsed a tidy bedroom. The bathroom featured mauve fixtures clumped in so tight she could barely turn around. She dabbed water and soap on the spot, which only made it spread wider. She leaned over the sink, holding the fabric to the mirror as she rubbed soap in a circle. The mirrored front of the medicine cabinet hung open an inch.

Cleo's hand moved to the mirror. She hesitated. She shouldn't. She wasn't the type to snoop in people's medicine cabinets. Their refrigerators, yes. Their bookshelves, most certainly. A bookshelf, Cleo believed, was the window of one's heart and soul.

However, they had come to investigate. Cleo opened the cabinet, and a plastic tube fell into the sink. She picked it up and recognized an injector, labeled with a prescription. She squinted at the letters, always so tiny and hard to read, expecting it to be Jefferson's or Jacquelyn's. She gasped when she read Dixie's name, highlighted in neon yellow. Two more tubular injectors wobbled on the narrow cabinet shelf.

This could be the missing syringe Gabby sought. The deputy would want to see this. Cleo gave thanks that she'd put her phone in her pocket. She pressed Gabby's number and held her breath until Gabby answered. Then she ran the water for cover and whispered what she'd found. "What should I do?" she asked.

"Get out now," Gabby ordered. "Please, Cleo. I'll be right over."

Gabby hung up. Cleo flushed the toilet and ran more water, thinking of Dixie's life-saving medicine, replaced with sugar syrup. To do that, the culprit needed access to the syringe and Dixie's home. Jefferson and Jacquelyn had both. With a tremor to her hand, Cleo replaced the plastic tube on the shelf. The cabinet creaked as she shut it, and again when she opened it right back up. She wanted a photo. What if Gabby couldn't get inside and someone destroyed the evidence? Cleo aimed her phone camera at the vials. She was messing with the camera, which always got stuck on video, when footsteps sounded in the hall. A step, a squeak, and then five more heavy tromps. The sound stopped just outside the bathroom door.

"Everything okay in there?" Jefferson's voice.

Cleo froze. She recalled young Jefferson reading to kids at the library. She thought of current Jefferson, a man who wanted to mime and perform poetry. Was she being silly? Foolish? Foolhardy? Gabby was on her way, and Pat was just outside. Cleo steeled herself. She took several deep breaths and swung the bathroom door open.

"Jefferson, this is wonderful!" she exclaimed brightly, pointing to the cabinet and borrowing the chief's presenting-a-theory technique. "You've found your mother's prescription! The police have been looking all over for it. They'll be delighted!"

Chapter Eleven

"It's like our mothers always said: *Trouble comes to those who go looking for it.*" Mary-Rose adjusted her rosy-red shawl and grinned, suggesting she approved of seeking out trouble. She and Cleo stood at the corner of Main and Catalpa, the park at their backs and a bright new day ahead.

Cleo might have protested, except Mary-Rose and their mothers were right. Cleo had gone poking at trouble, and now it had spotted them. She watched with unease as a rusty Toyota jerked into reverse.

"Oh dear," Cleo said, her sparkly sense of a fresh new day dimming. She'd woken with such hope. Yesterday, when Gabby and the chief arrived, pounding at his door, Jefferson had dutifully turned over his mother's prescription, as well as himself for questioning. Cleo had stayed up late, hoping to see Gabby and get an update. When her deputy neighbor didn't return, Cleo assumed police were busy solving the case, which meant she could get back to her business. *Library business.* She'd been heading over to check on the renovations when she ran into Mary-Rose. And now Jacquelyn.

"Maybe Jacquelyn just wants to give us an update," Cleo said.

"Uh-huh," Mary-Rose said, watching the sedan buck backwards. "If you're lucky, she'll chew you out silently, in mime. That would be pretty elaborate, though. How do you act out, *You went to my house bearing Trojan pie, rifled through my medicine cabinet, and got my husband arrested*?"

"Jefferson was only taken in for questioning," Cleo clarified. "Unless he's been arrested since."

Another driver—going forward in the correct lane— beeped at the careening Toyota. He was rewarded with a series of rude hand gestures, flung out the open window.

"Look, she's miming already," Mary-Rose said mildly.

Cleo groaned. She'd made unfortunate eye contact with Jacquelyn as the Toyota passed. The drama professor hadn't looked happy then. Cleo didn't expect a pleasant greeting now. "You should go, Mary-Rose. Go enjoy your errands."

"No way I'm leaving you alone with her. She could be a killer, for all we know." Mary-Rose firmed her stance in red rubber boots speckled with mud.

The Toyota jerked to a stop, a back wheel bumping up over the curb. Cleo and Mary-Rose stepped off the sidewalk into soft grass.

"You!" Jacquelyn sputtered. Dark hair frizzed around her face, like a gathering tornado. "You caused me a lot of trouble."

"Jacquelyn," Cleo said. "I'm . . ." She almost said she was sorry, but was she? *She* hadn't done anything wrong. Well, not really. The medicine cabinet had been ajar, and there were extenuating circumstances to good manners. "How is Jefferson?" she asked instead.

"How is he? Like you care! He spent the night with the police, the fool!" Jacquelyn released the steering wheel long enough to slap it with both palms. "I had to leave my conference, catch a red-eye flight, and drive all the way back down from Atlanta after I learned—hours too late—that my husband was 'helping the police with their inquiries.' Like I don't know what that means. They're trying to pin it on him. On *us*!" She puffed in exasperation. "I missed my conference talk to get here. Now I have to track down a decent lawyer in this Podunk town."

Mary-Rose huffed indignantly. A couple with a poodle strolled by, all glancing back nervously at the Toyota, parked halfway over the curb, and its sputtering driver.

"It's good of you both to *help* the police," Cleo said, careful to stress that they were helping. "They've been looking for his mother's medicine. I suppose they asked you previously? Maybe you forgot? It's such a stressful time."

Jacquelyn's knuckles whitened over the steering wheel. A messy pile of papers and books filled her passenger seat. Boxes obscured the backseat, and to-go coffee cups littered the floor and console. "Yes, it must have slipped our minds," Jacquelyn said tightly.

Cleo realized that presenting a sympathetic theory could backfire on an interrogator. She'd just provided Jacquelyn with an explanation.

"These small-town police," Jacquelyn sputtered on. "Why would we tell them anything? They're out of their depths and grasping to place the blame on the easiest target: Jefferson. My husband is an innocent."

Cleo noted that Jacquelyn hadn't said he *was* innocent.

"You took advantage of him," Jacquelyn continued. "Tricking him into letting you in, pretending like you cared, letting him think you were nice little senior ladies coming by to visit. You're a meddler, you and that friend of Dixie's."

Cleo stepped back. The words stung worse than a slap. She didn't like to think that she tricked anyone. "We brought by a blueberry pie. We do care," she said. "We wanted to see how you all were doing."

Jacquelyn glared back. "Jefferson's mother let him share her epinephrine prescription because we didn't have insurance to pay for it until *I* got my college job. It was the one kind, maternal thing that woman did for her son. *You* made it into something bad."

"I didn't . . ." Cleo started to say. "I'm sorry," she said truthfully. She did feel bad for Jefferson, at least for the sweet, sensitive boy she'd once known. Jacquelyn said nothing, prompting Cleo to fill the silence with perky chatter. "All facts are good," Cleo said. "The more information the police have, the quicker they can identify the perpetrator. If they can eliminate Jefferson, they're that much closer to the truth, and we'll all be safer. My goodness, Jacquelyn, a murder happened a few steps from your home. You must be nervous."

Jacquelyn maintained her stony glare. "I'm busy and irritated," she snapped. "I don't have time for any of this. I *certainly* didn't have time to go around terrorizing my mother-in-law, like that foolish police chief suggested. Why isn't Amy-Ray being hauled in for questioning? You know, I found her prowling around the property this morning when I got back to town. I bet she was the one sneaking around before too. I *told* the police, a few days before her death, Dixie railed at Jefferson and me, accusing us of tromping on her violets under the kitchen window. *I* had no reason to go over there. Jefferson wouldn't dare step on his mother's precious flowers. Someone was prowling around before her death, and it wasn't either of us."

"So you think it was Amy-Ray? Did you see this prowler?" Cleo asked, ignoring Mary-Rose's nudge and whisper of "Looking for trouble."

"I am too busy to keep to anything but my own business," Jacquelyn snapped. She revved the gas. The car bucked backwards. With a huff, Jacquelyn wrenched it into drive. "You'd be wise to mind your own business too." Her left hand moved from the steering wheel, the index finger uncurling in a slow, ominous point. Just as slowly, as if each word was its own command, Jacquelyn said, "Stay. Away. From. Us!"

Mary-Rose backed up, tugging Cleo's jacket. Cleo stood firm, eyes fixed on the pointing finger, which was now curling back. The window rose, tires squealed, and Jacquelyn Ames peeled out, cutting off the sole car peaceably rolling down Main Street. The other driver tooted his horn. The responding blare curled around the corner.

Mary-Rose inhaled deeply. "Well! If you ask me, she's a more likely suspect than her husband. She has . . . what shall we call it? Verve? Determination?"

She had verve, all right, and anger. Cleo had no doubt that Jacquelyn was good at research—and planning too.

However, that didn't make her a killer. "I hope I didn't put the police onto the wrong direction," Cleo said, her sunny feeling now clouded over.

"All you did was go visiting, with a pie," Mary-Rose said. She winked at Cleo. "And go looking for trouble."

* * *

Mary-Rose set off on her errands. Cleo continued across the park alone, dwelling on Jacquelyn's words and Amy-Ray's prowling around the property. She intended to ask Gabby about Amy-Ray. She'd like to visit Dixie's daughter too. Cleo wondered if Amy-Ray liked pie.

When she reached her destination, however, thoughts of murder and suspects drifted away. Cleo stood in front of the Catalpa Springs Public Library, transfixed by the beautiful sight. The blue tarps patching the roof were long gone, replaced by sturdy metal panels. Where the toppled oak once stood, a graceful redbud now grew. The wraparound porch curved unbroken, and painters had freshened up the exterior with a pale palm-frond green that set off the thick ivory trim.

Cleo patted the porch railing affectionately, thinking about all the building had seen. It had begun life in the late 1800s, built as the fine home of a family named Tipple. Alfred and Emmaline Tipple had made and lost a succession of fortunes growing peaches and raising ten children here. Cleo sometimes imagined all those little feet running the halls. She pushed open the heavy front door, wondering what Emmaline Tipple would make of the renovations.

Surely the original owner would approve. A local wood-worker had replicated two decorative corner pieces around the doorframe to the reference room, peaches carved in bas relief. Inside, he'd mended and replaced the built-in bookshelves. The wood glowed in rich mahogany tones, awaiting a final coat and seal. Paint-test splotches dotted the walls. Best of all, no tree limbs poked through the ceiling, which boasted plaster in elegant swirls and an antique chandelier donated by the Historical Society. The cast-iron lamp had once hung in this very space, then the Tipples' dining room. It had come home.

Cleo felt *she* was returning home too. Her entire life, she'd been coming to this library, since the day her mother carried her in as an infant. She's spent her entire working life here too. Wonderful decades had flown by. *Five decades.* That was Cleo's not-so-little secret.

The grand reopening coincided with Cleo's fifty-year service anniversary at the Catalpa Springs Public Library. By coincidence, the contractor had picked the day as his sure-to-be-done date. Cleo hadn't mentioned her work anniversary to anyone. She didn't want others making a fuss about it. However, it was a huge deal to her, marking a massive milestone and an even bigger decision.

The library would reopen, but Cleo Watkins wouldn't be returning full-time to the circulation desk. She'd continue captaining Words on Wheels, making way for Leanna to eventually take over main library operations.

Cleo ran her hand along a dusty shelf, thinking the temporary closure had been a blessing in disguise. With Words on Wheels as their sole library, Cleo had discovered how many people benefitted from the bookmobile. She'd always taken getting to the library for granted, but a lot of folks couldn't visit easily. Kids whose parents juggled multiple jobs. Neighbors, young and old, who lived far out in the rural reaches, without transportation. Lonely souls who might otherwise be forgotten in nursing homes or hospices. Plus, it was just plain fun. People lit up when they saw Words on Wheels approaching. It was like driving an ice-cream truck in a heat wave, only better because books were a thrill in any weather.

Cleo spun slowly, standing in the hallway, breathing in sawdust, paint, plaster, and varnish as sweet as perfume. The sawdust got to her, and she sneezed.

"Bless you!" came from somewhere on the other side of the building. Moments later, Leanna followed. "Pretty snazzy, isn't it?" Leanna smoothed her pale denim overalls, the knees sporting patches decorated with embroidered flowers. Her long, honey-colored hair was tied up in a polka-dot scarf. Cleo thought of Rosie-the-Riveter in cat-eye rhinestone glasses.

"Gorgeous!" Cleo allowed herself to gush. "Did you see the carved peaches on the doorframe? Mr. Hernandez did a lovely job."

Leanna had seen the peaches, of course, but they both gazed up to admire again. Strips of paint samples poked out of Leanna's pockets. She'd been researching late-nineteenth-century colors and a palette that would appeal to the Tipples and modern designers. She favored a porcelain white for the hallway, a blue-sage green in nonfiction, and a surprisingly bold blue for the kid's room. The Reference and Reading rooms would get coats of peachy cream. "Concord ivory,"

Leanna's paint chip called it, although Cleo didn't get "ivory" or anything "Concord" about it.

Cleo and Leanna stepped over wrinkled dust cloths. "The painter is coming back next week, after the sawdust settles down," Leanna said. "Then we can let everything dry and air out well before opening night." She ticked off her fingers in a silent calculus of days. Cleo had found herself doing the same.

Leanna began listing the handyman roundup for their new tech center, her voice swelling with pride. The library would serve as a community hub again, with computers for kids and job seekers, genealogists, and even "cybrarians." Cleo smiled at the last term. A cyber-librarian linked into libraries and archives across the globe, like an astronaut, an information explorer. Information flew fast through Leanna's systems too. Cleo liked fast. Zooming through the Library of Congress or surfing NASA's space photos was as thrilling as speeding down the highways in Words on Wheels.

The phone rang at the main desk, and Leanna jogged over to answer it.

Cleo smiled at the sound. The library was truly coming back to life. She listened to Leanna saying agreeable things. However, when her young colleague returned, Leanna looked as sour as a lemon in vinegar.

"We're getting a visitor," Leanna said through a groan. When she said the name, Cleo let out a groan of her own.

Chapter Twelve

"Mr. Whitty said he has thrilling news," Leanna said. She frowned. "Do you think he means it?"

Before Cleo could express doubt about good news from Mercer Whitty, Leanna swung toward sweet optimism.

"Ooh . . ." Leanna said, eyes brightening. "Maybe he finally read that proposal I wrote up about the summer reading program. Do you think he's going to fund it? It's a perfect match for the Whitty Family Foundation. I know it seems early to start thinking about summer, but it's not really. Those kids will go through a lot of books. We'll need to make sure we have enough for every age group and different subjects and . . ."

Leanna burbled on. The summer reading program did match the stated purpose of Mercer's family founding. Cleo, however, doubted that a kids' reading program thrilled Mercer. She'd witnessed Mercer fall head over smitten heels for Belle Beauchamp and the bookless BOOK IT!

"I should warn you," Cleo started to say.

Leanna was distracted, busily shaking out a paint-speckled

drop cloth. Dust plumed. Cleo's nose twitched as footsteps thumped across the front porch.

The front door creaked, and Belle Beauchamp stepped in with a sunny smile. Mercer Whitty sidled up next to her, the library board secretary nervously slipping in behind him. The secretary avoided Cleo's eye and skittered into the reference room.

Leanna put down the drop cloth. "Warn me?" she whispered.

Cleo didn't have time to answer.

Belle strode their way, little clouds of dust puffing up under her heels. "Hey, Cleo," she trilled, coming to a stop by the circulation desk. "Mercer told me I simply *had* to come by and visit. He wouldn't take no for an answer, would you, Merc?"

A sly grin rose under Mercer's turtle-beak nose. "I *can* be convincing."

Belle gave him a twinkling laugh before turning to Leanna. "I've heard *all* about you, Cleo's li'l mini-me librarian. Why you're as cute as a button and so is this old place. How quaint!"

Mercer ran a finger over a dusty shelf, nose crinkling. "It's filthy in here."

"Excuse our dust!" Cleo said brightly. "We're in the final flourish of renovating, as you know."

Mercer sniffed and turned to Belle as if Cleo hadn't spoken. "*Quaint* is perhaps the kindest word. Even after all this mess is cleaned up, what are we left with? Stuffy. Trite. Dull. We are mired, stuck in the smothering quicksand of the old, I am sorry to say." He didn't look sorry.

He gazed at Belle like a puppy in love, wide-eyed and bouncy in his snakeskin loafers. "In contrast, BOOK IT! is the very height of modern," Mercer simpered. "You see why I feel you're the *perfect* person to help us out. We are in desperate need of your innovation and branding skills."

"You're too kind!" Belle said, touching his arm and making him quiver. "Let me take a look and see what we're dealing with." Belle strode through the library, Mercer loping behind, Cleo and Leanna dragging their heels.

Leanna tugged at Cleo's sleeve, holding her back as Belle and Mercer headed into the kids' room. "Miss Cleo, what's going on?"

Cleo whispered back. "It's like we saw the other day. The man is infatuated with Belle and her bookmobile. I didn't want to worry you at the time, but he talked about Belle applying for our part-time opening. I tried to discourage them both, saying it didn't sound like a job she'd be interested in." Mercer seemed to have found a way around that.

Leanna groaned.

Belle strode back to the main hallway. "Yes, I can help! I'll be your consultant. It's good y'all are still in the construction phase. You're poised for success. Once I'm done, you'll be so brand new, you won't even recognize this place."

"No!" Leanna sputtered.

Cleo patted Leanna's elbow. "What Leanna means is, we're just fine, thanks so much anyway. We're in no need of fixing or consulting. Now, thank you all for coming. We won't keep you." The final phrase was her mother's polite version of *"Shove off."* Any gracious southern lady would recognize it as such.

Cleo waved an open palm toward the exit, her version of kicking unwanted visitors to the curb.

"Wonderful!" Mercer said, ignoring Cleo. "Let me show you more, Belle—may I call you Belle? We'll be working so *closely* together."

Mercer could move fast when he wanted. He swooped into the reading room and pointed to a table piled high with boxes and cords. "The so-called technology center will be here," he said. "Already, I see how your bookmobile has better offerings than what we have planned. This is so . . . boring, tired."

Leanna jumped in. "It's not finished yet! It will be really great and interesting." Cleo's beloved protégé was an introvert on top of shy. Leanna usually held in her words and feelings, but if pushed too far, she sputtered like a boiling kettle. Cleo put out a comforting hand. It was too late. Leanna was steaming over.

"We'll have laptops patrons can use in the library," Leanna said, talking fast. "New databases to access newspapers and journals, and a kids' station called All Hands on Tech. We got a state grant and a matching grant and some money from a will and . . . and it's all going to be amazing! I mean, really interesting." Leanna sputtered to a halt. "Sorry," she said. "No, I mean, I'm not sorry, I'm . . ."

"Sorry? Not sorry?" Mercer said. "Words, young lady. Think about your words."

Cleo saw Leanna's mouth open, about to form an automatic "sorry."

"It will be lovely," Cleo said quickly. "We're bubbling over with enthusiasm. We'll have some cutting-edge resources for those who want them and good, old-fashioned quiet spaces for readers."

"See?" Mercer said, turning to Belle. "Quiet. Old-fashioned. Like worn-out pajamas. This is exactly why I *must* hire you, Belle. What was the title you prefer? Creative consultant? Innovator?"

"Wait a minute," Cleo started to say.

"A minute?" Mercer held up a gold wristwatch and bobbed his head for a few seconds. "Okay, we waited a minute. Now what?"

"Mercer, you're such a card!" Belle laughed.

He didn't question the logic of that. He was too busy blushing.

"Mr. Whitty," Cleo said in her briskest of librarian's tones, "as you are aware, our renovations plans have already been approved by the *full* library board. We will not be making any changes at this late hour."

Mercer had teeth like little piano keys, Cleo noted. They were tight and square, and he flashed them at her before glancing back at his watch. "Hardly a late hour, Mrs. Watkins. It's only nine thirty-six."

Cleo held in a frustrated huff. "We do *not* have a job opening for an *innovator*. Our current opening is for a part-time librarian, experience and degree required, to be chosen by the full board and head librarian." Cleo was the head librarian. She had no intention of hiring Belle. Belle seemed nice enough and misguidedly enthusiastic. However, she was in no way qualified. "Ms. Beauchamp is welcome to apply, of course. We'll be giving all applicants full and equal consideration."

"Belle won't want that mundane, part-time job," Mercer declared. "As I've already informed the board, my foundation will fund a contract consulting position so that Belle can help you ladies whip this place into proper shape. Why reopen at all if your new is already outdated? The board is enthusiastic. Thrilled, in fact. Belle and I spoke with several members at that ridiculous wake, and they are all agreed."

Cleo's mouth hung open—catching flies, her mother would say. Cleo snapped it shut, since she certainly didn't have anything nice to say either. The board secretary popped her head around the doorframe, eyes wide as a bunny's in headlights. She ducked back.

Mercer's fingers had come to rest in a church-steeple pose. He blushed at Belle. "All I need to know for the contract is the title you prefer."

Belle gave a little clap. "I've been thinking. I had the *best* idea. *Innobrarian!* Isn't that cute! It's 'innovator' mixed with 'librarian.'"

Leanna slumped into a chair. Cleo's head spun. Reasoning with Mercer seemed hopeless. She tried appealing to Belle directly. "Belle, it's very kind of you to consider us, but I'm afraid we can't accept. Leanna and I—the main library staff— are happy with the direction of our library. Besides, we can't steal you away from the Claymore Library. It wouldn't be right."

"I hear you," Belle said in a sugary drawl. "So many of my clients say the very same thing. *'We're not ready. We're happy the way we are . . .'* Your concerns just prove you need what I call 'shock innovation.' Don't y'all worry. It's like getting a shot. It'll be over before you know it, and all for the better. We'll have a great time! Look at all the fun we had bookmobiling together! Ooh . . . I have some ideas for your old bus too. If we take out some of those bookshelves, you'd have all sorts of fresh space."

Before Cleo could respond, Belle spun on her heels and strode to the door. "Gotta go! I'm meeting my own specialty consultant. Mercer, honey, once you get that innobrarian contract written up, give me a call and I'll scoot right over."

"Good day, ladies," Mercer called out as the front door creaked open, and the board secretary slunk out behind him.

"No, it's not a good day," Leanna muttered to the closing door. Leanna continued to sputter, so agitated her glasses slid off kilter. "How could they call our library dull? *'Shock innovation'*? An *'innobrarian'*? This is absurd." She stomped her sneaker. "I knew that bookmobile with no books was going to be trouble! Those two just can't picture our finished product. Once everything's all set up, everyone will love it. Right?"

"Of course!" Cleo said, more confidently than she felt. "I'll talk to the board. At least half of them hold seats because they love libraries. They'll understand our side." The other half were there because of their money, and Cleo feared they'd be harder to sway. They'd likely see Mercer's offer as a benefit, a *free* consultation. But free could cost the library, the bookmobile, and Cleo's legacy too. Cleo needed to clear her head, and she knew what would help: talking out the troubles with Henry Lafayette.

"Will you be okay working alone here if I pop out for some air?" Cleo asked.

Leanna was busy rooting, head deep in a packing box. Her voice came out muffled. "As long as those two are gone, the library and I will be just fine."

Chapter Thirteen

O utside, the day still looked sparkly. The temperature hovered just above the level of chilly air-conditioning, and a single cotton-ball cloud dotted a bright blue sky. Cleo reminded herself to be wary. At Main Street, she looked both ways, scanning for Jacquelyn and her Toyota. At the park, Cleo picked up speed, anxious to get to Henry's. Consumed in her thoughts, she strode by the bubbling fountain with hardly a glance. She cut a diagonal across the lawn and veered away from a patron prone to lengthy chats. Cleo even passed an adorable infant without pausing to fawn. When she reached the other side, she stopped short.

Henry's shop and home occupied a corner brick building. Sun hit the gold lettering spelling out the shop's name, "The Gilded Page." The wood panels along the front gleamed in a deep ebony paint, reminding Cleo of Old World bookstores she'd seen in photos and postcards. It was lovely, except her view was becoming blocked.

A red pickup hauling a silver Airstream pulled up. *BOOK IT!* Music filtered from the camper. The truck honked. Cleo frowned, head lobbing to her shoulder, as the shop door opened and Henry emerged. The truck and camper reversed, obscuring Cleo's view of her gentleman friend. A few moments later, the pickup and camper pulled away. The street returned to silence. The view was back, but Henry wasn't in it.

Cleo adjusted her bifocals and told herself she'd misread the situation. Henry had probably gone back inside. She crossed the street, avoiding a slow-moving SUV searching for parking. A "CLOSED" sign hung jauntily across the door. Henry often forgot to flip his sign over. The antiquarian book market wasn't a booming one anywhere, let alone in tiny Catalpa Springs. Henry did most of his business transactions online. In the back of the shop, he had his book "surgery," where he mended geriatric books, fixing broken spines and brittle glue and touching up paint and pages, often offering his services and skills for free. He and Mr. Chaucer lived upstairs in a cozy apartment lined with bookshelves and well-stocked in cozy reading spaces.

Cleo knocked and waited, reading the shop hours she knew by heart. "Monday through Friday—when open. Weekends and holidays, nights, special occasions, and inclement weather—at whim." Had whim taken him off with Belle? Heaven forbid he was smitten like Mercer. Teenage jealousy rose in Cleo. She tamped it down, recalling Belle's words before leaving. Belle had mentioned meeting her "own" specialty consultant. Cleo sighed, an ember of jealousy remaining, stoked by disappointment.

A raspy bark came from inside, followed by anxious whimpers. Cleo went to the picture window and tapped on the glass. She smiled and waved at Mr. Chaucer, who goggled up at her, head bobbing in recognition. With effort, the elderly pug launched himself up his ramp, specially made for access to his window-box seat. When he reached the top, he waggled his curlicue tail, turned in a circle, and plunked down on his satin pillow. Within moments, his eyes drooped into sleep.

Cleo wished she could spend the afternoon napping. She cataloged her options. She could go back to the library and help Leanna, although she was no help with computer setup. Or . . . The perfume of fresh-baked delicacies wafted down from the Spoonbread Bakery. Some strawberry shortcake spoonbread would calm her nerves. The sweet, pillowy cross between cornbread and a soufflé might spark a helpful idea, and strawberries were fruit. Her doctor wouldn't have to know.

Cleo was halfway to the bakery, anticipating sweet delights, when she spotted the good doctor, sitting at the one of the outdoor patio tables, smack in front of the entry.

That doctor! She was everywhere.

Cleo turned heel and headed toward a nearby neighborhood. It was no use being among yummy baked goods if she had to stick to health food. She walked on, letting her feet choose a path that passed by a little clapboard home once owned by her late Auntie Audrey. Cleo slowed to picture the cozy kitchen. She wished her aunt was still there. Auntie Audrey was always generous with her sampler boxes of chocolates and with good advice.

A cool cloud of melancholy swept over Cleo, until she realized her aunt would always be with her. So would her wisdom. A smile spread across Cleo's face and into her heart as she whispered one of Audrey's favorite tips for taking on an adversary. *"Slay them with sweetness."*

Cleo smiled wider, picturing her aunt rampaging through a chocolate box, poking and nibbling until she found a favorite flavor, coconut cream or chocolate cherry. Aunt Audrey didn't mess around with candies or situations she didn't like. There was a second part to her advice too. *"Then knock 'em cold with the truth."* Audrey's old one–two.

Cleo felt as light and bright as the day. She had a plan. She'd sweet talk the board members and then hit them with data about best library practices. Leanna could help with the latter. They'd come up with sensible, written goals and guiding principles for the library and bookmobile. Cleo became so wrapped up in plotting, she didn't notice that she was strolling straight into a coffin.

Chapter Fourteen

"**M**iss Cleo, hop!"

A young girl's voice. Cleo blinked and refocused, realizing she was outside the elementary school. Happy screams and excited words and laughter filled the playground. Cleo stared at her feet. She didn't hop. A coffin, clear as the day, stretched out before her.

The chalk outline covered three sidewalk squares, divided into twelve numbered blocks, some decorated in pink-chalk skulls. A coffin hopscotch? *A Halloween leftover,* Cleo told herself. The skulls were actually quite cute, grinning wide, with eyes outlined in flower petals. What wasn't cute was the little black coffin lying in square six just beyond Cleo's shoes. It had writing on it. White jagged letters that looked disturbingly familiar. Cleo stepped farther into the grave.

"Miss Cleo, stop! You have to hop that square. Number six. If you don't hop, you get turned into a ghost." Little girl imitations of ghostly *whoos* followed, peppered with giggles.

Cleo made herself turn away from the coffin. She smiled at a familiar freckled face framed in fiery red curls. Zoe, age nine, was Mary-Rose's grandchild and one of Cleo's favorite young friends.

"Like this," Zoe said. With a gust of wind carrying the scent of grape bubblegum, Zoe hopped by, grabbing the little coffin as she passed. It had been awhile since Cleo played hopscotch. At least two decades. She was trying to recall the rule, when Zoe tossed the coffin again. It rolled toward square seven, hit a sidewalk crack, and bumped askew to land against Cleo's shoe.

"Sugar!" Zoe said, her grandmother's favored alternative to cussing. "Miss Cleo, can you toss back our hopscotch shooter, please and thank you?" Behind Zoe, two other little girls shifted up in line, ready for their turns.

"Zoe," Cleo said cautiously. "What is this game?"

"Hopscotch." Zoe replied in the flat tone kids use when thinking adults as dense as petrified stumps.

Cleo smiled. She'd asked for that. "I meant, where did you get this design for the outline and this little . . . toy?" Cleo reached down and picked up the object. It was wood, painted black, only a few inches long but heavy in her hand. The words sent a chill up her spine. *Finders weepers. To whoever finds this, welcome to your next home.*

Cleo stared at the words, willing them to change. They were too similar, in sentiment and handwriting, to the awful notes they'd found at Dixie's. Whatever this was, it wasn't a toy. Cleo found a fresh tissue in her purse, gently wrapped the wooden coffin, and tucked it in her coat pocket.

"Hey," one of the other girls protested, stomping a high-top sneaker. She had buzz-cut dirty-blonde hair and jeans with holey knees. *Mothers used to have to patch those,* Cleo thought. Now the young folk bought frayed and ripped pants on purpose. "That's our shooter, ma'am. Can we have it back? Please?" The girl stepped forward, holding her palm flat out toward Cleo.

"I'm sorry, dear," Cleo said, wondering how she should explain the situation to the kids. "I have a friend who's a policewoman, and she's looking for things like this. It's very important. You made an important discovery."

The third friend nudged high-top girl. "We've still got the other." She reached in her own pocket and another coffin sailed past Cleo, landing on square eight. She whooped and flew past Cleo, a cascade of ebony braids bouncing behind her, up the chalk blocks and back again, grabbing the toy coffin as she went.

"Kayla wins!" Zoe declared, raising the girl's hand. "Champ!"

Kayla gave a toe-touching bow just as the school bell rang. "Lunch!" they squealed in chorus.

Now Cleo did hop. She jumped in front of the schoolyard gate. "Girls," she said, having to bend only slightly to reach their level. "This is very important. I'm a friend of Zoe's and—"

As she'd hoped, Zoe confirmed this with a vigorous nod and "Yep!"

"I need to know where you found these toys. The little wooden, um . . ."

"It's a vampire casket," Kayla said. "Like Dracula sleeps in during the day." All the girls giggled, and talk scattered into an elaborate fantasy world of castles and girl warriors with flying horses and superpowers and—

Cleo gently cut in to ask when and where they'd found the vampire casket.

"This morning, on the way to school." Zoe glanced anxiously beyond Cleo. Cleo heard a stern voice announcing the recess was over.

"It's Mrs. K. She's looking mad," the high-top girl warned.

"Please," Cleo said. "Kayla, could I borrow the one you have? My policewoman friend will want to see it too."

Three sets of skeptical eyes looked back at her. Lunch was important. Finders keepers was important too. Cleo straightened and glanced over her shoulder. Mrs. K. strode their way. High-top girl was right. The principal did not look pleased.

"Why do you and your police friend want our vampire casket?" Zoe asked, hazel eyes narrowing. "Are you detecting?" She turned to her friends. "Miss Cleo is like that lady my gran watches on TV. Miss Marple. She fights crime."

"Like Wonder Woman?" Kayla asked.

"Yeah," Zoe affirmed. "Like her. Kinda."

"Girls!" Mrs. K. rapped a pen against the metal gate. She looked taller than usual to Cleo, her hair a steel helmet in its no-nonsense crop. Her expression suggested she might give them all detention.

"Mrs. K.," Cleo said with forced brightness. "I've been keeping the girls. They're helping me out." She turned to the girls and gave them a conspiratorial "Shh," a finger to her lips and a wink of her eye.

Three eyes winked blatantly back. The girls filed past,

Kayla first. She nudged Cleo's hand as she passed, turning over the coffin.

Zoe went by last. "In the park. By the fountain," she whispered. "That's where we found the first one. The second was by the flower lady's shop, waiting by the door. We're not the only ones who have 'em. There's some boys who have one, and they say it's cursed, but we don't believe that. It's like an Easter egg hunt . . . for vampires!" She ducked her head and edged by Mrs. K. to join her friends. They took off across the lawn, running and laughing, the last ones in the stately brick building.

Cleo had attended this same school. Her mind time-traveled back to the clank of metal lockers, the squeaky waxed floors, and old-sock mustiness of the dreaded gymnasium. She'd been a good and dutiful student, especially in subjects that relied on reading.

"What did you need help with?" Mrs. K. asked, lingering behind the fence.

Cleo thought fast. On-the-spot lying wasn't her best subject. Standing before the principal, she was sure Mrs. K. would catch her out.

"Nothing important," Cleo said, and she quickly changed the subject. "I've been meaning to ask you what the Who-Done-Its selected for this month's reading. I'll need to get myself a copy. *If* I'm still your moderator, that is."

To Cleo's surprise, a blush rose on the stern principal's cheeks. Mrs. K. stammered that *of course* Cleo was still their moderator.

"But we're not *reading* exactly," Mrs. K. said, the flush

spreading. "We're, uh, doing things a little differently this month. We're watching the TV adaptation of *Big Little Lies*. We'll be discussing it afterward. Reading the original book is . . . uh, optional."

"Oh," Cleo said, unable to fully hide her shock. Reading optional for a *book* club? Working out that logic could hurt one's head. Cleo didn't want to try. She needed to get going. The wooden coffins felt as heavy as lead in her pocket. Mrs. K. looked like she wanted out of the conversation too. Simultaneously, they announced that they shouldn't keep the other.

Yet Mrs. K. hesitated at the schoolyard gate. "I don't suppose . . ." the principal said.

Cleo could guess what was coming. She raised her eyebrows encouragingly.

"Would the library have a copy of that book, the actual book?"

A lesser librarian—and less polite book-group moderator—might have lengthened Mrs. K.'s squirm. Cleo saw an opportunity to promote more than reading. Mrs. K.'s sister sat on the library board.

"I believe we have a copy," Cleo said, acting thoughtful but recalling the patron interest in the bestseller, which had sparked again with the TV adaptation. "I know I had it in the bookmobile until recently, when I swapped it out for newer releases. It'll be in the main library. As you know, we don't officially reopen for a few more weeks. I'd be happy to track it down, but I am having a bit of difficulty right now." A few minutes later, Cleo had talked up the library's renovation plans, pouring on the sweetness before admitting her concerns about hiring Belle Beauchamp as a last-minute consultant. "I'm afraid her ideas could be detrimental to both our main library and mobile library," Cleo said. "Under her *consultations*, we'd likely have far fewer books for patrons like you to enjoy."

Cleo was relaying Mercer's rude library insults when Mrs. K. interrupted. "That pompous little man! I'm sure *you* know what's best for the library, Cleo. I'll speak with my sister. I can't guarantee she'll do anything. Meg didn't inherit the family backbone." Mrs. K. straightened her own spine. Her nose wiggled, which turned into a sniffle and a sneeze that nearly knocked the sturdy principal over.

"Bless you!" Cleo said as sneezing continued for five more eruptions.

"Hay fever" Mrs. K. said after an apology. "Ragweed, mold . . . this is the worst time of year for me." She rummaged through pockets, muttering about needing a tissue. She came up empty.

"Here," Cleo said, reaching in her own pockets. As she was extracting a tissue, a coffin flipped out and landed on the grass. Cleo quickly thrust the tissue at Mrs. K. and bent to pick up the coffin, but when her hand reached the ground, it was already gone.

Mrs. K. held the distressing object at arm's length, as if it might reach back and bite. "You got one too?" She dropped it into Cleo's extended open palm and wiped her hand on her slacks. "Whoever's doing all this has a sick, twisted sense of humor. It's a bully, for sure. I do not tolerate bullies—in my school or my town."

The coffin felt even heavier in Cleo's hand. "I got this and another one like it from the kids," Cleo said. "They found it in the park. Did you find one? When? Where?" Cleo returned the coffin to her pocket, pressing hard on the Velcro flap to seal it in.

Mrs. K. rubbed the tissue at her nose. "Not me. Iris Hays. She's subbing for us today in social studies. Probably talking about painting instead, like always. She never sticks to the lesson. She found some awful paper coffin on her windshield. She thought it was a ticket or an advertisement. Then she saw it had her name on it and some cruel message about '*mold*ering in her new home.' Another member of our book club got one too." A bell rang in the school. Mrs. K. glanced at her watch.

"Who?" Cleo persisted.

Mrs. K. exhaled loudly. "You didn't hear already? Pat Holmes. As if that blessed woman needs more worries. I saw her on the way to work this morning and she'd already gotten herself into a state. She said she was going to call you, Cleo. She thinks you're some sort of super-sleuth who can solve our problems. I told her to pull herself together. There's no use getting all worked up by silly superstitions and childish threats. That's the worst thing to do, in fact. Bullies feed off fear." She blew her nose loudly and turned back toward her school.

"I'll be by to pick up that book," Mrs. K. called back. "Make sure no one else takes it out first. I want an upper hand on the TV show."

Cleo, busy rummaging in her purse, murmured a vague "Okay." Mrs. K. had reached the school doors by the time

Cleo found her phone. It was turned on, Cleo was pleased to see. She often forgot to do that. The trouble was the volume. Mute with vibration notification. Cleo recalled feeling odd sensations earlier that she'd attributed to unease.

She stood beside the hopscotch grave and saw she'd missed four calls: Three from Pat. One from Henry.

Cleo listened to the messages, her concern growing with each one.

Chapter Fifteen

"Cleo! I thought you were hurt, dead even!" Pat rushed at Cleo and embraced her in a hug scented with lemon cleaning fluid.

"No, thank goodness," Cleo said, taken aback at Pat's concern and the rib-crunching embrace.

Cleo had walked straight to Pat's cleaning company, a dour cinder-block building on the southwest edge of downtown. Pat had been at her desk, sipping tea, which she'd spilled in jumpiness when Cleo rang the buzzer.

Cleo couldn't recall ever visiting the cleaning office. She rarely came to this corner of town, although it was only a handful of blocks from the library. It seemed far away somehow, an odd triangle set apart by an abandoned railroad spur, now taken over by weeds, palms, and thorny vines. Cleo looked around, thinking of her mother's rule for visiting: *Always say something nice.* The office appeared to be a former garage, the floor, walls, and ceiling done in solid gray cement. Cleaning rags formed a little mountain in a wheeled cart. Industrial-sized tubs of Lemon Brite Bleach ringed Pat's desk.

"What a lovely, open office," Cleo said, grasping for a compliment. "You have lots of light."

Pat tugged her hair back, tying it with a rubber band that made Cleo cringe, feeling the tug to her own hair roots. "Too much light," Pat said direly. "Too open. Anyone could be hiding out in that weedy mess of a railroad track, looking in at us." She motioned Cleo in and locked the door behind her. "When I couldn't get you on the phone, I was worried sick. I got a death threat! I thought maybe you did too, or worse." Her hands and voice quavered.

"I'm sorry," Cleo said. "I had my phone ringer off. I was at the library working and then went for a walk to clear my head."

"I wish I could clear mine." Pat returned to her desk, where message slips soaked in lemon tea. She scooped them up and jabbed the soggy pile over a message spike. "Did you hear? The police let Jefferson go—let him go! Now *everyone's* worried. Some of my cleaning ladies checked in, and you won't believe the things they're hearing around town: dead frogs, evil omens, death threats, coffins with names on them like I got . . . It's not safe out there. You shouldn't have walked over, Cleo."

Pat turned wide eyes to the gravel lot, empty except for a dented white van bearing the company logo: "Holmes Homes: We Clean Your Grime When You Don't Have Time."

"Let's get out of here," Pat said, turning the "OPEN" sign to "CLOSED." "We can go over to the house. All of my ladies are out on jobs, and I can forward calls to my home phone. I need to tell you about what I found. You'll know what to do. The police weren't any help. They implied that the death threats made Jefferson Huddleston look *less guilty*. Of all the crazy things."

Pat clicked off lights and led the way out the back, across a weedy lawn to a tidy pale-brick rancher. Cleo followed behind, eyes scanning. *Everyone getting death threats?* The wooden coffins in her coat bumped at her side. She vowed to get them to Gabby right after she left Pat's.

Pat jangled a metal ring thick with keys. The backdoor led into a little mudroom, with no mud to be seen, and on to a lemon-scented kitchen. "It's not glamorous like Dixie's place," Pat said.

"I'm sure I'd much rather be here," Cleo said.

Pat offered Cleo a seat at an enamel-topped table and turned on an electric burner ring under a kettle. "Tea? I only have herbal. I know—I'm weird. Caffeine makes my heart race and my hands shake, and you know, I don't want to tempt fate with my family history of dying young."

"Herbal would be lovely," Cleo said firmly. "Good for your heart too, I'm sure."

Pat rummaged through a cupboard, apologizing for the mess, pulling out tea boxes and listing their faults: "too old, too zingy, not so good . . ." Cleo gazed around the kitchen. Here was a case of a mess apology when none was needed. Pat's kitchen was spotless and uncluttered to an extreme. The parquet floors gleamed, as did the Formica countertops, maroon with glitter speckles that reminded Cleo of her mother's kitchen. Unlike Cleo's counters, busy with favorite cooking tools, books, magazines, and to-do notes, Pat kept only a cookie jar, a vintage seventies Betty Crocker cookbook, and a mason jar stuffed with tightly folded squares of paper. A chalkboard-style label on the jar read "Happy Thoughts."

How nice, Cleo thought, watching Pat disparage the tea selection. Pat *did* have positive things in her life, and possibly even cookies. Cleo set her mind to listing good things in her own life. She was alive, as Pat had pointed out. That was very good indeed. There was Rhett, of course. She loved her cat. Words on Wheels most definitely brought joy. Getting in the captain's seat was such a thrill. The library—it had been coming along so well . . . Worries about Belle and Mercer wormed into her happy thoughts. Cleo turned her mind to her family, picturing each loved one, from her sons to her grandkids, her sisters, and cousins.

And then there was Henry. Her gentleman friend had brought unexpected romance to her senior years. His voicemail explained why he'd gone off with Belle earlier. Belle wanted to toss out some books at the Claymore Library. She wanted his opinion on whether they were "dumpster old," "thrift store old," or "worth something." He'd signed off in dire tones and promised to call Cleo when he got back to town. Soon, he hoped.

Cleo checked her watch. She took out her phone and made sure the volume was up. She didn't want to miss him again.

"Here. Sorry it took so long. My stove is acting up." Pat put a mug in front of Cleo with a shaky hand. "Sorry again for clogging up your voicemail."

"No worries about the messages," Cleo said, knowing Pat would worry anyway. "I'm sorry about that note. Tell me about what you found."

The tea was watery lemon. Cleo swirled the teabag around. The water remained pale. There was no sugar in sight.

Pat took a deep breath. She'd gone over to the office at six thirty sharp, she said. She'd been searching through her keys—she had too many—when she looked down and there it was, lurking up against the door. "My heart, Cleo! It almost stopped! It's like you found at Dixie's. It said, 'Welcome home, Pat.' My name was on it! It was addressed to me! It was about this long and looked like . . . oh, I should have taken a photo."

"That's okay," Cleo said, although it clearly wasn't. A chill crept up her neck. The notes Pat and Iris had received sounded like the paper coffins they'd found at Dixie's.

"I'm going to stop by the police station after this," Cleo said, keeping her tone brisk and businesslike. "I'll ask Gabby if she'll show me the note. I have some coffins to show her too, I'm sorry to say."

Pat gasped. "Oh no! We've been targeted, Cleo! Jefferson must have realized we didn't just drop by to visit yesterday. He's trying to scare us off. I *told* the police I was worried about him, but they brushed me off." Pat hadn't touched her tea. Her fingernails tapped at the white enamel tabletop.

"I didn't get one personally," Cleo specified, hoping this didn't seem like bragging. "At least, none that I've discovered yet." She told Pat about the kids finding the wooden coffins in the park and by the florist's and their report of other kids having them too. "That would explain what your ladies are hearing. People are finding threats around town."

The phone rang down the hall. Pat ignored it. "The police wanted to know *when* I found the note," Pat said. "The chief got grumpy when I told him it was definitely right before seven."

Cleo thought she knew why. "I saw Jacquelyn this morning. She stopped to fuss at me. She wasn't happy with our visit or with Jefferson volunteering to speak with the police. She was up in North Carolina at a conference and had to fly back to help and find them a lawyer. It seemed like she'd just returned to town. She also said she found Amy-Ray outside Dixie's house when she got home. If she's telling the truth, then Amy-Ray was in town early this morning, Jacquelyn wasn't, and Jefferson was with the police."

Pat frowned, putting it all together. "So Jefferson and Jacquelyn will claim they couldn't have left the notes around town early this morning. That's *convenient*! I'm not sure I believe them. Jefferson had his mother's prescription, and he could have hired someone to leave the notes to cause confusion. He must know people. Students. Mimes. Theater types. Maybe that's why he was so eager to spend all night with the police and why she left town." Pat gave a single, firm head jerk, as if she'd just solved the case. Before Cleo could take another sip of tea, however, Pat was contradicting herself. "No. That would be too complex, wouldn't it?"

The killing was complex. Cleo mulled the lengthy planning, the escalation of Dixie's fear. "I wonder about these new threats," she said. "I assumed the killer hated Dixie." Seeing Pat's face crumple, she said, "It's awful, but it seemed so personal, so tailored to Dixie. Why then leave out coffins for anyone—kids!—to find? Why threaten you and Iris and—"

"Iris?" Pat cut in. "But that doesn't make sense. She's my

second choice. My second pick for most likely murderer after Jefferson."

"She's not shy in her dislike of Dixie," Cleo agreed.

Pat rubbed her temples. "Yes, but there's more. I remembered it last night. You said there was sugar in place of Dixie's medicine? It's like that book." In response to Cleo's querulous look, she said, "Oh, that book. What was it called? The Who-Done-Its read it a couple years back. Remember? The killer was a nurse who replaced the victims' medicine with saline. It was an awful book. Sorry! I shouldn't bad-mouth a book in front of a librarian. I wish I could remember the title. *Her Last Shot? Bad Medicine?* It was before you started giving us book lists of choices."

Cleo recalled the book now. *"Her Last Shot,"* she confirmed. She remembered who picked it too. "Iris Hays chose it, didn't she? I remember because the group got in a bit of a tiff about it."

Pat got up and paced her tidy kitchen. "We'd have to go back through the club records and check for sure, but I think so. Mrs. K. keeps the list. I got myself pretty worked up last night, worrying. I almost called you, but it was past midnight. I got it in my fool head that Iris would be coming for me next." She straightened the "Happy Thoughts" and cookie jars and refolded an already folded kitchen towel.

"No," Cleo soothed. "Why would she target you?"

Pat pushed back her bangs, her broad brow wrinkled. "I used to help Dixie clean properties she listed. I didn't have anything to do with hiding the mold in Iris's house, but she might blame me anyway." She attempted a smile. "Dixie would tell me I'm being silly."

Cleo could see why Pat might worry. "If Iris did kill Dixie, why would she be so vocal about disliking her? A ploy to throw us off?"

Pat circled the table. "Exactly! She could be doing the same with that death threat she supposedly received."

They had more watery lemon tea and sugar-free cookies that came from the refrigerator rather than the cookie jar. A half hour later, Cleo said she should be going. She wanted to see Gabby, and now she had even more to tell her.

"Tell her about the book-club book!" Pat said again, as Cleo left. "Be careful, Cleo! It's scary out there!"

Chapter Sixteen

Cleo met Gabby at the police station. The young deputy drooped at her desk.

"Sorry!" Gabby said, unsuccessfully covering a full-face yawn. "This is good evidence, Miss Cleo. I appreciate it, truly. I caught a case of the yawns. We were up half the night talking with Jefferson. Then Jacquelyn barreled in with a fancy lawyer, threatening to sue. After that the phones went mad with half the town and beyond calling in threats." Gabby rubbed her eyes, sparking another yawn.

The balmy temperature in the station couldn't be helping with her sleepiness. Cleo extracted the folding fan she carried in her purse, useful in all seasons, from summer sultry to winter overheating. A radiator clanked busily by Gabby's desk. A fan whirled on a shelf behind the deputy, ruffling her curls and the stacks of evidence bags littering her desk.

Other than the competing fan and radiator, the police station was quiet. Cleo remarked on the solitude. The chief was out on so-called important business, Gabby reported, likely a late lunch and a nap. Sergeant Tookey was out running down more threats, real and imagined.

"I don't see a connection among those who've gotten personalized threats," Gabby said. "Do you?" She slid a handwritten list across the desk to Cleo. It included the postman, an auto-mechanic, a teenage boy, a hairdresser, the sole male member of the Who-Done-Its, and Pat and Iris.

Cleo couldn't either, except for the three Who-Done-Its.

"There are more of those general threats too, like your kid friends found," Gabby said. "Plus bad omens." She waved wearily to what she deemed the "superstition" stack at the edge of her desk. "Like this," Gabby said, holding up an evidence bag, lip curling in distaste.

"A deceased frog?" Cleo fanned faster. She liked frogs and didn't like to see them dried up and smooshed.

Gabby sighed. "Yep. A lady found it behind her car. She considered it a message from either the killer or the underworld— she couldn't decide. I didn't want to be rude, but here's a death I can solve right away. I mean, you can see the tire tracks on this poor creature! Then there's this. Can you guess what it is?" She held up a bag filled with twigs.

"Camellia branches?" Cleo guessed.

"The devil's pitchforks," Gabby said with a sigh. "See how they're all three pronged and pointy? A man found them on his sidewalk and got worried. Nerves are spreading. They're contagious, like a bad flu. I'm afraid we're about to have a pandemic. People are seeing the bad and scary where it doesn't exist. Mailboxes left open, damaged medicine boxes at the pharmacy, a perfectly natural wasp nest." As she vented, she sealed Cleo's coffins in individual evidence bags and efficiently labeled them.

Cleo noted Gabby's neat printing. Gabby would make a good librarian. She was methodical and detail-oriented, and even in the age of automated everything, good handwriting was a plus.

Gabby placed the coffin bags in a pile of similar items made of paper and wood. "I don't get it," she said. "The person doing this is angry. Or flat out mad. Why target everyone and anyone?" Gabby stretched her arms over her head, locking her fingers, her gaze far away out the tall windows.

The police station occupied a downtown building. The staff desks were upstairs, and from Gabby's corner nook, Cleo could see out over Main Street and the leafy fringe of Fontaine Park. It was a pretty view, which Cleo found herself scanning for evil omens.

Gabby yawned again and listed everything she wished she could make happen all at once: stakeouts, surveillance, fingerprint analysis of all the notes, a sniffer dog . . . "Or I could do all this paperwork," she groaned, dismally eyeing her desk.

"You won't do anyone any good if you wear yourself out," Cleo said in her best grandmotherly tones. "You'll think more clearly after a full night's sleep and a good meal. Have you eaten today?"

Gabby nodded to a box that once held granola bars and was now stuffed with their empty plastic wrappers and a banana peel.

Cleo tsked. "Come over to my place after work. I promise,

we won't talk about murder if you don't want to. I have chicken and dumplings to reheat. It's nothing special, but—"

"It sounds wonderful," Gabby said. She squinted toward the wall clock. "I can leave at six, and if you have more ideas about this murder, Miss Cleo, I want to hear them." She grinned. "Even if you are, technically, still a suspect."

Cleo smoothed her curls and said primly, "All the more reason for you to come to dinner, dear. I might just confess."

Gabby was still chuckling as Cleo left.

* * *

"Shh . . ." Cleo held a finger to her lips and pointed to the sleeping deputy. Gabby slumped in Cleo's most comfortable porch chair, socked feet resting on a stool, head nodding to her shoulder, a sleepy Persian stretched across her chest. Rhett raised an eyelid and frowned, as if reiterating what Cleo had said: *Don't wake the slumbering human bed.*

Mary-Rose gave a mime-worthy performance of tiptoeing in and silently easing shut the screen door.

It was nearly eight. The chicken and dumplings had been devoured, the dishes done. Gabby and Cleo had talked about their families and holiday plans and suspects over their meal. They'd been sitting on the porch enjoying coffee—decaf for Cleo, full-throttle for Gabby—when Gabby's eyelids began to droop. Cleo had let her sleep, fearing that if she woke her, Gabby would run back to work.

The night was pleasant for sitting out on the porch. Thick clouds blanketed in the day's heat and a still silence. Occasional whispers of rasping branches and rustling leaves made

Cleo glad for police company, even if that company was ever so delicately snoring. Cleo felt a little silly admitting it to herself, but she was waiting for another guest to arrive. Henry. He hadn't called. Cleo wondered if he'd forgotten. Or if he was still out with Belle Beauchamp . . .

"I came by to check on you," Mary-Rose whispered. "I heard that book club of yours was getting death threats." Mary-Rose eased herself into a wicker chair beside Cleo. "That club attracts ire. I've said it before."

"You've said they're prone to food fights," Cleo corrected. She assured her friend it wasn't the entire book club. "Only Pat, Iris, and Myron, the tall man. The only man."

Mary-Rose took that as good news. "Well that's less than half of them then, and not you, thank heaven."

Gabby groaned and fluttered an eyelid open. "How long have I been sleeping?" She slowly pulled herself more upright. Rhett remained stubbornly reclining. Gabby gave him a kiss on his head and ruffled his fur. "Oh, hi, Mary-Rose! Sorry, I'm being awful company."

"I'm glad you're here watching out for Cleo," Mary-Rose said. "There's a strange atmosphere around town. People are acting paranoid. Can y'all believe, I couldn't sell one slice of honey pie to a local today? They were all associating honey with bees—which is logical, of course—but then they moved on to calling bees killers. The florist accused me of hawking murder pie. So rude! I'm going to have to change up the pie special for the month. What do you all think? Caramel or s'mores?"

Cleo was momentarily made speechless, both by the extent of the fear and the stunning idea of s'mores pie.

Mary-Rose was describing the pie to Gabby: graham cracker crust filled with creamy chocolate and topped with marshmallow meringue. "The marshmallow gets torched so it tastes like a campfire," Mary-Rose said. "It's a thing of beauty."

"S'mores," Gabby said decisively. She sounded less sure when Mary-Rose asked if the police were closing in on a killer. "You didn't hear me say this—and don't go spreading it around—but no, not really."

"Have you at least cleared Cleo off your list?" Mary-Rose asked.

"Not officially," Gabby mumbled.

Mary-Rose pursed her lips. "Cleo, until you're cleared, I'll relent on enforcing your sugar ban. If you'd like a honey pie, you're welcome to come out to the Pancake Mill and get yourself one, on me."

Cleo turned to Gabby. "She's only saying that because she has leftover pies she can't sell."

"Not entirely true," Mary-Rose said. "Gabby, you're welcome to one too if you clear Cleo's good name."

"Now that's incentive." Gabby grinned. She stretched her legs and tried to ease Rhett off her chest. The big Persian stuck tight. "I need to get going, Rhett," Gabby said. "Otherwise, I'll sleep on your porch all night." Rhett escalated his purrs.

A real motor added to the rumble, a belching diesel. Tires crunched on Cleo's gravel driveway. A branch scraped metal, a sound like fingernails on a chalkboard to Cleo. She needed to prune that branch! A horn blew, and Cleo winced. Her grouchy neighbor to the north would not be happy.

Cleo wasn't happy either when a singsong drawl cut through the darkness.

"Yoo-hoo, Cleo!" Belle Beauchamp called out. "It's us!"

Two figures came up the pathway, Belle light on her clicking heels, Henry trudging and lugging two oversized canvas shopping bags.

"I brought you some books and your honey!" Belle trilled.

Mary-Rose gasped and leaned forward in her seat. Cleo got up to greet the new visitors, secretly pleased by Belle's acknowledgment of Henry as her "honey." And books? She always liked gifts of books, although she wouldn't have expected them from Belle Beauchamp.

Henry set down the bags, which bulged with the edgy outlines of hardcovers. He looked about to give Cleo a hug before Belle swooped between them, affectionately patting Henry's shoulder. "I had to twist this one's arm to accompany lonely me out to a *business* dinner. We should *all* go out soon, seeing as how you and I are work sisters now, Cleo." She flashed a brilliant smile, tugging Henry closer.

Cleo took heart in Henry's expression. The sweet man looked as miserable as Rhett on a trip to the groomers. "I saved . . . er . . . volunteered to take some of the Claymore Library's older books," he said, eyes aimed at the bags at his feet. "These are handwritten genealogies and county censuses from the 1800s. Some valuable history in these."

Belle grumbled that they were old and musty and would attract moths. "Cleo, we'll have to check your library for moth bait too."

Cleo shuddered and not because she worried about insects.

"My manners!" she said, changing the subject. She belatedly introduced her porch companions. "Gabby Honeywell, my favorite neighbor. Mary-Rose Garland, my favorite friend," Cleo said brightly.

Gabby managed to rise, Rhett still stuck to her with clawed determination. She shook Belle's hand. Mary-Rose gave a little wave, keeping her distance.

"Garland, you said?" Belle asked. "When I was a kid, I went to a summer camp run by a Garland." She described a Mrs. Malva Garland, who turned out to be Mary-Rose's aunt in-law.

"Mary-Rose, you worked at that camp, didn't you?" Cleo said.

Mary-Rose rather grudgingly acknowledged she had. "For a few summers, before William and I married.

"Small world!" Belle exclaimed. "I wonder if we met back then? I can't recall, and I do pride myself on my memory. But I shouldn't keep you ladies. Mr. Henry, shall I drop you off at home for a nightcap?"

"I, uh . . ." his blush flared above his beard. "I can't. I need to speak with Cleo."

Belle left with perfumed kisses all around, her cheek smacks landing most loudly on Henry. Only Rhett avoided a kiss. He flattened his ears as she approached and flapped his tail. "You're a feisty fellow, aren't you? Like my little horse, Lilliput," Belle said. "I'll have to get y'all together someday. Mascot playdate!"

Rhett's eyes went wide, although Cleo thought he might actually enjoy playing stalk-and-pounce with a mini-horse.

Belle left to the bang of the screen door and clicking of heels. The diesel engine spluttered to a roar and eventually rumbled off. In the garden, the silence settled back in.

Henry sank into a chair. "I don't want to sound rude, but is she *really* going to be working with you, Cleo? She has no respect for books—or boundaries. She practically kidnapped me. I finally insisted that I needed to get back to walk my dog. I said I was intending to see you too, but she's like an interrogator. She got me to admit that we didn't have any set plan." He rubbed his beard, which looked as frazzled as he sounded. His hair puffed out over his ears in mad-scientist style.

Cleo knew all too well how persuasive Belle could be. She murmured comforting sounds.

Henry yawned, sparking a chain reaction in Gabby and Rhett too. "If there's any good outcome," he said, "I rescued those books, and I can warn you too. Her library practices are, well . . . you saw her bookmobile. The library over in Claymore is faring no better."

Cleo didn't want to ask for details. It was too near bedtime, and she already had enough troubling thoughts to fuel nightmares.

Mary-Rose had been silent, nose to the screen. From down the street, Belle honked, a blare through the quiet night.

"I recognize her," Mary-Rose said, turning to face them.

"From camp?" Cleo said. Mary-Rose had a good memory for people.

But her friend was shaking her head no. "From last week! The voice at the farmers' market. Cleo, Gabby, remember how I told you about the slap I overheard when I was, uh, indisposed?"

Cleo might have smiled at Mary-Rose's porta-potty eaves-dropping, except the words sent a chill up her neck. "Belle? You think that was Belle Beauchamp yelling at Dixie?"

"I *know* it was her. I recognize that voice."

Mary-Rose slowly repeated what she'd heard. Goose-bumps rose up Cleo's arm with every word.

"'You'll get what's coming to you. You'll be sorry.' And then . . ." Mary-Rose slapped the side table, hard. They all jumped. Rhett's tail puffed. "Then she slapped Dixie smack on the cheek. I saw the mark left after."

Chapter Seventeen

Rain dove down the gutters and flew over the awning. The weatherman had predicted a chance sprinkle, convincing Cleo to leave her umbrella at home.

"It's a gully washer," Cleo said, huddling with Henry under the awning of the Spoonbread Bakery. Two nights had passed, with more threats discovered each of the following mornings, coffin notes left in the park, on the street, on doorsteps, and in mailboxes. Cleo's tiny town was on edge. Cleo felt it too.

To lift her spirits, she'd met up with Henry at the bakery for a Friday breakfast treat of warm scones and too many coffee refills. Cleo buzzed from caffeine and plans for a busy morning ahead. She'd added a break to her bookmobile schedule and planned to use it at the library. She wanted to get as many renovations finalized as possible before Belle could wedge her way in. Cleo mentally ticked off the to-do list, from final touches to party planning. Anxiety pinged through her core. Who would want to celebrate if a murderer was still among them?

"For once, I'm glad I'm not driving," Cleo said, looking out on the soaked scenery. "The road is a river."

"Mr. Chaucer will be feeling smug he stayed home." Henry zipped up his oilskin raincoat. He adjusted his hat, felt and brimmed. "Ready to make a run for it?"

Cleo assumed they wouldn't be actually running. Chivalrous Henry had offered an umbrella escort to the library. They dodged little rivers in the street and massive puddles in the park. Raindrops gathered force high in the trees and landed like water balloons on the umbrella.

"Still think rainy weather is nice?" Henry asked, as they sidestepped a night crawler the size of a snake. Spanish moss hung like bedraggled Rapunzel locks.

"I do," Cleo said. She'd confessed over breakfast about how she enjoyed a rainy day. Rain saturated the colors in the garden. Rainy days were also the best for staying inside and reading, not that she had time for that. They pushed on, the wind puffing spritz at their cheeks. Henry held the umbrella low and tilted, blocking their view until they nearly reached their destination.

Cleo, being shorter, spotted the trouble first. She stopped abruptly. Henry kept going a few steps. When he realized he'd lost Cleo, he backed up in a hurry. A raindrop rolled down the umbrella and onto Cleo's nose. She took no notice. She stood at the walkway to the Catalpa Springs Public Library, where two things were definitely not right.

One was Lilliput. Belle's mini-horse mascot wore a red slicker. The coat had slipped upside down and billowed under his dappled belly, brushing the grass. A long, thick lead tethered him to the garden's new planting, the slender red-bud, now bent to reclining. Although standing in lush grass, the little horse strained at his lead, grasping for the blades just beyond his reach.

Then there were the lights. The library glowed. It would be an inviting scene on a wet autumn day, except no one was supposed to be there. Leanna was at class. The handymen weren't scheduled until later. Cleo had counted on a few hours alone with her work.

"Belle," Cleo said in a tone Rhett might use for a hiss. Cleo took off without waiting for her umbrella escort. Henry caught up on the porch, where he shook out the umbrella and his jacket and murmured words surely meant to soothe, if Cleo had heard them. She pushed open the door to bright light and a chipper trill.

"Cleo! Henry! Why, how wonderful of y'all to join us!" Belle breezed across the drop cloths in a wave of lilac perfume. She wore a tweed jacket, beige leggings, and riding boots, and grasped Cleo's shoulders, swiveling her about in a series of head-jostling air kisses. Belle did the same to Henry, except the kisses smacked on skin.

"Ah, Cleo." Mercer Whitty sidled up behind Belle, dapper in his pinstripe suit, pumpkin-orange bow tie, and suede loafers that wouldn't survive a puddle. "We didn't think you'd be here so early," he drawled.

Clearly not. Cleo looked around, counting heads. It wasn't just Mercer and Belle. It was practically the entire board, five members plus Mercer, the president. The only person missing was the often-absent Tipple granddaughter, a descendant of the original owners of the building.

"We were, uh . . . hoping you would show up Miss Cleo," chirped the secretary, her blush betraying a clear case of nerves and fibbing. Two members Cleo had counted as book-loving allies avoided her glance. The remaining two, the money members, as Cleo thought of them, made blustery protests about this being a "private" board meeting.

"Private?" Cleo demanded. "I'm the head librarian. Our board constitution says I must be informed of any meetings, as must the public, with minutes kept for the public record."

The secretary held up a notebook. "I posted a photo of us on Facebook! I've been taking notes. Here!" She thrust the notebook at Cleo and stepped back as if Cleo might bite.

Cleo frowned at the woman's shaky handwriting but most of all the odd words: *Tiger Team Work. Blast branding. Extreme organization + streamlining = profit/patrons.* Her temples thumped as she read text underlined and highlighted in little stars.

"*Long-term outlook:* Full-time *innobrarian = profit*'?" she said, reading the words out loud.

"That's me!" Belle chirped. "Remember? Innovation plus librarian equals . . ." She waved open palms encouragingly, and the board members chorused "innobrarian."

Cleo hadn't been questioning the made-up term. "*Full-*time?" she repeated. "I understood Mr. Whitty wanted to hire a temporary consultant, although I see no need since we're doing just fine. There's no full-time position open right now, or a need for one." Her hands twitched, yearning to shoo everyone but Henry out into the rain. Leanna would be adding on hours when she finished her studies. Cleo was holding the position for her. She had it all planned.

"We're about to have a full-time opportunity,' Mercer said. "That's why I've invited the board here—to see Belle's vision. They have. They've generously accepted my offer to fund this important position. Belle will guide our library design, innovation, outreach, activities, and mobile ventures."

"By mobile ventures, I mean bookmobiles!" Belle said, clapping her hands. "I have all sorts of ideas to snazz up this place and your bookmobile, Cleo. Like, thinking outside the box, what if it's not even a bus? What if we had a tiny stagecoach for Lilliput to haul around the park?"

Cleo didn't like conflict, except in books, and even there it made her nervous. She took a breath, working to steady her voice and shaky hands. "Surely, I should have been consulted about this *position*," she said.

"You are now," Mercer said, his snapping-turtle smile daring her to object. "Don't worry, Cleo. We'll follow the proper hiring procedures. We'll be posting the job advertisement so anyone can apply. Of course, we already have a talented and experienced candidate. Your previous job ad mentioned preference given for candidates applying from within the institution. We'll add the same to this advertisement. Lucky for us, Belle will have that advantage now, being our consulting innobrarian."

"Y'all are so sweet," Belle trilled. "So's the salary! Mercer, you're both a visionary and a doll."

Cleo gawked at the board members. Why was no one

saying anything? Some did have the grace to turn away from the flagrant flirting. The secretary hid behind a hardback, while another member studied his shoes.

"I'm your consultant for the time being," Belle said. "Let me prove my worth. Cleo, you're just in time. Handouts, people! I have paper!" She handed around color copies. Cleo stubbornly—childishly—stuffed her hands in her pockets, refusing to accept one. Henry ended up with two copies. Cleo frowned at the pie charts he held. The wedges contained words. *Actionables. Product. Profit. Innobrary.*

Belle's voice had switched from syrupy to brisk, a stream of numbers and percentages.

"How do we measure success?" she asked the group. "By boots in the door, I say. By limiting our costs, by which I mean decreasing our outlays for high-priced, outdated inventory."

"Inventory?" Cleo asked.

"Books," Belle said in a dark tone Cleo might use when referring to gum or termite infestation. "Once books are read, they're done, right? I mean, who reads a book twice—or the out-of-date ones, for that matter? Plus, folks can lose paper books, or their kid or—say, mini-horse—might rip a page or spill something on them, or they get moldy or moth-eaten, or . . ."

She turned to Cleo with raised eyebrows. "Or a patron keeps a book out for over forty years, and the library staff has no way of retrieving either the book or the late fine. Unacceptable! Paper is the past! I say we limit the heavy, space-wasting paper books. That'll make 'em more valuable. Like diamonds. Think about it: What are diamonds? Plain old carbon, same as paper. They're valuable because there aren't a lot around. Now, if we decrease books by just thirty to forty percent, and divide that by an estimated patron increase of . . ."

Numbers and figures flew. Cleo's head spun in horror and grim realization. She recognized what Belle was doing, and successfully too: her version of Auntie Audrey's one–two punch. Sweet-talking and facts, although in Belle's case, Cleo suspected the so-called facts were fiction.

"Where did you get these figures?" Cleo demanded.

Belle didn't break her smile. She pointed to the pie chart. "Right here, of course."

"But where did you get—"

Belle cut Cleo off with a terse "Market analysis. I did it myself. It's right here on the chart. See?"

"Brilliant," Mercer said adoringly.

Belle ushered the group toward the main reading room.

Cleo caught up with the lagging library lovers she'd considered her allies. Mrs. K.'s sister Meg was among them. The principal was right: Meg hadn't gotten the family backbone. Meg blinked at Cleo like a field mouse facing a famished fox.

Cleo forced herself to smile pleasantly. She wasn't upset with the board members. She couldn't even fault Belle, really. Like a fox, Belle was just doing what came naturally.

The other book lovers were the nervous board secretary and a thirty-something, stay-at-home dad who relentlessly served on committees and boards.

"I know this wasn't your idea," Cleo said softly.

They shrugged as one.

"It's not so bad," Meg said in a quavering voice edged with surprising defiance. "No," she blurted. "I take that back. It's good. A win–win! We get a free consultant to help finish these renovations right *and* the Whitty Family Foundation will pay for a new full-time staff member."

The secretary bobbed her head. "Yes, yes! We saw spreadsheets earlier. With the money Belle saves and Mr. Whitty grants us, we can do all sorts of innovative things. Inno*bra*tive, I mean." She giggled.

Cleo winced. "But what about our library and bookmobile? People depend on us for *books* and much more. We can't destroy what's good for the sake of breaking a mold or looking flashy."

"Make libraries fun again!" the young father proclaimed, missing Cleo's point entirely. "Like BOOK IT!"

"Libraries *are* fun," Cleo countered, wondering if he'd actually seen BOOK IT! and its lack of books. She goggled at the usually sensible folks before her. With just a few alien words and pretty charts, they'd lost all reason. It was like they'd been swept up in a cult. Cleo had read about cults and group mind control. She'd never seen it happen firsthand.

"But books," she said, keeping her voice calm, careful not to agitate the possibly cult-afflicted. "Surely you all agree that we don't need *fewer* books in our *library*."

"We'll have books," Meg said with a little giggle. "Don't be silly, Cleo! We'll have more resources and product than ever."

Cleo edged closer to Meg, sniffing discreetly, checking for

any hint of detectable drug or drink. She smelled nothing but the lilac perfume that lingered after Belle's hugs.

"Mr. Whitty explained it when he called us all last night," Meg continued, her voice taking on an edgy trill. "You see, we're all competitors—every library, I mean. We're competing for clients. Clients are what *you'd* call our patrons or readers. If we don't change, then we'll lose out anyway. Our clients will go over to Claymore. A lot of folks go over there anyway to shop at the big-box stores."

The young father agreed that he did just that. "You should see all the activities they have for kids now over at the Claymore library. My children love that little pony, and on weekends there's sometimes a farmer who brings by mini-goats and a micro-pig and cotton candy and—"

It sounded more like a miniaturized petting zoo than a library. Cleo bit her tongue to keep from demanding where his children got actual books. Her nose twitched. Belle's perfume swept in a moment before its wearer.

"What are all y'all doing over here in the corner?" Belle asked, grabbing Cleo by the elbow. "Cleo, I have to show you, I found the *best* paint colors! Now, I simply *adore* your color swatches. That's why I think they'd really pop if we went a teensy bit brighter. What do you think of neon peach fizz and a graffiti mural? We'll use words, like in BOOK IT! You liked those, right? You said so . . ."

Many decades ago, Cleo's Granny Bess had taken young Cleo aside for a serious talk. Not about the birds and the bees, but about the perils of politeness. Her wise grandmother warned that being too nice could sometimes be like stepping in quicksand. Go a little too far, wiggle a little bit too much, and you got yourself stuck.

Cleo felt herself sinking deeper, but what could she do? Yelling out reason would get her nowhere with this crowd.

Belle waved toward the west wall. "We'll remove those bookshelves. That'll give us all sorts of space for our light display. Fun, right? We'll have to turn down the lights so the illuminated words pop, but that's okay. Folks won't want to sit around and just read once we're done!"

Cleo would have slapped a hand to her thudding heart, except she was being tugged away toward the front room.

"Now, here," Belle said. "How many nonfiction books does anyone need? I was thinking, we clear this out and . . ."

Cleo closed her eyes and thought again of wise Granny Bess and that long-ago conversation. Her grandmother had offered a solution. The nice and polite of the world didn't have to become brawlers and bullies, her grandmother said. But sometimes—just occasionally, in dire times only and for the greater good—they could employ a little deception. Cleo summoned deception.

"Lovely ideas," Cleo drawled. She was pleased to see shock on a few faces, most of all, Henry's. Good. She must sound properly believable. She continued, clasping her hands in feigned eagerness. "Belle, you and I should talk much more about these . . ."—Cleo glanced at the nearest pie chart—". . . these action plans. We'll get Leanna too and have a proper action meeting."

Belle opened red-painted lips, but Cleo kept on speaking, louder and firmer. "Oh, but we can't do that yet, can we?

173

Leanna and I will not be properly prepared. We'll have to do a pre-meeting to prep for our meeting." Cleo knew she couldn't hold Belle off forever. She just needed some time to think. There had to be a way to sway Belle or Mercer or, better yet, the entire board. She wanted to consult with Leanna.

Cleo smiled sweetly at Mercer. "Of course, more meetings mean more times Belle will have to come all the way over here to see us."

Mercer looked as pleased as a pig in mud.

Cleo caught Henry's eye and winked. He nodded back, a knowing smile spreading.

Chapter Eighteen

"Oh no," Leanna groaned. "She's here! It's started, hasn't it? Our undoing!" She stood in the library foyer, looking dismal yet bright in her polka-dot yellow raincoat, candy-cane boots, and cable-knit tights. The library door groaned behind her.

"I'm afraid so," Cleo said in a low voice. "I arrived to find most of the board here this morning. They liked Mercer's idea of hiring her as a consultant. He's fully funding it all, so they would." She didn't want to mention the threat of a full-time "innobrarian" right yet. Leanna already had a lot to take in.

"What is that awful, ugly color?" Leanna spluttered, pointing to sofa-sized splotches dotting the walls. Her pointing moved down the hallway. "That one's worse. This isn't a Victorian color! It's not *library* calm. It's clown house!"

Cleo was glad that Jefferson, even in his murder-suspect circumstances, wasn't around to hear Leanna's clown insult. But Leanna was right. Only a clown—the kind who terrorized cemeteries and the pages of Stephen King novels—could live with the neon-orange and shocking yellow.

"That's called Electric Peach Fizz," Cleo said, taking Leanna by the arm. "The other is Sun-Gazer Surprise." She mouthed *Outside* to Leanna. Although she was keeping her voice down, there was no need. Belle was in the back, and twangy tunes blared from a speaker set up on the circulation desk.

"What?" Leanna said, still squinting into the neon.

"I need some air after all this exciting paint," Cleo exclaimed loudly, in case Belle could hear them. She pushed the heavy door open with a satisfying shove and led the way around the curve of the porch, passing by the wide window that looked into the fiction room. Inside, Belle merrily measured the room size, likely imagining it free of shelves. Outside, the clouds were wringing out their final drips. Raindrops tap-danced on the metal roof and rumbled down the gutters.

Leanna looked as droopy as the Spanish moss. "We have to put up with this until the reopening? I won't want to reopen if the library looks like a demented clown house. This is the worst!"

"Not quite." Cleo decided to get the bad news over with fast, like ripping off a bandage. "I'm afraid there's more. Mercer proposes to fund a full-time 'innobrarian' position with Belle in mind. Unfortunately, she's interested."

Leanna groaned and leaned on the railing, staring out over the garden. "Why is it always this way? Why do the pushiest, loudest people with all the money always win?"

"No, no," Cleo said, fearing she didn't sound very believable. "We can fight this."

Leanna kept her face turned to the garden. Her voice quivered. "We fought to get the library back, Miss Cleo, and just when it's almost done, almost perfect, we get this? What if it turns into something like her noisy carnival bookmobile? It's *almost* worse than not having a library."

Cleo felt terrible and partially responsible. She hadn't acted quickly enough with the library board. She'd gotten distracted by the murder and the threats. *And by my own self-interest,* she thought. She'd wanted to clear her name and solve the awful puzzle of the case. Cleo admitted how Belle had outfoxed her with sweet talk and pie charts.

"I blame myself," she said. "I let myself get wrapped up in Dixie Huddleston's death when I should have been entirely focused on the library. I foolishly thought if we hurried and got our renovations finished, everything would be set and safe."

Leanna spun around. "No, Miss Cleo! It's not your fault. It's *hers* and Mr. Whitty's too. Why can't he just ask her out if he likes her so much?"

Cleo wouldn't speculate on Mercer Whitty's love life. "I have a plan," she said, wishing it was more than a half-formed desperation move. Nonetheless, Cleo pitched it in battle terms. She'd recently read a novel set during the Revolutionary War and was up on her fighting terminology. "We'll appear to fall back at first. We'll sound agreeable, a feint. Our mission will be to delay her, hopefully long enough to get most of our major renovations through. If we have to concede some ground on paint color, that's okay. We can always change the paint later. We'll concentrate on preserving the most important parts, the heart of the library: our books and programs. Meanwhile, we'll begin our main thrust, showing Belle what working in a library really means."

Leanna nodded. It was a polite nod, Cleo assessed. An unconvinced nod.

"How do we show her what she's already seen and not understood," Leanna asked, skepticism clear.

"We put her to work," Cleo said.

"Like take-your-innobrarian-to-work day? You really think she's going to suddenly fall for indexing and receiving? Circulation procedures? The literacy program? Outreach to the schools? Our rural bookmobile efforts?" Leanna kicked at a stray magnolia leaf, sending it tumbling down the porch.

Cleo ran her hand along the railing and a line of raindrops. "Actually, I don't think she'll be very interested at all. But we might convince her that she doesn't want a job here, that she's looking for something else as her second career."

Leanna managed a wry smile. "We can always hope, can't we?"

"And act," Cleo added firmly. "I'll do my best to sway the board. Sweetness and facts—it's a tactic of my very wise aunt that I didn't implement soon enough. You concentrate on your studies . . . and lying low."

"Those I can definitely do." Leanna gave Cleo a quick hug. "Call me when the coast is clear, okay?" She was down the steps in a flash, stopping only to scoot around the corner and ruffle Lilliput's mane. The little horse stood under the porch overhang, his red slicker righted and his long lead tethered to a sturdy crabapple. Someone had stepped in and straightened the toppled redbud sapling. *Some things could be set right,* Cleo thought. She just hoped the Catalpa Springs library—and Leanna's future in it—would be among them.

*   *   *

"Monday?" Belle tapped her knee-high boot when Cleo returned inside. "Leanna doesn't have any time today or this weekend? I thought she was only a part-timer and a college student. What's she have going on that's so important?"

"All sorts of busy things," Cleo said with peppy vagueness. "Leanna's a real go-getter and so looking forward to our pre-meeting meeting. Don't worry. We'll still have time before the grand reopening. Speaking of which, what do you think we should serve for snacks?"

Cleo had a policy on food and beverage in the library. It was simple. Neither was allowed, a restriction that went double for gum. However, the grand reopening was a party, and Cleo felt they had to serve *something*. She was considering safe items that wouldn't harm books, like dry crackers and pretzels. Dry roasted nuts. Celery sticks? Cleo worried only Pat would enjoy that menu.

Belle let her tape measure snap back into its holder. She'd been in the kids' room, brainstorming ways to bring in more noise. *Speakers . . .* Belle had been muttering when Cleo checked on her. *Surround sound . . .* Cleo found surround sound unsettling, even in movie theaters.

"Ooh," Belle said, clapping her hands excitedly. "You know what I love? Fondue! It's so retro it's hip, isn't it? Do you have a fondue pot? My folks have must have a dozen around the house. I could bring 'em all. I think we might even have one of those fountains, a chocolate fountain, but I bet it would spurt cheese too."

Cleo suppressed a shudder and an automatic *No!* Fondue? Liquid cheese? Molten chocolate, sliding off apple slices dangling from little forks? She did adore fondue, but there was a reason it went out of fashion. It was a hazard.

"Now, I know what you're thinking," Belle claimed. Cleo hoped not.

Belle proved a mind reader. "You're thinking fondue will smear all over your precious books. But hear me out. Folks don't go far with fondue. They hover around the pot."

Cleo opened her mouth to protest. It hung open as she realized she could see Belle's point. "Why, yes," she said in amazement. "Fondue could work. It's more festive than what I had planned too."

"See?" Belle said, giving Cleo's shoulder a friendly slap. "I do have some clever tricks up my sleeve, Cleo Watkins."

She did have tricks, surely. Cleo reminded herself not to let down her guard. Her stomach rumbled rudely. It was long after noon, nearly one, and Cleo was starving. She usually started her pre-lunch snacking around the brunching hour.

"Got that covered too!" Belle said, patting her own slim belly. "You're too hard a worker, Cleo. I called and ordered us some lunch from Dot's Drop By. She makes the best food."

This was true, but Cleo knew her cousin Dot did not deliver. Had Belle convinced Dot to run over in the rain? Cleo was torn, bristling at the thought of putting Dot out and salivating at Belle's description of what she'd ordered.

"Two of those gigantic chocolate chip cookies. Sweet tea, of course. And for the pièce de résistance, the Friday special is a biscuit sandwich with fried chicken, pimento cheese, and pickles. I got us both one."

Cleo's stomach rumbled happily. "That's very thoughtful," she said. "I can go pick it up. Dot's my cousin, and I know she has a hip that acts up in stormy weather."

Belle made a *pish* sound. "No need for any of us ladies to get our hair messed up." She ran a manicured hand over her immaculately sleek bob. Cleo could feel her own white waves actively frizzing in the damp air. Belle tucked a shimmering lock behind her ear. "I have a delivery boy," she said slyly, just as the door moaned open.

Cleo couldn't help but smile at the sight of Mercer Whitty pushing his way in. The board president held a large paper sack in one hand and a cardboard drink holder in the other. Rain had turned his thinning hair into lanky strings dripping at his earlobes. In a more generous mood, Cleo might have felt sorry for him. Not today.

He wouldn't have noticed anyway. Belle was buttering him up with sugary thanks. "You're so sweet, Merc," Belle drawled, taking the bag and drinks and heading toward the staff room.

"I can stay and help you ladies," Mercer offered eagerly.

"No need," Belle said, already over the threshold to the staff-only room. "Miss Cleo and I are getting on just fine."

A frown clouded Mercer's face, his small eyes narrowing. He turned the frown toward the wall with the shocking paint sample. "What *is* that?" he said with clear distaste.

Belle gave him a sparkly smile. "Got your attention, didn't it?" She disappeared into the break room, her perfume and a "Thanks, hon!" sailing behind her.

"Electric Peach Fizz," Cleo said dryly. "Belle picked the color." She enjoyed the conflict evident in Mercer's reptilian features. "Thanks for dropping lunch by!" She shut the staff-room door firmly behind her. A groan sounded down the hall, the front door announcing Mercer Whitty's inglorious exit.

Belle had already spread out the goodies on the long wooden table that served as an organization and picnicking space. Cleo savored the first bite of biscuit, pimento cheese, and Dot's fine fried chicken, washed down with a sip of properly sweet tea. Belle nibbled at the biscuit and poked at her phone.

"Sorry," Belle said when she finally put the device down. "These things are a blessing and a bane, aren't they?"

"I often forget to check mine," Cleo said.

"Keep it that way," Belle said, raising a dill pickle to punctuate the point.

Cleo sipped more tea and decided now was a fine time to ask. "So," she said in her best mild small-talk tone, "how did you know Dixie Huddleston?"

Belle's head jerked up. Just as fast, she looked back at her phone, snatched it up, and started poking at the screen again.

Cleo waited patiently. While she did, she sampled a bit of cookie and concluded, once again, that her cousin was a genius.

Belle looked up after a few beats. She cocked her head.

"Who?" she asked, then quickly took a big bite of biscuit sandwich.

"Dixie Huddleston," Cleo said, enunciating loudly. "You were at her wake." Cleo knew folks who made wakes a hobby, going to every open reception they could, regardless of whether they knew the deceased. She didn't picture Belle as a recreational mourner. She also knew that Belle couldn't have forgotten Dixie. According to Mary-Rose, Belle had slapped Dixie at the farmers' market just last week.

"Oh, how silly of me!" Belle said. "Her . . . Yes, I knew her as Dixie Oakley, way back when. I wouldn't have gone to the wake, honestly, but Mercer invited me, saying I should meet the community and some library board members. I thought I should play nice and go. That was some wake, wasn't it? She certainly had a lot of friends." She sipped her tea and returned to her phone.

"She made some enemies too," Cleo said, hoping to provide Belle with an opportunity to vent.

Belle glanced up. "Hmm? Like you, I hear. She's the one who had that overdue book, isn't she? I read about it in the paper and asked Merc. He told me you'd tried all sorts of things to get that old book back. That must have grated on your nerves. Did you ever get it back? The book?"

"No," Cleo admitted, not appreciating how the conversation had turned on her. She tried to get back in the interrogator's seat. "You knew Dixie when you were young, you said? How? You aren't from Catalpa Springs, are you?"

Belle made a noncommittal noise. "That was such a long time ago. We 'seasoned' ladies shouldn't be made to reveal our ages, should we?" She smiled conspiratorially and leaned in a little. "Tell me, what makes that book so special, anyway? Is it valuable? Do you even remember what it's about?" Before Cleo could answer, Belle sat back. "I suppose it doesn't matter. It'll be old now anyway. Write it off, I say."

Cleo did wish she could remember more about *Luck and Lore*. She certainly wasn't ready to write it off. It was the principle. Besides, books didn't lose their value with age any more than people did. In other circumstances, Cleo might have given a rousing speech. Instead, she forced herself to remain silent.

As she hoped, Belle filled the void. "Rude of her to keep the book so long. I know, I shouldn't call her rude, her being so recently dead and all." Belle crumpled a piece of wax paper. "Which is a shame, don't you think? Or do you? You can tell me, woman to woman. I heard folks saying you were out to get her. Is that true?" She turned her crumpling energies to more wrappers, stuffing them in the larger paper sack.

Cleo studied Belle. Why was she being so evasive? "But you knew Dixie personally," Cleo said. "I heard you two had a *disagreement* at the farmers' market last week."

Belle had cleared her place, pushing her cookie toward Cleo. She brushed crumbs off the table and shoved back her chair. "Who told you that? Small towns, I swear, they're like gossip tornados. Every little thing gets swept up and twisted around. Sometimes I wish I hadn't left Atlanta."

Cleo didn't feel she could press more about Dixie. "Why *did* you leave Atlanta?" she asked.

Belle had squished her lunch sack into a tight ball. She

threw it into a nearby trash can with such force the can tipped and rattled. She twisted her lip. "You're lucky, Cleo," she said. "Holding out this long in your domain. In my work—my former work—a woman over sixty is considered as useful as a dinosaur in heels." She sighed, shrugged, and looked at her watch, a bright but chilly smile returning. "Can you believe what time it is? Lilliput will be demanding his afternoon apple treat. I'd better get him home or he'll eat the garden down."

Cleo was relieved to see Belle leave. She was even more intrigued by her abrupt departure and her strange reluctance to talk about Dixie Huddleston.

Chapter Nineteen

Afrer Belle left, Cleo got her quiet time in the library. It wasn't the same as she'd imagined earlier in the day. She found herself wandering from room to room, taking in details to store in her memory in case they disappeared. Her mind kept spinning around Belle, about what Belle's innovations might mean to the library and bookmobile, about why Belle didn't want to talk about Dixie.

Faced with too many questions she couldn't answer, Cleo turned to doable tasks. She shelved several boxes of books, telling herself that filled shelves would be harder to remove. She tidied the reference room and cleared out some empty computer boxes. She called Leanna, who seemed to be taking lying low seriously. Two calls went straight to Leanna's voice-mail after the chipper greeting: *Hey, you've reached Leanna the librarian. Leave me a message.* Cleo left a message, saying the coast was clear at the library and that she'd be around until about five.

Eventually, Cleo got caught up in her tasks and pleasant diversions, like reacquainting herself with favorite books.

Time sped by and when Cleo glanced at a window, she was surprised to see darkness settling in. Evening came early this time of year, and Cleo preferred to be home before dark, cozied up with Rhett. Her cat would be grumpy from a day shut in by rain. Cleo was switching off lights, preparing to leave, when she heard footsteps on the porch.

Leanna, she imagined, thinking she could stay a little longer to strategize with her colleague. Cleo returned to the wood-paneled reference room, eager to show Leanna the progress. She tidied a bit more, rearranging books on the fine oak table in the center of the room. She registered the groan of the front door opening. She turned around just in time to see the hallway go dark.

The stomp of feet followed. They sounded large and loud, and they were accompanied by a curse in a voice that was most definitely male and not Leanna.

Jefferson. Cleo froze, recalling Jacquelyn's anger. Was Jefferson coming by to chew her out too? A flutter shot up her core. The police hadn't arrested Jefferson, but that didn't necessarily mean he was innocent. She tiptoed to the door and eased it closed. There was no lock, and the overhead light could only be turned off by a switch on the hallway side of the door.

"Hello? Anyone home?" Jefferson's voice bounced down the hall. "Where are the lights in this place? Yoo-hoo, anyone here?"

In the gap under the door, Cleo saw the hall lights flicker. On, off, and then on again. Footsteps came closer, and the lights in her room flickered too. Before Cleo could decide what to do, the door inched open, and Jefferson's round face poked around.

"Miss Cleo! There you are. I tried your house, but you weren't there."

Cleo was relieved that Jefferson didn't seem upset with her. In fact, he looked so happy to see her, Cleo's leeriness waned. However, quick as a switch, his cheeriness dimmed. "The lights in here are confusing. I couldn't see and bumped my knee in the dark. Didn't you hear me calling when I came in?"

"I must have been caught up working," Cleo said brightly, wishing their positions were reversed. He blocked the door with his bulk. She moved behind the oak desk, keeping up a friendly chatter. "I'm meeting someone. She should be here any moment." She didn't know if Leanna had gotten her messages or if she would be coming by. Cleo's phone, which her kids and grandkids had gotten her for emergencies, was out in the hallway.

"It's just you here, then?" he asked.

Cleo didn't want to answer that. "My friend is practically here," she said, waving a hand toward the door he blocked. "Why don't we go out on the porch and wait for her? It's a lovely night."

"It's rainy. I offered a mime workshop in the park, but no one signed up. It was free! Free costumes, free face paint. No one would stop." He rubbed his cheek, and Cleo noted waxy white in the five o'clock stubble that didn't fit his baby face. He stepped farther into the room. "It wasn't just the rain. Rain doesn't stop miming. It's because people don't trust me, isn't it? They think I hurt Mother."

His shoulders fell so low they almost disappeared. His lip quivered. "I couldn't have hurt her. I told you, and you understand, right? The police said they did, but now I think they were lying. I was only trying to help by talking to them too. It didn't help me. Now everyone thinks I did it. I heard people saying so."

Sympathy swept over Cleo. Behind his big bulk and his scruffy face, Cleo could see the kid in Jefferson. His baby-fine hair stuck out in scattered disarray. His clothes were rumpled from his khakis to his jacket, and he carried a sour odor of anxiety. If the poor man really was innocent, he'd have to endure harsh suspicion that would never lift if the culprit wasn't caught.

"The chief is casting a wide suspect net," Cleo said. She forced a smile. "For heaven's sake, he even suspected me."

Jefferson's chin shot up. His eyes narrowed on her.

"Of course, I didn't hurt your mother!" Cleo quickly clarified, regretting her attempt at camaraderie. "I'm telling you that because I understand what you're facing. Folks have been muttering about me too. You have to keep your chin up and believe justice will be served."

"That's the trouble," he moaned. "I don't believe that at all! The chief, he keeps saying he knows why I did it. It was so easy for me, he says. I had access to the syringe, I had motive, I wanted Mother's house. She didn't like my miming and . . ." His list trailed off in a sniffle.

From what Cleo could tell, all of that was true. She'd thought it herself and could add some more items to the list. Jefferson knew his mother's superstitions, her fears, her allergies. Dixie had bullied and berated him for years. Cleo surreptitiously surveyed the room, looking for possible defensive weapons.

The reference room housed lots of large, heavy books, but a librarian shouldn't harm a book. Bookends would do. The nearest set was a cast-iron pair shaped like open books. If she could heft them, she could throw them. Cleo had played South Georgia amateur softball in her youth and felt she could still muster a mighty pitch. She rolled her throwing shoulder, telling herself that if those bookends somehow missed their mark, she could lunge for the decorative bronze bust of Jane Austen over by the window. She didn't like the idea of hurling around such an important literary lady, but she thought Miss Austen would understand.

"No one really understands," Jefferson muttered. "Jacquelyn's practically living in her office, saying we never should have moved to Mother's cottage. Amy-Ray's acting like she owns the place, after deserting us all for years. Now someone's threatening me and no one cares."

Cleo halted in her bookend appraisal. "What?" she said. "You've been threatened, Jefferson? What do you mean? What happened?"

He tugged on his ear and shuffled his feet. "You won't believe me."

"Try me," Cleo said.

"Someone left a paper coffin on my car. It had my name on it. The chief said I put it there myself, but why would I do that?" He lurched toward the desk separating them. Cleo jerked back, but he grabbed her hand. Two cold yet sweaty palms clamped on hers. "I need help, Miss Cleo. I heard about you solving the murder last spring."

Jefferson had, until recently, lived out of state. Was her reputation reaching beyond Catalpa Springs? Beyond Georgia? Cleo's curiosity got the best of her. She eased her hand from his grasp and asked how he'd heard.

"Mother," he said, blushing. "She called and told me. She said you might decipher crimes, but you'd never figure out how to get that overdue book back." A smile crept in. "She loved to play jokes."

Dixie loved to taunt and tease. Cleo kept that thought to herself.

"Someone was messing with Mother. Now they're messing with me. That coffin! I need your help. The police aren't going to help me. No one else is." He stuffed his hands into his pockets and paced the room.

"Coffins have been appearing around town," Cleo said, careful not to sound like she was agreeing to help. Jefferson had just offered a very compelling list of reasons to remain leery of him. "What did the coffin you found say?"

"I don't know, something like *Jefferson H., this is not your home. Get out.*'"

Cleo frowned. The message wasn't quite right. The other notes welcomed recipients to their new home, the grave. "Odd," she said. "You're sure it said '*not* your home'?"

"I'm sure! Look, I'll show you. I took a photo before giving it to the police—like they cared." He reached into his back pocket, fiddled with the phone, and then shoved it across the desk. "See?"

Cleo took the phone and stared at the photo. Not only was the message off, so was the paper and writing. The paper was black like the others, but glossy. The printing was distinctly different too, a loopy cursive unlike the jagged printing she'd seen on the other notes. "It's not right," she murmured.

"You can say that again!" Jefferson said. "Someone's following me too. I feel it. I felt it coming here and at the house—Mother's house and our cottage." He raised a trembling chin. "I'm extra-sensitive to extrasensory vibrations. I felt something the night before Mother died. I went outside, thinking I'd heard something. I wish I'd gone over. I might have saved her."

Cleo handed back his phone, thinking as she did. "Jacquelyn said she saw your sister around the house this morning. Did you or Jacquelyn see Amy-Ray the night before your mother's death?"

Jefferson shook his head. "No. I didn't actually see anything, any of the times. That's why everyone says I'm crazy or making stuff up. It's just a *feeling*. Will you help me, Miss Cleo? I know it's a lot to ask, but you were always so nice to me as a kid, letting me come in here and do the story hour."

Cleo felt torn. She wanted to believe he was innocent. Her heart said so. However, her rational, sleuthing side warned her to keep her distance. He was making pleading gestures, palms pressed as if in prayer.

"Hello? Miss Cleo?"

Leanna's voice cut through the quiet.

Jefferson's whole body twitched. "I have to go," he said. "If there's anything—anything at all—you can find to help me, Miss Cleo, I beg you!"

He turned and lumbered out the door.

Cleo hurried after him. She heard Leanna gasp and met her young assistant in the hallway.

"What was *he* doing here?" Leanna demanded. "Are you okay, Miss Cleo? Did he threaten you? We should call Gabby." Leanna patted her pockets, seemingly in search of her phone. Cleo's protégé unfortunately took after Cleo in cell-phone forgetfulness too.

"It's okay," Cleo said, reaching out a hand to halt her search. "Jefferson wanted me to help him. He says he's innocent."

"That's what any guilty person would say," Leanna countered. "I know enough about criminals to know that." She went to the front door and locked it. "Miss Cleo, remember what happened last time you went sleuthing around? You almost got killed."

Behind the sparkly cat-eye glasses, Leanna's eyes were pleading. Cleo's sleuthing hadn't only threatened her own safety. She'd put Leanna in grave danger too.

"I don't want to have to worry about you again," Leanna said, reversing their roles and sounding like the sensible elder facing a reckless youngster. "If you stick your neck out, the killer's going to take notice. You could be a target!"

Cleo didn't know what to say. She felt bad enough already. Her sleuthing hadn't achieved much yet, other than accidentally finding the second note at Dixie's. She hadn't narrowed down the suspects. She hadn't even managed to clear herself. Perhaps she should tell Pat their sleuthing was off. It was too risky, too distracting . . . too fruitless. Pat would be disappointed, but that was preferable to attracting the attention of a killer, as Leanna said.

"I wouldn't know what to do in the library without you, Miss Cleo," Leanna said with a twist of a smile and a mock chastising finger waggle.

Cleo smiled back. "Oh yes, you would," she said without hesitation.

Chapter Twenty

Gabby predicted it. Nerves spread like flu. Cleo touched her forehead, worrying she'd caught the bug. Last night, walking home from the library in the misty dark, she'd felt as if someone was watching. It was, like Jefferson said, the neck-prickling sense of a presence nearby and not a nice one.

Cleo had walked faster, head swiveling, jumping when raindrop-heavy branches reached out and touched her. At her door, she'd fumbled with her keys, her heart thudding when the lock stuck, as it often did in damp weather. Even safely inside, with the doors locked and Rhett purring on her lap after dinner, she listened suspiciously to every scraping branch and rustle in the shrubs.

In the sunny Saturday light of the following morning, she felt silly. Looking out over her pretty back garden, Cleo found it easy to explain away the sounds. She'd surely heard only the wind or raindrops or four-legged visitors.

"Maybe it was your friend the armadillo," she said to Rhett. Her cat twined around her ankles, angling for a second breakfast. Cleo poured herself a second cup of coffee.

"Or your girlfriend across the street," Cleo suggested. Rhett flopped on the floor, feigning disinterest in a neighbor's pretty petite calico.

Cleo peeked out the backdoor, telling herself it wouldn't hurt to look around outside. She pulled yellow rubber boots on under her bathrobe and headed out the front. The air sagged with cool moisture. Rhett followed as far as the steps, where he stopped, sat, and eyed the drippy landscape with frowny-faced disgust.

Coffee cup in hand, fluffy hemline gathering dew, Cleo trekked around her yard. Over the years, she'd expanded her flower beds so that the lawn remained only as a carpet of pathways and oval accents. No footprints other than hers showed in the wet grass. However, a nighttime visitor could have kept to the thick mulch bordering the beds. Cleo retraced her route, scanning the shrubs and flowers that fringed her foundation. Here and there, a stalk was bent, another broken. She told herself the storm was to blame, but she couldn't help thinking about the broken stalks outside Dixie's window.

"Stop being silly," she said aloud.

"Silly?" Gabby's voice floated over their shared fence. Her face popped up a second later, ringed in a headband that matched her pink exercise top. "What was that, Miss Cleo?"

Cleo definitely felt silly now. "I was giving myself a talking to, and you caught me," she confessed.

Gabby grinned. "You'd be the only person I've caught then." She rolled her neck and said she'd been doing some yoga. "*Trying* to do yoga. This case has me all knotted up in my muscles and my mind."

Cleo could sympathize. "You didn't hear anything in our gardens last night, did you?" she asked, quickly adding, "Wildlife? The cat next door? The wind?"

Gabby narrowed her eyes. "I'll be right over."

Gabby traced Cleo's path around the house, stopping to pet Rhett, who got up only so he could flop back down at her feet.

"I'm imagining things," Cleo said. "Jefferson came to the library last night and—"

"Jefferson?" Gabby had been sniffing a sweet olive, a shrub with tiny, unassuming flowers that emitted a knock-your-socks-off perfume. "Was he bothering you? Is that who you think was prowling around?"

Cleo hadn't pictured Jefferson as the prowler. She tried to now but imagined him leaving big footprints or waxy white nose paint on the windows. "He only put the idea in my head," Cleo said, telling Gabby about his feeling of being watched.

"He told us about that," Gabby said in a skeptical tone. "Did he show you the supposed threat he found? Come on! The writing's all different. So's the paper. We wonder if he didn't write it himself."

Cleo sighed. "Poor Jefferson. I think he's desperately frightened, of the killer and being accused." Cleo bent to deadhead some violets. She kept her eyes on the flowers as she acknowledged, "Unless *he* is the killer. In that case he's a much better actor than he seems."

"He does have motive, means, opportunity, and theatrical training," Gabby said. "We don't have enough firm evidence to arrest him yet, but he's a better suspect than you. He and Jacquelyn both are."

Cleo plucked another spent flower. "I should be happy I'm no longer at the top of the list."

"You never were for me," Gabby said, her nose back at the sweet olive. "We've gotten a few other reports of prowlers. One call turned out to be kids dressed up like Grim Reapers. Little ghouls! The others weren't caught or even seen. They were more feelings, like you're describing. People are worked up, that's for certain. They hear the wind and think it's a ghost."

"That's probably what I heard," Cleo said, but she felt vexed. She tugged out a weed by its roots and took aim at another. "Someone is leaving those notes around during the night. What about Amy-Ray? Have you spoken with her? Jacquelyn told me that she saw Amy-Ray snooping around Dixie's home."

Gabby had heard all about that too, from Jacquelyn, from their lawyer, and from Amy-Ray herself. "Amy-Ray admitted she dropped by a few times, but she claims she was nowhere near Catalpa Springs on the morning of the murder. We've been asking around. No one reports seeing her here. Her roommate says she was *probably* home, and her coworkers say she was her normal, grouchy self that day. She works at a naturopathic clinic in Claymore, a place called Healing Hands." Gabby ran her fingers over dewy fern fronds. "I can't see why she'd kill Dixie now. She has a job and no financial troubles, seemingly."

Cleo thought about Dixie's lovely home. Jefferson and Jacquelyn wanted it for their mime school. "The house?" Cleo speculated. "Amy-Ray was awfully keen on claiming it as her own." She immediately rebutted herself. "But like you say, why now? And why go to such elaborate lengths to terrify Dixie? Creating fear seems like a main motive, maybe more than material items or money."

Gabby shrugged, turning it into an elbow-bending stretch. "You're right, whoever did this wanted Dixie afraid." A beep sounded, and Gabby glanced down at her watch. She'd once told Cleo that the watch did everything from tracking her steps and heartbeat to taking calls and sending emails. Cleo didn't think she'd want that much monitoring and office work on her wrist. "Sorry," Gabby said. "I have to run. Run to work, not the fun kind of running. Promise me you'll call me anytime—night or day—if you think someone's creeping over here, Miss Cleo." She patted her hip. "I'll come armed in more than Spandex."

Cleo watched her neighbor jog around their fence. She'd intended to visit Amy-Ray, but between the library and other suspects, she hadn't had time.

"No time like the present," she said to Rhett, who still sulked on the stoop, glaring at the damp grass. He perked up in the kitchen when she offered him an extra helping of Tuna Delight, a bribe that let her sneak out the door without facing the special grumpy look Rhett Butler reserved for getting left at home.

* * *

Cleo called to invite Henry along. She did so from her driveway, sitting in her vintage convertible, letting the engine warm to a purr. She hadn't had her car out recently. It would be good to take it for a drive. The 1967 cherry-red Ford Galaxie convertible had previously belonged to her father, who'd kept it meticulously waxed and cooped up in the garage most of the year. Cleo never could understand the latter. The little car handled like the wind and demanded to be driven. She planned to zip over to Claymore and be back before eleven for her scheduled bookmobile stop in the park.

Henry waited outside his shop. He got in and greeted Cleo with a lingering peck on the cheek. His beard smelled of sandalwood and cinnamon. Cleo deduced that he'd had a treat from the bakery. She revved the engine to cover her rumbling tummy. In her hurry to hunt down Amy-Ray's work address, she'd forgotten to eat, a practically unheard-of problem. She touched her forehead again, wondering if she really did have a bug.

Henry buckled up. "I brought supplies," he said. He drew a paper sack from his jacket pocket. "Cinnamon scones."

Cleo could have kissed him.

"And hot pepper."

Cleo had been checking her mirrors. "Hot pepper? Tabasco?" Henry liked hot sauce on pretty much everything savory and sometimes tucked a peanut-sized bottle in his jacket pocket.

"Pepper spray," Henry said darkly. "In case this turns into a visit with a killer."

Cleo hesitated, hand on the stick shift. Just yesterday she'd questioned the wisdom of her sleuthing, and rightfully so. On the other hand, they intended to visit a business that boasted calming Saturday morning healing services from a full staff. "I don't think anything bad will happen to us at the

Healing Hands Clinic," Cleo said, shifting firmly into first. Still, she was glad for Henry's company and for his thoughtful supplies.

Catalpa Springs soon passed behind them. They crossed the low, slow Tallgrass River, through tall pines and marshy meadows. Then the landscape changed for the uglier. Cleo didn't like to label anything homely, but if Claymore could know her thoughts, she felt it wouldn't mind. The biggest town in Catalpa County was always expanding, and rarely for the nicer. Billboards spouted like hives on the outskirts. Shopping centers and parking lots mushroomed outward, deserting their abandoned predecessors. Neighborhoods fell into shabbiness, and new versions popped up. The roads always seemed to change.

Cleo found herself in a turn lane she didn't recognize. "I swear," she complained, "every time I'm over here, I feel like they've moved entire buildings. Wasn't that supercenter on the other side of the road before?" She managed a James-Bond-worthy lane maneuver and added, "We're looking for Hilldale Court and Healing Hands. Amy-Ray is listed as a 'healing professional.'"

Henry saw the street as they were about to pass it. Cleo swerved again. Her heart had just returned to a normal beat when she spotted Healing Hands. The dull cement building resembled Pat's cleaning company except for its odd flare. Shiny sculptures of upturned hands, red and taller than Cleo, flanked the door. Music greeted them as they approached, soothing sounds of pan flutes, rushing water, and crickets. A real cricket chirped back.

"What's our strategy?" Henry asked. His right hand was in his pocket, along with the pepper spray.

Cleo hadn't decided yet. "I just want to have a little chat, see what sort of person she is."

"See if she confesses to killing her mother and terrorizing Catalpa Springs?" Henry asked as the music melded into birdsong.

"That would certainly make this a worthwhile trip," Cleo replied.

Henry chuckled and held the door. Cleo entered to the startling likeness of Dixie reborn. Amy-Ray stood in the lobby, wearing lavender surgical scrubs and an unwelcoming expression. Stiff-looking armchairs ringed the walls, nearly obscured by a wild array of plants. Cleo reached out to touch an orchid and discovered it was plastic.

"We're not open yet," Amy-Ray said curtly. She pointed to the door, implying they could go out the way they came. She aimed her next words beyond the pass-through to the back of the office. "Who unlocked the front early?" No one responded.

Amy-Ray turned an unwelcoming frown to Cleo and Henry. "Who are you here to see?"

"You!" Cleo exclaimed, as bright and fake as the plastic orchid. "Do you remember me? Cleo Watkins. The librarian in Catalpa Springs. I was a . . ." Cleo hesitated. Claiming false friendship was a fib she couldn't stomach. "I knew your mother very well," she said truthfully. "My friend Henry and I were driving by and had heard you worked here. We wanted to pop in and make sure you're doing all right. Such a difficult time . . ."

"Watkins?" Amy-Ray said, her left lip curling up in what Cleo decided was a grin. "You're that librarian who was forever chasing after Dixie. Good effort! Forty years? Ha!"

Dixie, Cleo noted. Not *mother, mama, mommy,* or *mom.* "You reunited with your mother recently," she said, keeping up her bright tone. "That's lovely."

Amy-Ray gave a bored sigh. "Yeah, sure. A lot of good it did me. Can I help you? Do you need an appointment? If so, our receptionist is in the back and can be with you in four minutes."

Cleo wished she'd brought a backup plan. Usually folks liked a friendly visit or at least pretended to tolerate it. Amy-Ray was turning, heading for the employees-only door. "Wait!" Cleo blurted out. "I need your help. The police think I murdered your mother."

Amy-Ray turned, eyebrow raised in interest.

"I didn't," Cleo said, feeling Henry hover protectively closer. "I need to clear my name. Can we talk somewhere for a minute? Four minutes, before you have to start work?"

Amy-Ray heaved with a sigh. "Fine. We can go in my office." She pushed through the employees-only door, letting it swing back for Cleo to catch.

"Is anyone else actually here?" Henry whispered, looking around warily, his hand tucked in the pepper-spray pocket. The back corridors branched off like a maze. Cleo wished she'd brought the scones, for comfort and to leave a trail of crumbs.

"Here," Amy-Ray said, opening an office.

Cleo stepped inside and smiled. Books! Packed shelves

filled every wall. "What a lovely office," she exclaimed, earning a genuine smile from Amy-Ray.

"What can I say," Amy-Ray said. "I guess I take after Dixie in this. I hoard books."

"Books don't count as hoarding," Cleo said, to which Henry agreed. Since Amy-Ray remained standing behind her desk and hadn't offered them seats, Cleo moved to the shelves and inspected titles. The collection ranged from natural medicine to music, with a few novels mixed in. Cleo spotted a new bestseller she'd recently stocked in Words on Wheels. The two available copies flew off the shelf. She said so to Amy-Ray, hoping to show their common interests. "I drive the bookmobile," she said. "This book is very popular with patrons."

"You have a *moving library* and you still couldn't pin down Dixie and that book?" Amy-Ray said, missing the bonding point. "Bet that drove you crazy. No wonder you're a suspect. I am too, you know." She shrugged. "I didn't do it either, if that's what you're really here to find out. Like I told the cops, why would I? I already won."

Cleo recalled Amy-Ray yelling just that at the wake. "What do you mean, you *won*?"

Smugness rounded Amy-Ray's face. She ran her fingers through her spiky hair. "By holding out all those years. I didn't go running home and begging Dixie to take me back. Nope. I never called, never wrote, never asked for money even when I needed it. It worked. Dixie came crawling to me when she decided she was dying. She *needed* me to forgive her."

"Did you forgive her?" Henry asked softly.

Amy-Ray shrugged. "Sure. It didn't matter to me. We made a deal."

Cleo wouldn't usually be so forthright, but she thought Amy-Ray wouldn't mind. "What did you get out of your deal?"

Amy-Ray grinned. "I said I'd take away all that bad luck she'd gathered by shunning her only daughter on one condition: that she let me move back home."

Cleo drew a sharp breath. *How tragic!* Going home was Amy-Ray's sole condition? Could it be that behind Amy-Ray's blustery exterior, she'd missed her home so much that all she wanted was to return?

Amy-Ray snorted laughter. "Oh, you are precious! The look on your face! You feel awful for me, don't you? That's exactly what I wanted. Everyone would know that Mother came begging to me, that *she* was in the wrong all along. That's how I won, and I was going to rub it in *every single day*. I was supposed to move in next week. It won't be as fun now, but I still get the house. Jefferson will know I won."

Finally, a *mother* had slipped out. Cleo felt Henry shift closer to her. Chills crept up her arm. Amy-Ray's desire for home wasn't tragic, sad, or sweet. It was selfish and manipulative. "Just like Dixie," Cleo murmured.

Amy-Ray chuckled. "I suppose I am, aren't I?" She pointed to a row of books behind her, resting on the windowsill. The point narrowed to a single volume, a maroon cover with gold lettering.

Cleo gasped. She pushed back her bifocals and blinked. If Henry hadn't caught her arm, she might have lunged. *"Luck and Lore!"* she cried. She was about to push on, despite Henry's hold, when a terrible thought made her snap back, pulling Henry with her. She recalled their earlier logic. If Dixie had been waiting with *Luck and Lore* and it was now missing, then her killer likely took it.

Amy-Ray was chuckling so hard a tear slid down her cheek. "Y'all have made my morning. This makes working the weekend worth it."

Footsteps hurried down the hallway. A colleague in penguin-print scrubs poked her head in, looking alarmed. "Amy, are you okay? I heard . . . laughing." The woman frowned in confusion. "Your acupuncture appointment is here too."

Amy-Ray wiped her eyes. "I see why Dixie had such fun with this, but I don't have time for it." She yanked the book from its companions and tossed it at Cleo. "Enjoy! Consider it a gift from Dixie."

Chapter
Twenty-One

B ack in the safety of her car, Cleo opened the book with a shaky hand. A station wagon pulled into the Healing Hands lot and parked beside them. Its door slammed and locks beeped. Rush-hour traffic rumbled by on the street. Cleo opened the front cover, looking for the bookplate. The Catalpa Springs Public Library marked all its books with a pretty sticker, a woodblock print of the library with its name and founding date forming the border.

No bookplate.

Cleo turned to the cover. No barcode. She checked the back inside cover. No checkout slip either. Dixie had checked out *Luck and Lore* when due dates were stamped on a card tucked in a paper sleeve. The borrower's name was written in too. Now a machine spit out return slips that looked like supermarket receipts, and privacy concerns wouldn't allow patron identities and reading tastes on full display.

"This isn't it," Cleo said, disappointment overpowering her earlier fear that they'd met a killer. "It's not the library's copy."

"It's interesting that Amy-Ray has this book," Henry said, ever looking on the bright side.

Cleo flipped pages. At the title page, she stopped and read an inscription in red ink. "To Amy-Ray. Good luck. Dixie."

"Not exactly maternal and gushy," Henry said, "but Dixie clearly valued the book and wanted her daughter to have a copy."

Unseemly vexation welled in Cleo. "Dixie went out and *bought* this copy, didn't she? She had enough money to buy books. Oh, I suppose I should be happy. At least she didn't *steal* it from another library."

Henry politely shifted the conversation. "I'll be interested to read it, to see what made this such a treasure."

Cleo handed it to him with a huff and started her car. "I still think it's more about *how* Dixie got her copy. She said her luck turned the day she checked it out, the day she stole my birthday wishes. If she'd truly wanted her daughter to have good luck, she should have given Amy-Ray the library's copy."

"Amy-Ray seems to be all about winning too," Henry said, stroking his beard.

Cleo pondered that as her engine hummed. "Amy-Ray said it wouldn't be as 'fun' to win the family home without Dixie there. But those two never got along, by all accounts. What if Amy-Ray realized she'd have more fun without her mother in the house? Everyone in town and her brother too would still know that she'd been victorious."

They both peered out toward Healing Hands. A figure in pale lavender scrubs watched from the front window. Amy-Ray saw them looking and waved.

Henry automatically waved back. "Let's get out of here," he said.

Cleo was more than happy to. She pulled into the busy street, intending to go back the way they'd come. She found herself in the wrong lane at a turn. She quickly decided it might be the right lane after all. "Won't this street take us past the Claymore Library? I suppose we should stop in so I can see what Belle's been up to over here."

Henry closed *Luck and Lore* and shifted uneasily. "If we must," he said grimly. "But if Belle is there, I'm bolting. She's been calling me, leaving messages, wanting me to come over and help her pick out more books to discard. I cannot be a part of book tossing!"

Cleo felt a teenage glee that sweet, sensible Henry hadn't succumbed to Belle's sway like Mercer and her library board. She parked on the street in front of the library, allowing for easy fleeing if necessary. She scanned their surroundings but saw no sign of a red truck, mini-pony, disco bookmobile, or flirty innobrarian.

As they walked up the steps, Cleo made sure to appreciate the good points of the Claymore Library. It was sturdy. A sign confirmed this, marking the seventies-era cement-block structure as an emergency hurricane and tornado shelter. Cleo thought she'd enjoy riding out a storm in a library. Books were an essential element of her emergency kit, along with nonperishables, cat food, flashlights, and batteries.

They entered through glass doors, and Cleo revised her earlier thoughts. A storm had swept through the Claymore Library, a Belle disaster. "Good gracious!" Cleo blinked into a bright, empty gleam. The last time she'd visited—maybe a year ago—bookshelves had filled the front room. She'd been a smidge envious of the many display spaces.

Nothing remained except a single pedestal holding a lone book. Cleo approached tentatively, feeling unsteady from the emptiness and the white marble tile, as glossy as oiled ice.

"What is this book?" she murmured. It was thick and cracked open. If Belle wanted to create a sense of anticipation, she'd achieved it.

"Wait until you see," Henry said darkly. "I won't give away the surprise."

Cleo suspected she wasn't going to like the surprise. She peered down at the book before drawing back with a puff of disgust. "It's a fake!"

The mock book was wooden and hollowed out to reveal a tablet, the electronic kind, flashing images of books. Cleo sighed. "You did try to warn me."

"I didn't want to go into disturbing detail," Henry said, looking around. "Besides, you have to experience it."

A weary voice affirmed Henry's statement before Cleo could. "You certainly do."

Cleo looked up to see Sara Martinez, fellow librarian. Sara was in her late fifties, a usually cheerful woman, well rounded in her reading and her figure, with a healthy sense of humor and a bubbly nature. She seemed deflated today. Cleo could understand why.

"Sara," Cleo said, down-pitching her tone to funereal. "I am *so* sorry." She didn't need to elaborate about what.

Her fellow librarian looked warily over her shoulders.

"You will be, Cleo. I hear she's coming for you next." She lowered her voice. "We need to talk, but not here."

Cleo had already seen enough of *here*. She and Henry followed Sara to her office, a closet-like space with a view of the back parking lot, a massive air conditioner, and ventilation pipes. Sara had made the space cozy with framed photographs of magnificent libraries, cathedrals of books from all over the world.

Sara closed the door behind them and offered them seats. Cleo and Henry sat with their knees touching each other and bumping Sara's desk. Sara kept her voice low. "I should apologize to you, Cleo. Our director sent a glowing recommendation letter for Belle Beauchamp to your library board. I tried to get her to tone it down or be brutally honest, but she's desperate to get Belle out of here."

Cleo bit her lip. "Thank you for trying," she said, although it hardly helped. Seeing Sara's anxious expression, she said, "Our board president is infatuated with her. I'm hoping it'll pass or that I can convince Belle that libraries aren't for her."

Sara sniffed and pushed back a curl among the bouncy layers framing her face. "Good luck with that. We can't get her to do any actual library work except for tossing out books. Oh, and she likes interacting with the public, but that's to throw parties and make the kids happy with candy and that little horse. The horse *is* cute . . ."

They all agreed on the cuteness of Lilliput. Cleo didn't bring up Lilliput's fondness for munching periodicals. She suspected Sara already knew.

Sara sighed heavily. "We got tricked. Our director was

lured in by Belle's résumé and her flashy presentations, all her charts and numbers. But that's the trouble—Belle thinks the value of libraries can only be measured in numbers. Libraries are so much more than that! They're for learning, refuge, relaxation . . . and fun too, of course. Libraries are tons of fun already!" Sara slumped back in her seat. "I'm feeling so scattered that I can't even come up with the right words."

Cleo said she understood completely.

Sara sputtered out more affronts, turning to Henry. "Mr. Lafayette, you were here when she tried to throw out our historical collection. I appreciate how you helped. We've managed to save a lot by stashing books in the back. She's not interested in the stacks. She doesn't think our 'clients' will go back there. But, oh, this is bad: now she wants to turn our nonfiction wing into a movie lounge. It's like she's trying to undo everything a decent library does! I hope she'll move on soon." Sara pursed her lips before adding. "Sorry! I know that means you might get stuck with her."

Cleo managed sympathetic sounds, holding in the groaning dread she felt. If a bigger library with more staff hadn't stopped Belle, how could she and Leanna hope to?

"I wish her parents had moved down to Florida like they wanted," Sara said. "Then Belle would be down there with them. I'm being awful! Her parents are nice people. Belle is too, just not when it comes to libraries. She changed so much after she moved up to Atlanta . . ."

Cleo had sunk into worries. She registered Sara's words and shook her head sharply to refocus. "You knew Belle when she was growing up here?" Sara was younger than Belle, but from the area. They could easily have known each other.

Sara fiddled with a pencil holder, an art-deco ceramic cat that Leanna would love. "Belle doesn't remember, or she *says* she doesn't, but we overlapped at a summer camp a few years. Not in the same cabin—I'm younger—but we little kids would sneak over and spy on the teens."

"I'd heard she went to a summer camp," Cleo said. "She doesn't seem like much of a camper. She's so polished."

"Not then she wasn't. You want to see photos of young Belle?" Sara stood, inching out from behind her cramped desk. "You'll think we're awful snoops, but I was telling the other librarians how different Belle used to be. They couldn't believe it, so we went looking for photos of her in the archives. We keep local yearbooks and newspapers, of course."

"Not awful at all," Cleo said, interest piqued. "You were researching, gathering information, doing what comes naturally for librarians."

Sara brightened. "Exactly!" She looked both ways in the hallway before leading them quickly to a back room. "Honestly," she whispered, "the more I think about Belle's childhood, the more sympathetic I feel. It's no wonder she puts on an armor of polish now."

Belle, picked on? Cleo could hardly believe it. She seemed so strong.

Sara was heaving books from a shelf, heavy paged yearbooks, asking how many photos Henry and Cleo wanted to see.

"All you have," Cleo said, shooting an apologetic look to Henry. He, however, was looking as interested as she was.

"Belle was bullied at that camp and probably school too," Sara said as she got out more books. "She was the awkward kid. The mean girls liked to trick her. I remember the popular, pretty girls laughing because they'd conned poor Belle into thinking a cute boy liked her. They'd steal her clothes, take embarrassing photos. Kids can be so cruel! I guess adults can be too."

Sara added a few reels of microfilm to the stack. "See how thorough our 'research' was?" she said, looking slightly embarrassed. "We got a bit carried away, but lucky for you, we didn't get around to reshelving it all. Speaking of which, I should get back to work." After a scan of the hall, she trotted off.

Cleo loaded the hulking microfilm machine, marveling at how far technology had come in her lifetime and her career. "I *am* grateful for technological innovations," she said, to which Henry heartily agreed. She positioned her bifocals on the viewfinder. Thankfully, Sara had left a sticky note attached to the reel, marking the relevant dates. As the film spun by, she could hear Henry flipping through pages.

"My goodness," Cleo said. "Look at this." She stepped back to let Henry see.

"Is that Belle?" he asked. Cleo had stopped on a newspaper article about the summer camp. The image was grainy black and white, showing a group shot of the campers, all girls, their names listed in the caption by row.

They swapped spots and Cleo counted the campers and rows once more to make sure she was looking at the correct person. "Sara's right. I wouldn't recognize her, and I like to think I'm good with faces."

"She's in these too," Henry said, pointing to some open year-books. "What a transformation to her hair and clothes. I wonder if she didn't get plastic surgery too? Her nose looks different."

Cleo studied the photos. Young Belle had darker hair. She was a bit plump by the harsh standards of society and Cleo's doctor. In each photo, her head dipped, and she seemed to sink into the background. "It's not only her physical appearance, is it?" Cleo said, flipping through an earlier yearbook. "It's her way of holding herself. She's head high and confident now. Bold. A presence. In these she looks like she wants to disappear."

"It's good she gained her confidence," Henry said. He added, "She gained a little too much . . ."

Cleo turned a page and was about to keep on flipping when her eyes caught on someone else familiar. "Dixie!" She jabbed her index finger at the page. "They were there the same year!"

She studied the photo, the years turning back in her head. "I remember Dixie wearing this very dress," Cleo said, marveling at the memory. The dress featured grapefruit-size yellow daisies smattered across a blue background. Dixie would have been twelve or so. "She was spirited," Cleo said. "Spunky. Always confident. Well, until the end."

Cleo tempered her rose-colored memories. Sara had mentioned popular girls playing mean tricks. Cleo could easily see Dixie being one of those bullies. In the photo, Dixie stood with two other girls, one blonde like her, the other a long-locked brunette. They had the confident, hip-jutting pose of girls who know they're gorgeous, at least on the outside.

Henry pointed beyond them, to the background. "Look at this. The image is fuzzy, but could that be Belle?"

They both leaned in, cheek to bushy beard. The figure in the far back, blurred by tall grass and the camera's focus, seemed to lean out of the frame. "It could be," Cleo said.

Henry straightened. "It wasn't a huge camp. We can assume they knew each other there, even if they weren't friends."

Cleo shut the yearbook. She remembered that she hadn't told Henry about inadvertently chasing Belle off by asking her about Dixie. She described Belle's odd, evasive reaction. "I can see why Belle wouldn't want to remember her, if Dixie was a bully. I wouldn't want to look back on that."

"Perhaps that was why she and Dixie had heated words at the farmers' market," Henry said. "If Mary-Rose is right."

Cleo had no doubt about Mary-Rose's memory. Childhood bullying could be a thorn that ached forever. It would be just like Dixie to wiggle that thorn around. "Dixie managed to insult and upset Iris Hays even more when she tried to apologize to her. She blamed Iris for being 'weak' and called her health problems her own fault. Maybe she did something similar to Belle."

They stacked the books, reeled the microfilm, and thanked Sara again on the way out. Cleo was happy to get back on the road and put Claymore behind them. Driving over the Tallgrass River, she slowed, glancing into the deep, green waters. Their visit hadn't made her suspect pool any clearer. If anything, knowledge of Belle's bullied past and Amy-Ray's supposed "win" only muddied the waters.

Chapter
Twenty-Two

Monday morning, Leanna followed Cleo out to the library's front porch. They stood at the railing, squinting in the sun. Cleo had the same eye-stinging feeling inside, where a fresh rash of shocking paint samples dotted the walls.

"Are you sure you should do this?" Leanna asked again. "What if you're only attracting Belle's *innobrating* attention to Words on Wheels? The bookmobile could be Catalpa Springs' last remaining reading refuge. We could keep the books on the road, always roving, so Belle won't be able to find them and throw them out."

Cleo glanced at her young colleague, worried Leanna might be feeling the combined effects of too many paint fumes and the dystopic science fiction she'd been reading lately.

"It'll be fine," Cleo said. "Belle needs to see real library work in action. I'll take her on my bookmobile stops this morning. Then she's going to bring BOOK IT! to the school's Fall Fest later on." She continued on over Leanna's muttering. "It'll be fun, and a good opportunity to show her how much the kids love books. I know her party bookmobile will get their attention, but so will Words on Wheels."

Cleo wanted to ask Belle about Dixie again too. Belle had taken the weekend off, except for ordering more paint samples and bombarding the library staff and board with emails containing pie charts and "actionables." The latter included acquiring ribbons and "glamorous" scissors for the grand reopening party and confirming the fondue menu, all of which Cleo promptly acted on. She'd bought yards of red satin ribbon and sharp new silvery shears, and had located a library cookbook with one hundred recipes for fondue.

"While I'm out, see if you can get the contractor over here, like we talked about," Cleo said. "His kids are big readers. I'm sure he'll agree that we can't possibly move those bookshelves." She winked at Leanna, reinforcing their plan to have the otherwise honest contractor declare the shelves unmovable. By fib or fight, she was determined to keep the library's shelves and their books in place. The Catalpa Springs Public Library couldn't become bookless like BOOK IT! and the gutted Claymore Library.

"Belle's not going to like this," Leanna said with a nervous giggle. "Not the shelves or your day of real work." She turned on her patent-leather flats and scooted back inside, calling out "Good luck, Miss Cleo," as the door groaned shut.

Cleo yearned for a dash of good luck. Bad seemed to have settled in like a stench over her lovely little town. Pat had come by Cleo's house yesterday, filled with news of more threatening notes. Gabby had spent the weekend running down reports of everything from bad omens to prowlers. All around town, folks were looking over their shoulders, acting twitchy, avoiding others or clumping in groups. Cleo had even spotted a lady avoiding sidewalk cracks and a man tossing salt over his shoulder.

Cleo picked up her purse and headed down the walkway. Her bookmobile gleamed in the sun, its name sparkling in opalescent green. Rhett lounged on the hood, indiscreetly grooming his hindquarters. Cleo clicked her tongue and he looked up. When she rattled a can of tuna treats from inside, he bounded in to join her. She put his snack in his traveling peach crate, and he hopped in. Cleo browsed the shelves and flipped through a book of five-ingredient casseroles while waiting for Belle to show up.

A horn honked a few minutes later. Belle pulled up with BOOK IT! The silver Airstream wore a string of blinking, hot-pink lights. Cleo went outside to greet her. She complimented the lights, which were pretty and quiet and didn't seem to threaten any books.

"Aren't they cute?" Belle said. Her pickup had four doors. Where back seats once stood, Lilliput now did. Belle hauled a long ramp from the cargo bed and put it up to Lilliput's mobile stall. The little horse pranced down, pausing at the end to bob his head and let Cleo ruffle his mane.

"That ramp is clever too," Cleo said, following Belle onto the library's lawn and making sure Belle hooked Lilliput's lead to a sturdy tree. With the rain, the grass had sprung up. It wouldn't hurt to have a natural mower go after it, although someone would have to come in later with a not-so-miniature shovel to clean up after the little horse.

Belle tapped her temple. "That ramp is bookmobile-mascot innovation in action. Now, where are we going? This should be a hoot!"

They boarded Words on Wheels and drove to a nursing home, where Cleo delivered audiobooks and a stack of large-print novels, and Rhett sopped up loving from friends old and new. They stopped at the homes of some residents who couldn't get out much anymore. Rhett mostly stayed in the bus for those visits, while Cleo and Belle drank enough ice tea and lemonade to float away. They then went to a work center for adults with special needs and dropped by a halfway house for recent parolees.

"I didn't like that last stop," Belle whispered as she and Cleo left the halfway house. "What if they robbed us?"

Cleo's mind flashed to Dixie, running off with *Luck and Lore*. "Those patrons have never stolen a book," she said.

"Not the books," Belle said as they rounded Words on Wheels. "They're not valuable. I meant our jewelry." She placed a protective hand over her long strand of pearls.

For several miles, Cleo issued a lesson on the invaluable worth of books, reading, and continuing education. "Look at the books we just delivered to the halfway house," she said as part of her lecture. "They're helping the residents turn their lives around. Those men have admittedly had troubles, but now some are studying for their GED and learning new skills."

"Half of those books we delivered were *fiction*," Belle said, her tone suggesting she'd just wrecked Cleo's argument.

Cleo persisted. "Fiction can shine a light on the world. It can provide an escape, joy, empathy, compassion—"

"TV provides an escape too," Belle said stubbornly. She reclined on the front seat, wedged into the corner, her feet banked against the safety barrier. "I need a nap. Your kind of bookmobiling is a lot of work."

Cleo confirmed that it was. "But fulfilling," she continued in cheerleader tones. "Look how many people *you* helped this morning. The school event will be lovely too. The kids have a half day today. They'll be so excited."

Belle groaned. "What age are they again? First- through fifth-graders? They'll be exhausting, but yeah, more fun than the convicts, I suppose."

All morning, Cleo had been waiting for an appropriate opening to ask about Belle's childhood experiences at summer camp. On the way back to town, she stopped at a crossroads and saw her chance.

"That summer camp you used to go to," Cleo said. "It's down the road to the right, isn't it? The Holloway Road?" Cleo let the bus idle at a stop since no other cars were around. She turned back to Belle.

Belle sat up and looked around before lowering herself back to reclining. "Yeah, I guess. It's been a few years, to say the least."

Cleo eased the bus forward. "I recently learned that Dixie Huddleston went to that camp. Is that where you first met her?" Cleo glanced in her mirror to see Belle jerk upright.

"Cleo Watkins, you are as persistent as a mosquito! Why

do you keep bugging me about Dixie?" Belle's tone was light but tinged in vexation. "What are you trying to do, pin a murder on me? That's sure thinking outside the box, but not the way I like it."

"She bullied you," Cleo said softly.

"She bullied you too, keeping out that overdue book," Belle countered. "She bullied a lot of people, and bullies should get their comeuppance. Now, if you'll excuse me, I'm going to check out the back of this bus. I see room for improvement. It's all cluttered! Too many books."

Cleo didn't approve of changing seats while the bus was moving, but she let Belle go. She drove slowly back to town, her mind spinning as fast as her wheels. Bullies did deserve comeuppance. They didn't deserve to be murdered.

* * *

"How'd it go?" Leanna asked as Cleo stepped out of Words on Wheels that afternoon. The schoolyard was already bustling with preparations for Fall Fest.

Cleo started to answer, but a yawn took over. Belle wasn't the only one who'd needed a nap. After dropping Belle off, Cleo had gone home and sacked out on the sofa with Rhett. She'd sneaked out while he was still snoozing. Her cat liked children, but not in hyped-up crowds.

"Our bookmobile morning went well enough," Cleo said. "I tired Belle out and myself too." She told Leanna about their stops, glossing over Belle's talk of "decluttering" her bookmobile. "The school festival will go well too, I'm sure."

"I hope," Leanna said, sounding the opposite of her words.

"It looks like BOOK IT! is back in party mode." Lights flashed over at the Airstream. Lilliput wore a sparkly crown, and Belle had restocked her supply of sudsy water buckets and giant bubble wands.

"The kids will like the bubbles and Lilliput," Cleo said, "but they'll love what you've put together too.

To compete in bookmobile cuteness, Leanna had brought twinkling LED lights and paper banners shaped like autumn leaves. She also had activity tables where the kids could make origami animals and write and draw their own stories. Of course, the children and their parents could also check out books. Cleo had a stack of forms to apply for library cards, although she liked to think that everyone in her town would already have a card.

Since Leanna seemed to have the setup covered, Cleo toured the other stands. The school cafeteria had set up a cart doling out healthy snacks and hot apple cider. A local artist would give instructions on braiding friendship bracelets. Another local artist was setting up a row of easels stocked with paper. Iris Hays. Cleo hadn't spoken to Iris since Dixie's wake. She wondered if Iris remembered or if her tipsiness had blurred it out. She was heading Iris's way when she heard her name.

"Cleo!" Pat Holmes chugged up the sidewalk, waving. "I need to talk to you!" Pat reversed course to come in the schoolyard gate. Cleo walked back to join her. They met up just as the bell rang and kids ran out in a screaming wave. Cleo smiled, watching the kids ripple outward. Some bolted straight to Lilliput. Others wanted first dibs at Leanna's activity stations and the games the school had set up.

"More bad news," Pat said glumly. "One of my cleaners got a note on her windshield this morning. It mentioned her and her husband by name, telling them to clean up their act or they'd be scrubbing floors six feet under. Isn't that awful? The lady won't go on any jobs alone anymore, and I don't blame her." Pat took a breath and looked bleakly out across the schoolyard. "What have you heard? Do you have any new clues?"

Cleo had already reported on her visit with Amy-Ray and receiving her copy of *Luck and Lore*. She thought about the book now and mentioned it to Pat. "I wish I'd had a chance to read it last night. I was so worn out, I fell asleep in front of the TV news and then went straight to bed."

"Will you replace the missing version with that one?" Pat asked.

"I know it sounds silly, but that book's not the same as getting back the library's original copy," Cleo said. "Please don't tell the police or that newspaper reporter—they'll say I'm obsessed—but I want the original. It's still missing, still messing up my rosters."

"You can sue Dixie's estate for the overdue fine," Pat said.

For a moment, Cleo thought Pat had made a joke, but Pat looked serious and worried.

"I don't know about this event," Pat said. "Should the school be putting this on when there's a killer around?"

Cleo smiled at her, wishing she had something to raise Pat's spirits and hopes. "I'm sure it'll be fine. No one's bothered the school. I was heading over to see Iris. Do you want to join me?"

Pat declined. "I don't think she likes me after that trouble at the Pancake Mill. I'll go to Words on Wheels. I need a new book. We're not actually reading a book for the Who-Done-Its."

Cleo's head was still shaking, thinking about the bookless book-club meeting, when she reached Iris.

The artist greeted her with a grin. "Why'd Pat run off? There're enough easels for you both to draw." She flipped back the paper on the tallest easel. "I have a sketch going already. I call it 'Just Deserts.'"

Cleo cocked her head and squinted at ink scribbled in freehand loops.

Iris pointed to the various blobs. "There's the woman, lying on the pantry floor," Iris said. "There's the bees . . ."

Cleo drew back. "Iris, this is a school event! This isn't appropriate!"

Iris smiled serenely. "We all have our outlets. You have your books. I have my art." Iris muttered words inappropriate for a schoolyard, picked up a pen, and added a dark cloud of scribbles over the prone figure.

Cleo backed away, saying she shouldn't keep Iris from her work. She stopped by a few other stands and then returned to the bookmobile, thinking Pat had had the right idea by avoiding Iris.

Pat was reading in the back of Words on Wheels. "You've had a lot of customers already," Pat said. "Kids, parents, and teachers. Your friend Leanna checked them all out since I didn't know how. I'm not being very helpful—with this or the investigation. I keep thinking, what if the person is right in front of us? Speaking of which, did you see that Jefferson is here?"

Cleo hadn't. She followed Pat's pointing to beyond the schoolyard fence. Now that she saw him, he was hard to miss. He wore a mime costume in black and white and held a red balloon. Cleo shivered. Iris, Belle, Jefferson . . . all they needed was Amy-Ray and Jacquelyn, and all her main suspects would be in plain sight. She looked down to the closer distance and saw Leanna bouncing back and forth between tables. "I better go help Leanna," Cleo said. "Stay and relax."

"I could use some time with books," Pat admitted.

Cleo looked forward to that too, book work in her case. She helped Leanna with loads of checkouts and chatted with parents, kids, and teachers about their book selections. Cleo had moved over to Leanna's origami table and was attempting to fold paper cranes with a fourth-grader, when she saw Iris stomping into Words on Wheels. Cleo hoped the artist would be nice to Pat. She considered going to mediate, but Mrs. K. strode up.

"This is ridiculous," Mrs. K. said.

Cleo looked down at her mangled paper crane. "The origami?" she asked. "It is a bit advanced." She didn't mention that the fourth-grader had just folded a crane and an elephant with no problems at all.

The principal frowned. "I meant the silly superstitions swirling around. Parents, shop owners, teachers—everyone—even here at a *school* where people should know better. The whole town's fixating on bad luck and omens. It's absurd."

Cleo put down her failed crane, thinking cranes were

supposed to be good luck. "I can see why people are frightened," she said. "There's a killer. The threatening notes are connected to Dixie's death."

"Are they?" Mrs. K. said. "How do you know? Is that fact, Cleo, or a supposition?"

Cleo again felt like she was back in school, getting scolded for faulty logic or math mistakes. She was about to contend that it was fact. Then she reconsidered. The coffin note had been beside Dixie, but there was nothing to prove the killer put it there. "I don't know," Cleo admitted.

"Well, *I* know," Mrs. K. said. "I know that whoever is leaving the threatening notes around town is a common bully who needs to be ignored." She firmed her already rigid shoulders and looked out over the crowd, as if ready to round up bullies and send them to detention. "I'm going over to check on that other so-called *book*mobile. All those soap bubbles are not appropriate around books, if there even are any books over there. Want to come?"

Cleo wouldn't mind hearing Mrs. K. stand up against bubbles around books. She tagged along. They were nearly to BOOK IT! when a scream cut across the joyful yells.

"Help! Help—someone help!"

Cleo spun around. She saw parents running, kids fleeing, a mini-horse galloping, and her beautiful bookmobile filling with smoke.

Chapter
Twenty-Three

Cleo wrapped her coat and arms tight to her chest. Her heart thumped hard, and her eyes still stung. A fireman in full gear stalked the aisle of Words on Wheels, a massive extinguisher strapped to his back. Cleo prayed he wouldn't have to use it. Smoke was awful enough for books. Fire and water would be devastating.

On the other side of the schoolyard fence, the crowd had grown. Kids ran in excited circles. Their parents clung to the fence rail, chatting excitedly. The young newspaper reporter had arrived to capture the aftermath of the chaos. Cleo saw sunlight glint against his zoom lens and looked quickly away. Only Lilliput seemed nonchalant, busily munching down the tall grass along the fence. Belle stood nearby, slightly apart from everyone except her horse, her attention on her phone.

Cleo glanced again at her bookmobile but just as quickly turned away. "How do you feel?" she asked Pat. She and Pat sat on the open back of an ambulance. Pat huddled under a thin, reflective blanket, the kind handed out in natural disasters. The crinkly sheet reminded Cleo of the microwavable snacks her grandkids liked. For a second, a welcome flash of panic struck her. Her grandkids would be coming for their Thanksgiving visit in just a few weeks. She needed to stock up on some of their favorite foods.

Pat rustled and readjusted the covering over her shoulders. "I'm fine," she said shakily. She gripped Cleo's hand, squeezing hard. Cleo's arthritic knuckles protested, but she didn't mind. She was glad Pat was okay. It was Iris she worried about more.

The artist lay on a stretcher several yards away. Two EMTs hovered over her, tending to a gash on her head and plying her with oxygen. More sirens approached.

Pat gave a raspy cough. "So much smoke," she said. "I'm sorry, Cleo! I don't know what happened."

"It's okay," Cleo reassured her again. "It was just a smoke bomb, they say." *Just!* Who would do such a thing? Who would hurt Words on Wheels, and at a school fest, no less? Cleo gave thanks again that no kids were on board. Her stomach tightened, taking in the schoolyard, now empty except for emergency responders and the immediately affected.

"Thank goodness!" Pat exclaimed. "Look, Iris is coming to."

Iris's hand fluttered to her forehead. Cleo exhaled in relief. Pat and Iris had been in the bookmobile when smoke started billowing out near the driver's seat. Iris had collapsed in fits of coughing, but Pat managed to pull her out the back emergency exit. In the process, Pat had twisted her wrist, and Iris had banged her head. Before the EMTs had shooed her away from Iris's side, Cleo had heard the word *concussion* volleyed around.

Pat bit her lip. "I tugged her too hard. It was the adrenaline. It's my fault she fell and went down on her head. I messed up again."

"You did the right thing!" Cleo assured her. Out of the corner of her eye, she saw Leanna pacing around Words on Wheels. A fireman looked out. Leanna gestured for him to pull down all the windows. He did, starting at the back, smoke puffing out as he went.

"Tell me again what happened," Cleo said. She kept hoping that words might shift and bring sense to the situation.

Pat released Cleo's hand and adjusted her crinkly blanket. "Like I said, Iris and I were already upset," Pat said. "Iris had picked out an art book from the New Reads shelf and found one of those coffin notes in it. She started complaining that it was all Dixie's fault. Of course, it wasn't! Dixie didn't leave the notes. She was a victim! I went up to see, and then suddenly there was this *pop* and smoke started coming at us. We couldn't breathe! I dragged Iris to the back, where the air was better, and we got the door open, and . . ."

Pat's shoulders rose in an apologetic shrug that sagged back to a slump. "I should have gotten us out the front door. It was closer but smokier."

"You did great," Cleo assured her. They watched in silence until Gabby strode up, bringing a glum Leanna with her.

The young deputy nodded briskly to Pat. "Mrs. Holmes, let's get you into the other ambulance. It's going to the hospital."

Pat protested, but Gabby insisted. "Do it for the library," she said. "I'm sure Miss Cleo wants to make sure you're okay. You and Iris can ride together and keep each other company."

Pat shot Cleo a worried look. 'She'll blame me," Pat said before she let herself be led off by a husky EMT.

Leanna took Pat's place at the back of the unmoving ambulance.

Gabby gave them what was surely meant to be a reassuring smile. "Everything will be fine. We'll just need to search and process the bookmobile and get your statements. I'd like to know who went in the bookmobile both this afternoon and earlier in the day."

Gabby was called off by the chief. Leanna produced a notebook from her backpack purse. The backpack was calico cloth, and the notebook had a cartoon cat on the front, appropriately reading a book. They filled up two pages with names. Leanna doodled on the next page, a wiggly mass of flowers all connected by the same line. Cleo was reminded of Iris's disturbing drawing.

She told Leanna about it. "I saw that drawing, and Iris went up a notch on my suspect list. But then she found a coffin in the bookmobile, and she was hurt. She wouldn't have done that to herself."

Leanna flipped the page. "Gabby asked who had access to the bookmobile earlier in the day." She pressed hard on her pencil and wrote "Belle Beauchamp" across the top of the page. She underlined the name twice and highlighted it in pointy stars.

Cleo drew a breath. It was true. Belle had been in Words on Wheels alone a few times during their long morning together, when Cleo was chatting or running a book in to a patron. Belle had gone to the back when they were returning to town too, presumably upset over Cleo's questions about Dixie and summer camp.

"Then you went home for lunch?" Leanna prompted.

Cleo smiled at her young colleague. "Yes. I went home, had leftover quiche, and took a tiny nap on the sofa with Rhett."

"How tiny?" Leanna asked, pencil poised over the page. Cleo thought her protégé was both an excellent librarian and a natural detective.

"More than tiny," Cleo admitted. "It was probably forty minutes or more. I was nearly late getting over here." She sighed, thinking she should have kept on napping. She and Words on Wheels could be safely home.

"The bookmobile was locked," Cleo said before Leanna could ask. "But . . ." She always felt safe parking Words on Wheels in her driveway. "The front window was open," she admitted. "It would have been easy enough for someone to break in." She pictured a faceless, formless prowler slithering in while she and Rhett snoozed, oblivious, not far away.

* * *

"You're the best statement-givers I've had all week," Gabby said, when she returned to find Leanna and Cleo bearing written lists and time lines. "We'll get Words on Wheels back to you as soon as possible, Miss Cleo. I called you a ride."

Cleo took calling a ride as a not-so-subtle hint that they should leave. She hated to abandon her bookmobile.

Gabby escorted them to the gate, grumbling about the crowd of gawkers and "that pesky reporter."

"I love the press," Gabby said, "Don't get me wrong. But that guy can make anything sound extreme and scandalous."

Cleo dreaded what he'd write about the attack on her bookmobile. Her dread swelled when she noticed he was chatting with Belle. Gabby was saying their ride should be here anytime.

"We can walk," Cleo said. It was only a few blocks and fresh air might clear her head.

Gabby grinned. "I think you'll enjoy the chauffeur service I called." She raised her chin, nodding beyond the crowd to where a station wagon was jolting to a stop. Henry jumped out, spotted them, and waved.

Cleo and Leanna hurried to the waiting car. Cleo had just gotten in and locked her door when the young reporter's flushed face appeared at the window. He tapped at the glass and yelled his questions when she didn't roll down the window.

"Cleo Watkins, a statement? Did you find another body? Were there omens you ignored? What do you say to those who call your bookmobile cursed?"

"Words on Wheels, *cursed*?" Cleo said with a huff. Her finger flew to the automatic window button. "Why, I have half a mind to—"

"Hold that thought!" Henry said, snapping on his seat belt. The station wagon wheezed to life. Henry hit the gas and the horn simultaneously, and they were off with a jolt. After an initial burst, Henry returned to his typical tortoise speed. He apologized for the possible whiplash. "I thought you might like time to consider your statement to the press."

From the backseat, Leanna chuckled. "I'd have enjoyed hearing it."

So would the reporter. Too much. Cleo reclined her seat a few inches and thanked Henry. He dropped Leanna off first and idled in her driveway until she was safely inside.

"Where to, madam?" he asked.

Home, Cleo thought. She always loved returning to her comfortable house and Rhett. She could invite Henry in, and they could sit on the porch and talk about topics other than smoke bombs, bullies, and murder. But she couldn't. "I should go over to the hospital and check on Iris and Pat," she said. "I feel responsible as head librarian and bookmobile captain. If you could drop me off at my driveway, I'll get my car and—"

Henry did something she'd never seen him do. Slowly, cautiously, and not at all gracefully, he looped the station wagon in a wide U-turn.

* * *

"They're kicking me out already," Pat said. Cleo and Henry found Pat sitting on the edge of an exam table in a cheery yellow room. She wore a hospital gown, wrapped and tied up tight.

"That's wonderful!" Cleo said. "You didn't think anything was wrong, and now it's confirmed."

Pat sighed and scraped back her bangs, half of which

remained swooped up in a cowlick. "Yes," Pat said, sounding glummer than she had at the scene of the smoke bombing. "There's nothing new wrong with me today, but who knows about tomorrow?"

"No one knows about tomorrow." Pat's doctor swept in, chart in hand. Doc Bliss lived in Catalpa Springs, and Cleo knew him as a fan of thrillers, biographies, and historical fiction. He flipped pages of the thick chart. 'Check, check, and check again. We have done every test, so you will be more than thoroughly checked out, Mrs. Holmes. One of these days, I'll prove to you that you're in fine health, for a woman of your age, of course."

Pat scowled.

"You're fine," Doc Bliss reiterated.

"If you say so" Pat muttered.

"Get dressed." Doc Bliss had the chiseled-chin handsomeness of a fifties film star. He bestowed a gleaming smile on Pat, which she missed by studying her socks. "Your friends are here to take you home. You'll feel better there. Call me if anything *serious* comes up, okay?"

He left with an efficient swish of his white coat. Henry tactfully waited in the hall while Pat got dressed. Cleo stayed on the other side of the curtain and kept up a happy chatter. "It's good to be checked out, just to be sure," Cleo said. "Peace of mind."

A scoff came from behind the curtain. A minute later, the cloth whipped open, jingling on metal rollers. Pat stepped out. A smoky smell stuck to her clothes. "Doc Bliss doesn't know if I'm actually okay. How could he? He barely listened to my lungs and refused to X-ray my wrist." She gave a little cough as if to prove he'd missed a dire disease. "He doesn't take me seriously. I came in for some blood work last week and saw my chart."

"Oh?" Cleo edged toward the door, hoping to encourage Pat to follow.

"It was in this same room," Pat said. "Doc stepped out so I looked. You know what he'd written on the very first page of my record? 'Chronic complainer'! Underlined!" Pat stuffed her socked feet into worn sneakers. "Sorry," she said. "I am complaining, aren't I?"

Cleo bristled for her sake. "No, *you* shouldn't be sorry. That was a rude note."

They met Henry and tried to check on Iris, but a "Do not disturb" sign dangled from her door.

"I didn't know they had those kinds of signs in hospitals," Henry chuckled.

"Leave it to Iris to get one," Cleo said.

Afternoon light was sinking away by the time they got Pat checked out. Cleo tried to get Pat to sit up front, but she declined. "I can stretch out back here," she said. "I've already interrupted your afternoon together."

"Nonsense," Cleo said gently. "Henry and I were worried about you. Did you happen to remember anything else? Any other folks who came in the bookmobile?"

Pat said she'd given that some thought. "The gym teacher popped in. A bunch of kids. Little kids. I don't think they'd have a smoke bomb! Some parents. Iris and me, of course." She leaned forward between the seats. "But there's something else. Just before the smoke went off, I heard whistling. I looked out and Jefferson and Jacquelyn were going by. I didn't see them come inside, but anyone could have sneaked in before, when you were busy setting up or looking at the other stands."

Henry pulled up to Pat's property. The cleaning office and house were dark. The abandoned railroad tracks seemed weedy and wild. "You'll be okay?" Cleo said. "Is Albert home yet?"

He wasn't, but Pat said she'd be fine alone. "I'm used to it. You two go and enjoy your evening."

Cleo tried to follow those instructions. She and Henry stopped by his shop and picked up Mr. Chaucer, and then they all gathered in Cleo's kitchen for a comforting dinner of leftover chicken casserole. They watched a mystery on TV, the pleasant kind set in a distant time and place. Everyone, from pug to cat, to Cleo and Henry, ended up falling asleep. Around midnight, Cleo awoke with a start. Henry was still fast asleep, his dog at his feet. Cleo drew a soft blanket over Henry and a smaller throw over Mr. Chaucer. She and Rhett went upstairs, Rhett's tail at tall sail, happily anticipating bed. Cleo's thoughts sunk low, to her bookmobile and Dixie and a criminal as elusive as smoke.

Chapter
Twenty-Four

"Oooh . . . good morning to you *two*!" Mary-Rose twinkled at Cleo, surprising her. Cleo's best friend sat on the porch swing, the *Catalpa Springs Gazette* open on her lap, a pie carrier at her feet.

Cleo was in her fluffy bathrobe and slippers. Henry wore the same outfit he'd come to dinner in the night before. It was just past seven, and he was stepping out to walk Mr. Chaucer. The pug waggled his back end at Mary-Rose. Cleo affectionately chided her friend for again failing to ring the doorbell.

"I must have sensed you had company and knew I should wait for a *discreet* time to knock," Mary-Rose said with a chuckle and a wink as man and pug scuttled down the front steps.

Cleo informed her friend that Henry and his dog had been chivalrously guarding her by falling asleep on her sofa.

"You're in good hands," Mary-Rose said. "I was mainly waiting to knock because I wanted you fully rested."

"That's nice," Cleo said, distracted. She tilted her head to get a better view of the pie. "Is that what I think it might be?" Toasted marshmallow floated like heavenly clouds. The crust appeared to be either graham cracker or gingersnap.

Mary-Rose confirmed Cleo's mouthwatering suspicion. "S'mores pie. It goes beautifully with coffee. Perfectly appropriate for breakfast. We're all adults. We can enjoy pie for breakfast if we want."

Cleo's joy quickly soured. She frowned at her friend. Why was Mary-Rose being so generous with sugar and pushing pie for breakfast? Cleo flashed back to Mary-Rose's gift of pecan jam. She'd brought that the morning after Dixie's death, treatment for Cleo's shock.

Cleo inhaled sharply, a hand flying to her mouth. "Did someone die? Iris, is she okay?"

Mary-Rose calmly folded the newspaper. "I assume she's fine. She survived the toxic mold. She can take a little knock on the head." She tucked the paper under her arm. "Let's go inside. Best you read this before Henry and that adorable little dog get back. You might say something unseemly."

The coffee pot burbled, and Rhett purred happily on Mary-Rose's lap. Cleo read, growing increasingly unhappy. Before Henry's return, she had indeed thought many unseemly things and tossed the newspaper in the recycle bin, the polite alternative to crumpling it up, stomping it with her slipper, and shoving it in the trash. By the time Henry and Mr. Chaucer returned, she'd reconsidered and fished it back out.

"Why, this is nice," Henry said, eyeing the plates of pie. Mr. Chaucer beelined for a dog biscuit that Cleo put out.

Rhett hopped down to demand a second breakfast, which Cleo indulged. If she was having a giant slab of chocolate pie, he could have another spoonful of Tuna Delight.

Cleo let Henry settle in, unfold his napkin, and enjoy a sip of coffee before she started sputtering. She slapped the paper on the table and pointed, turning away as Henry read.

"'Bad-Luck Bookmobile Strikes Again?'" Henry read. "'Librarian questioned in prior death on scene of bookmobile bombing?' Oh dear . . ."

"You can say that again," Mary-Rose said. She stabbed a hunk of graham-cracker crust. "You could sue that young man for libel, Cleo. Or take the high road and ignore it all, which I'm sure I personally wouldn't do, but would recommend. In any case, no one will take this seriously. Catalpa Springs is a town of sensible people who know and love you."

Sensible folks who'd sunk into superstition and fear, Cleo thought. She ate more pie and allowed herself a moment of self-pity wallowing. It was hard to maintain, given the pleasant company and sweet treat.

"I shouldn't complain," Cleo said. "There are certainly worse things happening around town."

"So true," Mary-Rose said. "Murder, threats, those awful paint colors in the library, although I did peek in the other day, and there's a peach color I rather like." Henry had put the paper down. Mary-Rose scooped it up. "No need to worry about the rest of this. In fact, don't even bother getting yourself a copy. No news is good news . . ."

"What is it?" Cleo asked, suspicious.

Mary-Rose pushed the pie platter in Cleo's direction. "You might need another slice."

*　*　*

By eight thirty, Cleo had called five library board members, ignoring her mother's rule of never telephoning before nine a.m. She dispensed with Aunt Audrey's approach of starting with sweetness too. Cleo went straight to the cold-hitting facts, countering the most shocking statements in Belle Beauchamp's newspaper interview.

"A public library cannot—*should not and will not*—have a first-class, paid-membership reading lounge," Cleo said, this time speaking to Mercer Whitty himself. She'd uttered versions of this sentence to other board members. Repetition hadn't dulled her outrage.

"A minor misquote, I'm sure," Mercer said. "In any case, it shows that Belle thinks outside the box. Who's to say our patrons wouldn't want a special reading room, an elite book lounge, as she called it?"

Cleo calmed herself by counting the cookbooks lined up along her kitchen counter. Sixteen. Rhett lay on a windowsill, his tail twitching at a bird outside the window. Mary-Rose, Henry, and Mr. Chaucer had returned home to "give Cleo space," as Mary-Rose put it.

"We already have a special reading room," Cleo managed to say without grinding her teeth. "We have the lounge area by the magazines and the historical research room containing special collections. *Any* patron can use those areas. A *public* library is free for anyone to use."

"Awfully literal this morning, aren't you?" Mercer grumbled. He was the only board member who'd sounded sleepy when answering the phone.

"I'm putting my foot down," Cleo said, stomping her slipper for no one but Rhett to see. Her cat threw his ears back. "Belle shouldn't have spoken for the library. We will *also not* be selling off books of a certain age, tripling our late fees, or outsourcing fine retrieval to a collection company. I'll be contacting the newspaper and clarifying all these points and more."

A yawn responded from Mercer's end. "You *should* speak with the newspaper, Cleo," he said. "I'm just looking through this week's edition right now. You're upset with Belle's enthusiasm? I'd suggest you start presenting a better image yourself. Why, just listen to this line, 'Murder-suspect librarian refuses to comment, hides from camera.' It's not a very flattering photo either. If you ask nicely, maybe Belle will help you with some image rebranding."

He hung up. Cleo fished the paper from the recycling, crumpled it page by page, and stuffed it in the trash.

* * *

"Think of it as a barbeque ambience," Sergeant Earl Tookey said. The first-prize winner of the southern Georgia regional smoke-off leaned back against the dashboard of Words on Wheels. Cleo had just gotten dressed and had been contemplating a third slice of pie when she heard a beloved horn honking outside.

Now she sniffed her way up the aisle of her bookmobile, her nose wrinkling. Rhett sat in the driver's seat, meticulously cleaning his claws.

Tookey sighed wistfully. "It would be a far nicer aroma, of course, if it were a hickory, peach, pear-wood combo with whole hog involved." He dug into a bag of hickory-smoked potato chips, took out a handful, and crunched.

Cleo reminded herself to be grateful. Iris was okay. Tookey had confirmed that the artist was getting out of the hospital this afternoon, if she hadn't left already. Pat's wrist was only bruised. Cleo had called her earlier. Plus, her bookmobile was back! Other than the lingering smell and a smudge on the back of her driver's seat, the vehicle and its contents seemed fine. "Is this where the smoke bomb went off?" she asked, pointing to the smudge.

"Yep," Tookey said. "It had a timer, a simple digital thing, like you'd use to time a roast." There was no way of knowing when it was set, he said, and no fingerprints to give away who'd left it.

"Why Words on Wheels?" Cleo said, not expecting the sergeant to know the answer. It was inexplicable. Who would target books?

He munched some more chips, eyes glazing over. Cleo suspected he'd gotten lost in food appreciation, but then he said, "Escalation? To spread more fear? We looked through that shelf over there." He pointed his chip bag in the direction of the shelf Cleo had stocked with autumn-themed books. "A few books had those coffin threats in 'em. I don't doubt we'll be getting reports from folks who checked out books. You might be too. That new newspaper reporter will probably be calling you as well."

Cleo looked around her beautiful bookmobile, wanting the bad air out. She reached for the nearest window, tugged it down, and moved on to the next. Tookey hurried to help. Cleo couldn't chide him for getting greasy potato-chip fingerprints on the glass. The entire bus would need a good airing and scrubbing.

The sergeant was heading back to work when he turned and gave Cleo a little grin. "This isn't official advice, mind you, but you should air this vehicle. Take her on a spin on the open roads. Windows down, a bit of speed . . ."

Cleo could practically feel the wind in her hair. She smiled in anticipatory bliss, but then narrowed her eyes. Was Sergeant Tookey goading her into another speeding ticket? Tookey, however, had a face of pure innocence and was saying that he and his fellow officers were way too preoccupied for traffic stops. "Murder takes precedence over speeders," he said.

"Your investigation of a smoke-bombed bookmobile takes precedence too," Cleo added.

"It's likely all connected," Tookey said, leaving Cleo with a dread that not even having her bookmobile back could cure. Later, she left Rhett at home in case Words on Wheels experienced any more incidents. She drove to the library and parked on the street, leaving the bus's windows open but locking the door. Leanna greeted her, looking jumpy with anticipation.

"Belle's not here," Leanna said. "I hope you don't mind. I

went ahead and told the painters to go for it with the peachy color we both liked."

Originally, Cleo had favored a pale neutral. But the fresh-peach color had grown on her, especially compared to Belle's blinding alternatives. Now that she saw it, covering two whole walls and the worst of the neon samples, she loved it. "It's gorgeous," she said. "A wonderful executive decision, Leanna."

Leanna exhaled with relief. "Thank goodness! I panicked, wanting *something* done in here. I got the contractor on our side. He came over and reinforced the brackets holding in the bookshelves. I told him, we'll padlock them if we have to." She took a deep breath. "Sorry. I'm nerved up. I read the newspaper."

"I called the board members already," Cleo said.

"You told them, right? And they agreed?" Leanna said. "They know we can't have a first-class paid-access room?"

"Most do," Cleo said, trying to focus on the positive. "Think of them as a glass half full."

"Half done for," Leanna mumbled. "I was saving the bad news. We had a bunch of book returns this morning, books checked out yesterday from Words on Wheels."

"Coffin threats," Cleo guessed.

Leanna nodded. "A couple people said they won't let their kids come near the bookmobile until we get this fixed. It's not our fault! Words on Wheels isn't to blame."

Cleo spent the rest of the morning scouring her bookmobile shelves. She found a half-dozen more threats, all in the new books shelves. She called Gabby, who came over on her lunch break with ham sandwiches from Dot's Drop By. Gabby promised to catalog the notes.

"I don't expect much useful evidence from these," she said. "None of the other notes have had any fingerprints besides those of the people who found them. We do have other leads. We finally got a call about a beehive break-in. The owner just noticed it, but he thought it could have happened a little while back. There was an incident at Iris Hay's studio too. Someone broke a window and threw moldy fruit inside."

"Moldy fruit?" Cleo considered the act. On the surface it seemed childish, a prank. Except . . . "Iris fears toxic mold."

Gabby nodded seriously. "The perp is spreading fear, getting bolder." She turned concerned eyes to Cleo. "You *could* shut down the bookmobile for a while until we figure out what's going on." Gabby read Cleo's look and exhaled heavily. "I know . . . you won't. But be careful, okay?"

Cleo planned to do just that. "I'm getting out of town. Words on Wheels has an appointment at Happy Trails Retirement Village this afternoon," she said. "Nothing's happened out there that I know of."

Gabby tactfully didn't mention Cleo's past incidents at the retirement community. When Gabby had gone, Cleo revved her engine and headed for the open road, taking Tookey's word that the Catalpa Springs Police Department would be otherwise occupied. She edged up the speed and let the wind clear her head and her smoky bus. Her arrival, however, was not as calming. Happy Trails was a gated community, and her favorite gate guard, Tamara, watched over the entry.

"Sorry!" Tamara said when Cleo pulled up. The young

woman hung out the window of the little hut that served as her guardhouse. The gate remained down.

"Really, I'm truly sorry!" Tamara repeated. "You know I don't like to turn folks away—well, okay, I kind of like doing that, but not you, Miss Cleo. It's just that . . . well . . ." Tamara bit her lip. "You're kinda banned."

"Banned?"

Tamara gave a helpless look. "For now. It's temporary. It wasn't me!" She named her boss, a flighty woman who would fear a fly's shadow. "She heard that you were bad luck. She said you were bringing around murder and crime. She said that Happy Trails—and mind you, I'm quoting here—'doesn't need any more of your troubles.'"

"But I have a bookmobile appointment," Cleo protested, knowing she was making her case to the wrong person. "People will expect their books."

She noticed Tamara's gaze drift over her shoulder toward the far distance, where the road disappeared into tall pines. Cleo squinted into her side mirror. A speck of red was fast turning into a pickup, and behind it, a flash of silver Airstream.

"Arrangements were made," Tamara mumbled, eyes avoiding Cleo's gaze. She lifted the gate. A few minutes later, BOOK IT! breezed by in the outside lane, horn tooting, Belle's hand waving out the window.

Chapter
Twenty-Five

C leo returned to town at a subdued speed. She parked
Words on Wheels behind the library and entered through
the back door. Leanna had gone to class. A lone painter, a
young man named Alex, worked steadily, head bobbing to a
headphone beat she couldn't hear. Cleo surveyed the space,
imagining the drop cloths gone, the painting complete, and
the hallway filled with books and happy patrons.

She could imagine it, but would it happen? Darker
thoughts seeped in. What if people shunned the library
and her, the bad luck librarian, as Happy Trails had just
done? What if Belle rolled in and swept aside all she and
her colleagues had worked to build? Fifty years of work—
gone—and her legacy with it.

Cleo stepped to the circulation desk and gripped the
familiar beveled front. No, she promised herself. No, she
couldn't help what people thought of her, but she could stand
up for library principles. *Library justice,* she thought, slapping
the wooden desk.

Alex looked over, his paintbrush still moving steadily on

the wall. He was so tall he hardly needed a ladder, and he was usually reticent to speak. He removed an earbud. "People came by. I told 'em you were closed, but some left messages anyway."

He started to replace his earbud.

"Where? What kind of messages?" Cleo asked.

"Oh, right . . ." He rummaged in the many pockets of voluminous coveralls. "These," he said, handing over three more coffins notes and what appeared to be an irate missive from a concerned parent. "A man came by too, looking for you. I forget his name. Short. Bow tie. Pointy nose. I asked if he found a coffin, and he got madder."

"Mercer?" Cleo asked. "Mercer Whitty? Sharp dresser? Thinning hair?" Being polite, she didn't mention Mercer's resemblance to a snapping turtle.

"Yeah, that's him," Alex said. He dipped his brush and expertly edged around a doorframe. "He said something about a shake-up or shaking? I wasn't really listening." He held the earbud to his ear. Cleo thanked him with a smile and let him get back to his solitude. She tried calling Mercer but twice got his answering machine. Her own voicemail had two messages from the newspaper reporter, asking for Cleo's response to the "recent report" and her "comments on the proposed radical shake-up of the Catalpa Springs Public Library."

Cleo's finger hovered over the redial icon. She chickened out. She rationalized her reticence, telling herself she should speak with Mercer first. *A radical shake-up?* Cleo walked through every room, remembering her nearly fifty years here. If Mercer's shake-up involved her, she would go out fighting.

Alex left at dusk, and Cleo locked up soon after. She walked home under a rumble of distant thunder and a few tentative raindrops. Cleo put up her hood, which protected her hair but muffled her ears. She recalled the feeling of being watched she'd had the other night and removed her hood. A few raindrops wouldn't hurt her. The streets were empty, whether from the weather or the faceless threat, she wasn't sure. By the time she turned up her lane, she'd convinced herself that she was being silly, a victim of the fear bug. Then she saw the form.

A figure, dressed in black, ran up the front steps of the bungalow on the corner. The mailbox slot clanked. The figure jogged back to the sidewalk. Cleo backed into a shrub, a sharp-leaved holly that jabbed needles at her neck. Her glasses were fogged and so was the view, the misty rain smudging out the dim light of a lone streetlamp. The figure disappeared down the next walkway, and another metallic clank reached Cleo's ears. She reached for her purse and rummaged for her phone.

The phone came to life with a shockingly bright screen. Cleo pushed back into the holly, praying the figure kept moving away from her. But not too far away.

Gabby answered on the second ring. Cleo whispered her location and what she was seeing. "Where are you?" Cleo asked, imagining Gabby at the police station, several blocks away. The deputy could get to Cleo's location quickly at a run or in her cruiser.

"I'm home," Gabby said, now whispering herself. "I can see him coming. Stay where you are. Do *not* follow him."

"Him?" Cleo asked, but Gabby had hung up. Cleo could

no longer see the figure. The homes on their street nestled behind picket fences, flowering hedges, and arbors of climbing roses and vines. Cleo stepped out from her holly hiding place and started up the street, toward home, Gabby, and the prowler. She wished she had Henry's pepper spray or a cane with a pointed end or . . .

"Ahh!" The prowler yelled, swung around, and lumbered back toward Cleo, pursued by Gabby. Cleo froze, knowing she couldn't outrun him and banking on Gabby running faster.

"Jefferson!" Cleo gasped, as his hood fell back, revealing his pale, panicked face.

He grabbed her shoulders. "Help me, Miss Cleo, help me." He ducked behind her, and Cleo could feel him shaking.

Cleo managed to extract herself from his grasp. Gabby helped, pulling Jefferson's arm behind his back and snapping on a handcuff.

"Help!" Jefferson cried again. "She pointed a gun at me! I'm just giving out invitations!"

"Right," Gabby said. "Invitations to the grave? *Welcome to your new home*?" Gabby clicked the other handcuff, speaking into the radio clipped to her jacket as she did. "Got him. Yes, sir, it's Jefferson Huddleston."

Chief Culpepper replied in blustery blurts and codes Cleo didn't understand. She put her hand on a nearby fence to steady herself. What a shock. What good luck. Relief swept over Cleo. Maybe the terrorizing was over. Sadness crept in next.

"Why, Jefferson?" Cleo murmured. She didn't want him to be the killer. He'd been such a nice kid, a good reader . . .

Porch lights came on in the nearest house. A siren approached and more lights appeared, along with more figures, crossing their arms anxiously.

"My bag," Jefferson said in a quavering voice. "Miss Cleo, please, look in my bag."

Cleo reached toward the small tote slung across his chest. Gabby stopped her, putting up a protective palm. "Let me," she said. She drew out a handful of postcard-sized papers and read.

"Oh, for heaven's sake!" Gabby exclaimed. She thrust a note at Cleo with disgust and got back on her radio.

Cleo read.

Pass the word. Mother's spirit will leave this world.
Clashes to ashes, cussed to dust.
You're invited!!

A closing line gave a date and time, Dixie's full name, burial plot location, and notice of further poetry.

"A funeral invitation?" Cleo said.

Gabby groaned as a police car careened to a halt beside them and the chief stepped out, tugging at his suspenders. He took one of the cards and read, head shaking. "I'm not even going to try to understand this one," he said. He turned to Gabby, who was unlocking the handcuffs. "Good work, Deputy. You've nabbed us a criminally bad invitation. When is this funeral? Saturday? We'll be there for sure."

* * *

Moss dripped from branches and padded the graves of Eternal Rest Cemetery. Ancient live oaks arched above the cobbled drive. Headstones buckled over roots, wedged in their rows like crooked teeth.

Cleo drove through the scrolled iron gates, glad she and her full convertible of funeral carpoolers were heading to the newer part of the cemetery. A low-lying area, too damp for graves, had recently been converted to a wildflower meadow overlooked by a marble-pillared columbarium. Mary-Rose sat in the passenger's seat, her arm out the open window, hand surfing the wind as if they were out sightseeing. Henry and Leanna sat in the back.

Cleo could feel Leanna fidgeting, knees bumping against the back of her driver's seat. On top of disliking funerals, Leanna had a research paper due and an exam to study for. However, Leanna, like the rest of them, felt a funeral could not be missed. Especially this one.

"I still can't believe Jefferson was prowling around, leaving invitations in mailboxes," Mary-Rose said. "Didn't he understand how that would scare people?"

"It scared me," Cleo said. "He claimed he wanted elements of 'surprise' and 'individual attention.' He also thought the mail would be too slow, and he needed to spread the word." She tapped her brakes. They were stuck in a funeral traffic jam.

Mary-Rose made a scoffing sound. "I saw Jefferson and his wife at the park yesterday in full mime getup, handing out more of these things. Not that anyone was taking them. They eventually tossed them around like confetti. I'm surprised so many people are even here."

Cleo smiled. "Are you really surprised?"

"Not really," Mary-Rose admitted. "People enjoy a spectacle, and I predict this'll be a good one."

A somber-suited parking attendant waved for them to park along the lane. The "event," as he put it, was a short hike away. They arrived to see Jefferson climbing the little hill to the columbarium. A pedestal stood at the top, with a microphone attached. "Testing, testing," he said between the microphone's squeals and squawks.

"Thank goodness!" Cleo said. "He's wearing a normal suit." It was pale gray, with only a ruffle to the white shirt displaying his love of flair.

Mary-Rose took in the crowd. "There's trouble already. That book club of yours. They're all together again." She pointed to the other side of the flower garden, where the Who-Done-Its stood as a group, Pat and Iris at opposite sides of the little cluster. Iris's choppy hair hived above a prominent bandage wrapped around her forehead.

"I should go say hello to them," Cleo said to her little group.

"I'll stay here," Mary-Rose declared. "It's higher ground. I can watch out for you, Cleo. Let's all meet up here at the end of the service or police action, whatever comes first."

Leanna drifted off to wander among the flowers. Henry accompanied Cleo.

"How are you?" Cleo asked Pat, the first Who-Done-It she encountered. She felt a little guilty. She hadn't been keeping up with sleuthing. Despite the smoke bomb, Pat was still eager to detect. She'd called Cleo yesterday, hoping to get together to study Amy-Ray's copy of *Luck and Lore*. It was a good idea and something Cleo kept intending to do.

The trouble was, she'd been stuck for days dealing with Mercer's staff "shake-up," which turned out to be mind-numbing meetings about the library's "image" and a staff bonding retreat on Friday. They'd retreated only as far as Mercer's country home, where Belle led exercises such as waving their arms and making free-form animal sounds, and walking Lilliput while blindfolded. Cleo had refused the blindfolding, citing her age and doctor's orders. Neither were true hindrances, but Cleo liked to keep her eyes open.

"I'm fine," Pat said. "How was the bonding retreat you had to go to? Did you learn anything useful about Belle?"

Cleo considered. There had been something. "We had to play a truth-or-dare game, and I asked her again if she argued with Dixie Huddleston at the farmers' market."

Pat clasped her hands. "And?"

"And she decided that we'd done enough team building," Cleo said. "That was a good outcome for me. I still find it odd that she's so evasive about Dixie. She must remember Dixie. You always remember a bully, don't you?"

Pat nodded solemnly. "She likely remembers every single thing Dixie did."

"You always remember getting pushed out of a smoky school bus too," Iris offered, leaning around Mrs. K. and the other group members.

"Sorry!" Pat exclaimed. "I pulled too hard!"

"Iris," Cleo said with forced cheer, "I'm very happy you're okay." She continued over Iris's mutters of not *really* being okay. "I heard you had some vandalism too? That's awful."

"Moldy fruit," Iris said darkly. "There's a vile person on the loose." She looked around at the crowd, as if suspecting everyone. "Police are all over this place, and they can't catch 'em. I bet they don't have any clue who bombed your book-mobile either. Did you bring it? Is it safe for the public?"

"It's safe," Cleo said quickly.

Pat whispered, "Is it really? *Did* you bring Words on Wheels?"

Cleo said she'd carpooled with Henry and friends. "The bookmobile is fine, although I'd like to hire your ladies to scrub it out," Cleo said, politely but firmly refusing Pat's kind offers to help for free. "The ladies are already scheduled to clean the library before the grand reopening. We'll add the bookmobile to the tab."

"The library party's still going on?" Pat flushed. "Sorry, I read the paper and heard some people talking, saying they wouldn't go near Words on Wheels, and I thought maybe people were avoiding the library too. Not me, of course! And I didn't mean your library is cursed or anything. That'd be absurd."

Iris gave a pointed snort.

Cleo pitched her tone to perky and positive. "The library renovation is coming along beautifully. We'll be all ready. Everything will be back in place."

"What about that overdue book you were chasing after?

Did you get that back?" Iris asked, a twitch of her lip suggesting she knew the answer.

Cleo's perkiness faltered. "Well, no . . ." Her gaze turned to the mound and the marble building where Dixie's ashes would rest. "Dixie won that one," she murmured.

She was saved from further uncomfortable conversation by a gong, this time from a real instrument, with the mallet wielded by Jacquelyn. Jefferson launched into a poem that might have come from a rhyme dictionary. "Dust. Must. Nonplussed. Stardust. Star seeker. Weaker . . ."

Cleo looked around, assessing the reaction and the attendance. Chief Culpepper was off to one side, talking into his radio. Gabby had a good view of Jefferson and Jacquelyn and the crowd. A group of realtors stood to one side, all except one engrossed by their phones. Who was absent was as interesting as who was here. Cleo looked around for a sleek blonde bob. She didn't see Belle. Mercer didn't seem to be here either. She asked Henry if he'd seen them. He hadn't.

"What about Amy-Ray?" Cleo asked.

They both looked around for Dixie's daughter, trying to be discreet in their head swiveling. Discretion, however, wasn't necessary. Up on the hill, Jefferson was raising a jade-colored urn in both hands, offering Dixie's ashes to the heavens. He pointed his face up too, his poem continuing. "Ashes. Flashes, Fake eyelashes . . ." A murmur rippled through the crowd.

Amy-Ray Huddleston sprinted up the mound. Dixie's daughter wore bright pink scrubs and white sneakers. Jacquelyn saw her before Jefferson did, and banged her gong in warning, but it was too late. Amy-Ray grabbed the urn from her brother and started to run back down the hill.

"I won!" Amy-Ray yelled, hugging the urn tight.

Jacquelyn, quicker than her husband, leapt at Amy-Ray. The tackle left them tumbling. Jefferson tripped behind. The trio rolled down the hill in a writhing bundle. The urn bounced after them, followed by the flailing funeral director.

Pat moaned. Iris touched her bandaged head and smiled. "That didn't take long to go bad, did it?"

Chapter
Twenty-Six

I n Cleo's experience, pie was a salve for many problems, including the bad aftertaste of a bitter funeral. At the gates of Eternal Rest, Cleo and her carpool companions turned away from town and sped for Mary-Rose's Pancake Mill. The pancake destination closed in the afternoon, which made the visit all the more relaxing. Cleo, Mary-Rose, Leanna, Henry, and a kitchen helper polished off half an apple pie and made good headway into a coconut cream. They walked it off by strolling around the natural spring, the resident peacocks trailing behind them.

No one wanted to be the first to make motions to go home, but after a second lap around the water, daylight was dimming, and there was little excuse left to linger. They'd already hashed and rehashed the funeral, from the fight to the police-supervised internment of Dixie's urn in the marble columbarium. A cemetery official had closed the ceremonies by looping a thick chain across the iron-gated doors to the final resting place, bolted with a padlock the size of a grapefruit.

Cleo dropped her riders off one by one, Mary-Rose to her house first, followed by Leanna. Then it was down to Henry.

"Home? Your shop, I mean," Cleo asked.

His smile lines flared. "Would Rhett forgive me if I asked you in for a nightcap? I have wine, port, decaf coffee . . ."

"I think Rhett will find it in his heart," Cleo said, smiling back. She drove the long way around the park, which would allow her to park right in front of Henry's shop. *The scenic route,* she thought, since it also took them past the library.

Cleo drove slowly, admiring the blinking orange lights in the florist's window. The bakery had replaced its Halloween jack-o-lanterns with pumpkins of all colors, decorated in paper turkey feathers. A few stores had gone straight to Christmas décor, which Cleo both loved and slightly resented. She wanted to enjoy all the holidays in their turn, to their fullest. She was remarking on an early Santa, when her foot jabbed the brakes.

"I agree," Henry said. "Way too early for Santa."

Santa hadn't led to Cleo's abrupt breaking. The library was to their right. A silver Cadillac stood out front, shining under the streetlamp.

"Mercer Whitty! That's his car," Cleo said. There was no mistaking the personalized plates, "1WHITT." Cleo eased her convertible forward. Inside the library, the chandelier blazed in the restored reference room. "What is he up to? He has no business being in the library after hours." Cleo feared he wouldn't be alone. Belle hadn't attended the funeral. Had she spent the afternoon doing heaven knows what to the library? Cleo's worries were confirmed when she spotted

Lilliput, trotting out from the backyard. The little horse reared and whinnied before disappearing back into the darkness.

Cleo swung her car in front of Mercer's. She peered across Henry, already anticipating the worst. What would it be? A rogue contractor, removing their bookshelves? A disco light in place of the antique chandelier?

"I'll go in with you," Henry said, anticipating her intent to storm the building.

She hoped he couldn't read all her thoughts. Mercer! After their "bonding" retreat, he'd promised to speak with Belle about toning down her most radical ideas, like the pay-to-lounge first-class reading room. He'd fielded complaints from patrons all week, he admitted. Cleo suspected Mercer would forget all about those complaints if Belle started sweet-talking him.

Lilliput blew an equine raspberry from somewhere in the dark as they passed. Cleo didn't have time to greet the little horse. She swung the front door open as if it weighed nothing at all. She stopped short in the hallway, hands on her hips. Darkness filled the hallway, broken by a light slicing under the reference room door and a slight sound. Cleo cocked her ear. What was that? Scuffling? Heavy breathing?

A fresh worry bubbled up. What if she and Henry were about to burst in on a romantic moment? Cleo almost turned around, but thoughts of inappropriate behavior in a library propelled her on. Still, she wanted to give fair warning.

"Hello? Mercer? Belle?" she called out.

Cleo knocked on the reference room door. When no one

answered, she pushed the door open. Henry pressed to her shoulder, grabbing hold when she nearly fell back.

Under the warm light of the chandelier, Belle stood, breathing in raspy bursts. Her platinum hair shimmered. In her hand hung a pair of scissors, the oversized pair Cleo had bought for the ceremonial ribbon cutting.

Belle dropped them. The scissors landed softly on the antique carpet.

Cleo's hand shot to her mouth, covering her gasp.

Mercer was indeed with Belle. He lay at her feet, a dark stain at his side blurring into the carpet's busy floral pattern.

Henry backed up, trying to pull Cleo with him.

"Wait," Cleo said softly.

"I found him," Belle said, taking a step toward Cleo. "He was here."

Henry moved to Cleo's side and thrust a protective arm in front of her. "We'll call an ambulance. Let's go, Cleo."

"You found him?" Cleo asked. "What do you mean, you *found* him? You met here? Was it an accident? Mercer could be . . . vexing." She caught herself about to slip into Chief Culpepper's I-understand routine. She did understand. Not about killing a man, of course, but about how infuriating Mercer Whitty could be.

"No!" Belle cried. "No, this wasn't me! I didn't hurt him!" She took another step in their direction. "Why would I hurt Merc?"

Cleo could think of some reasons. Had Mercer nixed Belle's plans? He was prone to mocking and had a biting tongue. He could be cruel. He was also infatuated. What if his adoration had taken a nasty turn to unwanted attention? Cleo didn't want to put either of these possibilities to a woman who'd just been holding bloody scissors.

"I understand," Cleo said, grasping for something to say.

Belle shook her head so vigorously her bob became a blonde blur. "Understand what? Cleo, I know you and I don't see eye to eye on libraries, but how can you think I did this? No!" She moved to the oak desk, her hand grasping the edge.

Henry lowered his arm and took Cleo's hand. "Let's go," he whispered. "We need to call the police."

He was right, but Cleo couldn't go. Her eye had caught on the book resting near Belle's hand. It was maroon with gold embossing and art deco designs. Her breath caught in her throat, and despite her shock—or maybe because of it—she took a step forward. *Luck and Lore: Good luck, death lore, and deadly omens of the Deep South.*

Was this the one? Cleo took another step. She spotted a library call number on the book's spine. Dixie's overdue book! She fought the urge to grab it, her stomach twisting as she again remembered their theory that Dixie's killer swiped this book. She retreated back to the doorway, nudging her purse toward Henry, whispering for him to find her phone. He took the bag. She could hear rummaging, contents dropping, and then Henry's voice, soft but urgent in the hallway.

"*Luck and Lore,*" Cleo said to Belle. "This is the book I've been looking for, the one Dixie Huddleston kept out all those years."

"Dixie again!" Belle huffed. "You are *obsessed* with that awful woman and this book too!"

"Were *you* obsessed with Dixie?" Cleo asked. "She was cruel to you at that camp, wasn't she? Did she try to apologize recently and make it worse?"

Cleo heard sirens. Help would be here soon, maybe too quickly. She wanted answers, and in Belle's stunned state, she might provide them. "Help me understand," Cleo said. "I can help you."

Belle replied with a sigh and a dull monotone. "I hated that camp almost as much as I hated Dixie." She turned to the nearest bookshelf, filled with thick leather-bound tomes recording the early years of Catalpa Springs. There were family trees and simple ledgers and records of times good and terrible, none of which should be forgotten. Belle drew out a county record, nose wrinkling. "This book is in wretched condition. I bet it has bugs. Dust mites. Silverfish. I tell you, Cleo, we need to freshen this place up."

Cleo wasn't going to argue about dust mites with a probable killer. She tried to return Belle to her own past. "What happened between you and Dixie at that camp?"

Belle shoved the county record back in place. "She was mean, that's all. Cruel. I wasn't the only kid picked on for having frumpy clothes and being shy and plain, although it seemed like it at the time." Belle turned back to Cleo, her beaming smile sending a chill up Cleo's spine. "And you know what? As much as I detested her, I wanted to be just like her. Isn't that pathetic? I realized how much she'd twisted up my life when I saw her again after moving back here. I'd spent so much time trying to be like her and her popular friends. What a waste! Where'd it get me? Back here, driving around in a cute-as-can-be camper, trying to impress people, and all I get is gripes. You know, those retirees out at Happy Trails did nothing but fuss when I showed up instead of you and your bookmobile the other day." Her pitch rose in mock complaint. *"Where are all our books? I want an audiobook, I want large print, where's my interlibrary loan?"*

Outside, car doors slammed. Henry touched Cleo's shoulder, whispering that the police were here.

Cleo talked fast. "What happened when you saw Dixie at the farmers' market? What did she say to upset you?"

Belle's snort might have come straight from Lilliput's lips. "I went up and said, 'Hey, Dixie,' and reintroduced myself. I thought I'd show her what I'd become, and she'd be impressed. All she remembered was the other me. The *old* me. She said, 'Oh, you're that dumpy girl from camp? I'm doing apologies and clean forgot about you!' *She forgot!* I hadn't forgotten about her."

"It doesn't matter what she thought," Cleo said. "You were very successful in your career. *Are* successful. Why, you have your bookmobile and innovating and . . ." Cleo trailed off, worried she'd just taken a wrong turn. "And your lovely little horse!" she exclaimed. *Everyone, even killers, loved their pets.* "He's a doll. A real cutie."

Belle exhaled and seemed to calm down. "He's a little spunk, isn't he? I always wanted a horse and my own bit of land. I need to start looking into that." She turned to the window. Cleo caught Belle's reflection in the wavy antique glass. Her gaze looked distant, pensive. Was she thinking of green pastures? If so, Belle didn't realize her next home would likely be prison.

"Cleo, Henry?" Gabby's voice sounded hollow in the foyer. "I need you to back out slowly."

Henry gently tugged. Cleo had one more question. "Why bring back *Luck and Lore*?"

Belle turned, her voice flat. "Cleo, don't you know me better than that? I have *no interest* in old books, and I have *no idea* how that old moth-bitten thing got here."

Chapter
Twenty-Seven

G ood cooking required an essential ingredient: a hefty
  helping of heart. Cleo's heart wasn't in breakfast, even
to whip up a batch of Sunday biscuits. She searched her
pantry, fridge, and freezer and came up with only deep-
frozen waffles. Ice crystals grew from the crevices. They
were hardly appetizing, especially for a guest.

Pug and Persian claws clicked down the stairs. Cleo put
on the coffee, thinking she could invite Henry to Spoonbread's, her treat.

Rhett and Mr. Chaucer trotted into the kitchen. The pug
looked as off-balance as Cleo felt. His human companion
followed, his hair ruffled and tufted, like Albert Einstein's
after an electricity experiment.

"I have dog biscuits," Cleo announced, "a large supply of
Tuna Delight, and coffee. I thought we might go to Spoonbread's after a boost of caffeine."

They both said, "My treat" in unison.

Cleo felt better with the coffee and especially the com-
panionship. It had been awfully nice of Henry to stay again.

They'd been awake until late, buzzing from the murder and the long wait afterward to give their statements. She'd slept fitfully, waking to thoughts of Mercer and questions about Belle and the mysteriously returned book.

Henry claimed he'd slept like a baby in the guest bed. He stifled a yawn and rubbed his eyes. Cleo recalled the sleepless nights she'd spent with her infants and suspected he *had* slept like a baby.

When they finished their first round of coffee, they left Rhett sunning in a window. They planned to stop by Henry's first so he could change into something less rumpled and drop off Mr. Chaucer.

The day was sunny and bright, with dewy jewels on the grass and birdsong in the air. They strolled past pretty picket fences and autumn planters, and Cleo could almost—*almost*—talk herself out of last night's doubts. *Of course* the case was closed, she told herself. They'd caught Belle red-handed.

"The book bothers me," she murmured to Henry at a cross street as they waited for a car to pass. Mr. Chaucer took the opportunity to sniff-inspect the signpost.

Henry reached over and squeezed her hand. "That book has bothered you for a long time. Now it's back. It's good."

"But Belle said she didn't have anything to do with it," Cleo said.

Henry clicked his tongue at his dog. When Mr. Chaucer failed to respond, he reached down and turned the pug in the direction of crossing. Like a windup toy freed from a barrier, the pug wobbled forward. "She said she had nothing to do with killing Mercer Whitty too," Henry pointed out. "Now I'm not a criminal expert like *some* people I know, but I've heard that criminals tend to lie about their guilt."

"But why would she bother?" Cleo persisted. "Belle doesn't care about books, especially old books."

"Maybe someone else returned it earlier in the day?" Henry said. "You and Leanna were out at the funeral and then the Pancake Mill. Maybe Mercer found it outside and brought it in?"

They'd reached the park. A group of early-morning walkers in velour tracksuits passed them, arms churning. "Good job, Cleo!" one of the ladies called back. "Hip, hip, hooray for our hometown detective!" another yelled, arm waving, not breaking stride.

Cleo felt heartened, not for the praise—although that was, admittedly, very nice—but because the fear seemed to have lifted. People were out enjoying themselves. The sun was shining, birds were singing, and a warm breakfast was on the way.

"I think I'll keep the 'CLOSED' sign up today," Henry said as they approached his door. He jingled through his keys, locating the proper one. Cleo admired the golden rays lighting up the Spanish moss in the park across the street. She never tired of such beauty. When she turned back, she realized Henry wasn't unlocking the door. He crouched low, a handkerchief in his hand. When he stood, his hand moved toward his jacket pocket before hesitating.

"What is it?" Cleo asked.

"I don't want to show you this," he said. Grim-faced, he held out his palm. Through the folds of the handkerchief, Cleo recognized the corner of a black paper coffin.

"No!" she exclaimed. "How can this be?"

"A leftover threat, that's all," Henry said, key skittering across the lock.

Cleo wanted to agree, but she couldn't. "But we were here last night to pick up Mr. Chaucer, after Belle was arrested. We would have noticed."

Henry unlocked the door. Inside, Mr. Chaucer trotted straight to the back book surgery and his breakfast bowl. Henry put the note on his workbench. He doled out dog kibble and opened the back curtains and generally delayed approaching the bench.

Cleo read it for them both: *Henry Lafayette. I'm not done, but you are. Welcome to your future home.* A shiver crawled up her spine. "Who would do this?"

"It's nothing," Henry said with stiff joviality. "In fact, it's good news. It proves that this coffin business is nothing but a prankster. We misinterpreted. We thought that because Dixie had a note with her when she died, her killer had left it. This will pass. No one will take these silly things seriously now, and the prankster will tire of them. Let's go to breakfast. It's a lovely sunny day."

Cleo didn't feel at all sunny. She didn't even feel like breakfast. "I want to call Gabby," she said. Her eyes prickled. Had she put him at risk with her detecting? Had she drawn the killer's attention?

"Okay," Henry said gently. "Let's call. But I'm sure it's fine."

Cleo dug out her phone. She'd turned it off last night in the police station, after fielding calls from concerned friends, family, strangers, and the newspaper reporter.

Henry bustled around his workshop as they waited for the phone to go through its succession of lights and sounds. A photo of Cleo's grandchildren filled the screen. She pressed the phone icon, but before she could call, she noticed her voicemail.

"Six messages," she said, easing herself down into a low-riding armchair.

"Probably congratulations," Henry said, still in stiff good humor. "Like those ladies walking this morning."

"It's Mary-Rose," Cleo said. "From this morning." Mr. Chaucer came over and leaned on her leg. She reached down and patted his forehead wrinkles. He panted up at her with worried eyes.

"Mary-Rose found a coffin too!" Cleo said when her friend's voicemail ended and the system droned on, giving the time and date of the next caller. Cleo kept listening. After the next caller, she gestured for Henry to bring a pencil and paper.

When the calls were done, she tallied up the list. "Mrs. K., the principal, got a threat. So did Iris and the male member of the Who-Done-Its and Pat too." Cleo tapped the pencil to the notepad anxiously. "The last message is from Gabby. She's already heard about the coffins. She wants to know if we know anything." Panic rose in Cleo, thinking of her friends, her book group, and Henry, all targeted. "We don't know anything," she said morosely. "We're no closer than when we started."

"Now," Henry said softly. "That's not true. We know Belle Beauchamp didn't leave these notes. She won't be meddling with your library anymore either."

Cleo hardly felt soothed, even when Henry made a sweet offer. "I'll go pick us up some scones and cinnamon rolls to go. Stay here and call your friends back." He kissed the top of her head. "I'm locking the door and leaving the guard dog."

Mr. Chaucer put his wrinkly head on Cleo's shoe and whimpered.

* * *

"There was a line at the bakery counter," Henry said, backing in the front door with two paper bags and a tippy cardboard holder with two coffees. He smiled when he turned around and noticed Gabby. The deputy had come over to pick up the evidence and check on Cleo. They sat in the front room in velvet armchairs, books all around. The little coffin, tagged and sealed in an evidence bag, lay on the low rectangular coffee table in front of them.

Gabby slid it to the far side of the table, going a step further to hide it under her coat.

Cleo could still feel its hateful presence.

"I called Mary-Rose," Cleo told Henry. "Her note had her name on it too. *'You're a goner, go away,'* it said."

"Childish," Henry declared. He laid out napkins and

antique dessert plates he retrieved from the back. "Coffee?" he asked Gabby, after handing Cleo a cup with her name spelled "Cloe" and "cream, no sugar" scrawled in ink across the side.

Gabby thanked him but declined. "I'm swimming in coffee. We were up half the night again."

Henry ripped open the bags to reveal the goodies inside. Cleo counted half a dozen cinnamon rolls and four scones. "Savory and sweet scones," Henry said. "Pimento cheese and ham, and then there's white chocolate, sour cherry, and pecan. I thought we needed some good thinking food."

"I should be a genius by now," Gabby said. "I keep crashing your breakfasts."

"We're glad you're here," Cleo said. She thanked Henry for his thoughtfulness and gave a savory scone her proper attention. Henry and Gabby went straight for the iced cinnamon rolls. Bakery scents filled the bookstore. Mr. Chaucer ambled up his ramp to enjoy the view from his window-seat pillow.

Cleo waited until everyone had had a few bites. "Well, did she confess?" she asked. She didn't feel she needed to specify who.

"Nope," Gabby said, licking a dab of icing off her finger. "In fact, Belle snapped out of that glazed look and sharpened up by the time we got her to the station. She called a lawyer down from Atlanta. We all stayed up waiting for him to arrive and instruct her to say nothing." Gabby sighed. "Before all that, though, Belle insisted up and down that she was innocent and had no reason to hurt Mercer Whitty. As I understand it, he was paying her a pretty penny to consult for you all. Why would she stab the golden goose?"

"Anger?" Cleo suggested. "Mercer might have nixed some of her ideas for the library."

Gabby raised an eyebrow. "Do you think she felt that strongly about the library? I know you and Leanna do, Miss Cleo—and rightfully so," she added quickly.

"Belle felt strongly about her career and image," Cleo said, trying to remember Belle's exact words. "She was picked on by Dixie and other popular girls. Although she remade herself to be like them, she still must have felt insecure. She might have snapped if Mercer touched a nerve, which, bless his heart, he did tend to do."

Mr. Chaucer snored, jolting himself awake. The little pug rose, turned in a circle, and flopped down as tightly rolled as a cinnamon bun. Gabby smiled at him. "The chief's adamant that we have our woman—for both murders. According to him, the notes are a separate issue. Someone with a cruel sense of humor. Maybe even a kid. He wants me to go question some teenagers today. That should be fun." She took another cinnamon roll.

"See?" Henry said. "Kids! Nothing to worry about."

"Do you believe that?" Cleo asked her deputy neighbor.

Gabby chased down bits of icing with a plastic fork, delaying. "Not entirely," she said quietly, after a long pause. "It feels wrong somehow."

"The murders are different," Cleo said. "One was elaborately planned. The other seemed spur of the moment. What if we have *two* killers in town, and Dixie's murderer is still out there?" She reached for a cinnamon roll but didn't feel comforted. "You should stay at my place again tonight, Henry," she said. "I haven't received any notes, and I live next door to an armed deputy."

Gabby rose, grinning and adjusting her belt of police gear. "I encourage that in any case," she said with a wink.

Chapter
Twenty-Eight

P olice tape crisscrossed the library door. Cleo stood on the walkway later that afternoon, staring at the unhappy yellow ribbon. Leanna paced the porch. She peered in windows as she went.

"When can we get back in?" Leanna asked. She paused outside the reference room, clutching the collar of her vintage coat, a wooly plaid of reds, oranges, and olive green.

For once, Cleo wasn't eager to return to the library. "Tomorrow at the latest, Gabby said. They might keep the reference room roped off for a bit longer, but that's fine by me."

"Fine by me too," Leanna said, resuming her pace. "Poor Mr. Whitty. I feel bad. I thought ugly things about him before he died. The police asked me about that. They wanted to know about the staff retreat at his house and if I was upset with him. I had to admit I was. I didn't want to lie."

"They asked how *you* felt?" Cleo asked. "The chief didn't sound suspicious of you, did he? Did he tell you he empathized?" Cleo went up to join Leanna on the porch. She glanced into the nonfiction section, where neon paint samples still dotted the walls.

Leanna cupped her hands to look inside too. "That paint!" she said, stepping back. "The chief told me he'd seen the color samples on the wall and understood why we all would be feeling 'unstable,' as he called it. He asked whether you and I were upset about the stuff in the newspaper too. But that was all Belle, not Mercer. I told him I couldn't speak for you but that Belle and I had different philosophies of library science." She raised her chin defiantly. The firmness withered as she admitted, "This sure isn't the way I wanted to get our library back . . ."

"Me either," Cleo agreed. "You should go home and rest. There's nothing we can do here for now."

Leanna said she had a research paper she could work on. "But what about Words on Wheels?" she asked, brightening. "The bookmobile isn't off limits. We could set up shop by the park."

The bookmobile was still off-limits in public perception, Cleo feared. It smelled of smoke, and word of the continuing coffin threats had spread around town. She'd heard whispers when she stopped in at Dot's Drop By earlier. Patrons who were usually friendly had shied away from her and avoided eye contact. One of her libraries was a crime scene. The other was bad luck on wheels.

Cleo patted Leanna's arm. "I think it's best if Words on Wheels doesn't go out today, out of respect for Mercer. I have a few home deliveries. Those folks will be happy to get their books. I'll take my car since it'll just be a few bags of books and audio materials and some returns."

Leanna scuffed her shoes, shiny flats with ribbon bows that reminded Cleo of Mercer's bow ties. "We're still at the mercy of whoever keeps leaving those coffin notes, aren't we?" She managed a twist of a smile. "Promise me you'll be careful when you're out? That's the most important thing. You're my only family, Miss Cleo. Well, you and Rhett too." She flushed at the sentiment, gave Cleo a hug, and hurried off.

Cleo lingered, a tear stinging her eye as she thought of all she held dearest and feared losing the most.

*   *   *

"Garlic wards off vampires *and* the evil eye," Mary-Rose said, pointing to a full-page illustration of oversized garlic cloves and toothy bats. "We should make some garlic necklaces, Cleo. I'm sure you have some string and a needle we could use. Oh, and look—burying onion peels in my garden will make me prosperous, and burying bourbon will keep rain away from a wedding. I wouldn't bury good bourbon before a wedding." She turned another page in Amy-Ray's copy of *Luck and Lore*.

Cleo yearned to tell Mary-Rose that her library copy of *Luck and Lore* had finally been returned. However, the police had sworn her and Henry to silence. They wanted a clue few others knew about, something to test the veracity of witnesses and suspects. Cleo had reluctantly promised. She couldn't break her oath, even though she saw no harm in telling her best and oldest friend.

Mary-Rose flipped more pages. "Ah, here's something on gris-gris spells and hexes. One of the ladies from the church auxiliary was just saying, she knows the cousin of a bona fide gris-gris practitioner down in New Orleans. She said we should get the gris-gris expert up to do a good-luck spell, but then there was another auxiliary lady who said . . ." Mary-Rose chatted on. Cleo's friend liked to know things and pass that knowledge on. Cleo decided maybe it was for the best that police orders forced her to keep a secret from Mary-Rose.

Cleo kicked off her shoes and rested her socked feet on the edge of the solid wooden coffee table. They were on her porch, enjoying the night songs of a mockingbird. The squeak of her front gate momentarily interrupted the melody. Henry had gone out for an after-dinner walk with Mr. Chaucer. Was he back already? Cleo waited for the little pug to appear in the puddle of porch light. Instead, Gabby came striding up, dressed in jeans and a leather jacket that looked suited for a night out on the town.

"I heard y'all out here and thought I'd check in," the young deputy said.

"And a good thing too," Mary-Rose declared. "Cleo and I were just saying, we might resort to garlic jewelry to keep ourselves safe. We'll stink. That'll scare off the vampires and criminals."

Gabby chuckled. "That's a plan. I want you both safe, my star neighbor and our star witness. Mary-Rose, the chief is building you up as our big chance to convict Belle of murdering Dixie Huddleston."

"The slap," Mary-Rose said, inhaling sharply. "The death

threat at the farmers' market. I've been reliving the moment, even the atmosphere of that HoneyBucket porta-potty so I'll be ready. Ooh . . . what if you got a HoneyBucket as a prop? I could reenact the moment in court."

Gabby eased herself into a seat, politely saying that a porta-potty reenactment probably wouldn't be necessary.

"Casserole?" Cleo offered. Mary-Rose had brought by enough baked ziti to feed a small sports team. Mary-Rose held fast to the tradition of feeding the grieving. Unable to track down a direct relative of Mercer, she'd brought food to Cleo, saying Cleo had suffered yet another shock. Henry had done his best to help out and was now walking off his two hefty helpings.

Gabby patted her flat stomach and said she'd had a salad. "I have to stay alert," she said, her brown eyes twinkling. "I'm staking out Jefferson and Jacquelyn's cottage tonight. Unofficially, off the clock, no overtime." She gave a little one-shoulder shrug. "I want to see if either of them sneaks out to, say, leave threatening notes around town."

Over on the porch swing, Rhett opened an eye. His eyes popped open, wide and round, when he realized they had a new visitor. He hopped off the swing and onto Gabby's lap, where she rewarded him with sweet names and pats.

"You're doing this alone?" Cleo asked, worried. "We could come too."

"Speak for yourself," Mary-Rose said. "My hubby's already worked up that I'm out after dark. His houseguest left this morning, so he's catching up on everything he missed, like two murders and a town threatening." She stretched and announced she should be going. "Henry will be back soon? You'll be okay?"

Cleo assured them all that she'd be just fine. "I can sit on my own porch without fear."

"I'll wait until Henry returns," Gabby said after Mary-Rose left. "I want to spend time with my favorite neighbor cat," she said. "And I won't be staking out that cottage alone. I'll have a friend with me." She ducked her head and emphasized the word *friend*.

"Oh . . ." Cleo said with grandmotherly interest. She'd like Gabby to find a worthy and doting significant other. She'd secretly hoped it would be her beloved grandson, Ollie, but Ollie kept leaving town and blushing something silly when he did see Gabby. Since Gabby didn't seem inclined to elaborate, Cleo returned to a safer subject: murder and its means. "Jefferson did have his mother's prescription," Cleo said. "Did you find anything else in his house? Any results from the lab tests?"

The police had gotten a search warrant for the cottage, Cleo knew. They'd sent out for testing the syringes Cleo found in Jefferson's medicine cabinet.

Gabby shook her head, twining a curl around her finger. Cleo noted that Gabby appeared to have on a fresh coat of mascara. Her hair was loose and curling over her shoulders. A surveillance date? That would certainly prove whether a young suitor was interested and committed.

"All the syringes contained medicine, just like they should," Gabby said. "We didn't find anything suspicious in the house, unless you count a whole lot of costumes."

"Any Grim Reapers?" Cleo asked, thinking of Dixie's omens.

"Mostly mime and clown stuff," Gabby said darkly. "Some Shakespearian ghosts, according to Jacquelyn. A bunch of wigs too. Not my thing, but no clear evidence that they're murderers. We got a handwriting sample from each of them too. Neither matches the writing on the coffin notes, including that oddball note Jefferson reported finding."

Pug claws clicked up the steps, human steps right behind. Henry greeted Gabby as she was heading out the door.

"Good luck," Cleo called after her. *Have fun,* she almost said, thinking of Gabby's "friend." Then she remembered the death threat on her own gentleman friend.

"Let's all go inside. It's getting chilly," Cleo said, prepared to hunker down for the night, the doors locked tight. She turned on more lights than necessary and peered out the windows as she tightened each lock. She was just checking the kitchen when her landline rang, the old-fashioned rotary phone in her hall.

Mary-Rose's voice came out breathless on the other end. "Now, don't worry . . ." she said, words that sent Cleo's heart racing.

Chapter
Twenty-Nine

"She was run off the road?" Cousin Dot tightened her apron ties and eyed her shop, as if every aisle might hide danger. "Is Mary-Rose okay? Was she hurt?"

"She *said* she was fine," Cleo reported, sorry she hadn't been able to personally verify Mary-Rose's fineness. She'd wanted to rush right over last night, but her friend had refused, saying all she needed was a hot bath and bed. Cleo had also begged Mary-Rose to call 911, but the stubborn woman refused that too, saying she'd only called to vent nerves and check that Cleo was okay.

"She said it *could* have been kids out speeding or a drunk driver," Cleo said. She stood at her cousin's deli counter, eyeing cookies the size of her head. Dot reached in with tongs and grabbed one.

"But you think it wasn't just kids," Dot said.

"It wasn't. Or if it was, they should be arrested. The driver followed a ways back, Mary-Rose said, right until she got to the curvy part of Fish Camp Road. Then the car got on her bumper, lights on high beam, actually tapping her tail end a few times. She didn't dare stop, but she eventually lost control and swerved off. The car kept going. Mary-Rose managed to get back on the road and drive home." Cleo's stomach tightened just telling the tale. She'd been in a similar incident last spring and knew how terrifying it was to spin out of control.

"Awful!" Dot exclaimed.

Cleo unclenched her fists with effort. "She just missed going into that swampy spot on the way to her house. She could have been seriously stuck." Or seriously injured. "I got her to call Gabby, unofficially. Gabby made Mary-Rose promise to come to the police station this morning and make a report. Mary-Rose didn't get a good look at the car, and she doesn't have an eye for vehicles anyway. She thought it was possibly a dark sedan or a Jeep."

Dot fished out another cookie, chocolate chip with shiny flakes of salt on top. Cleo used to think she'd never tolerate salt on a cookie. Now she couldn't do without it.

Dot set about wrapping each cookie in neat waxed paper. She added them to a hefty paper lunch sack, listing the items already inside. Ham and pimento-cheese sandwiches on potato rolls, two bags of chips, and two dill pickles.

"Do you want extra pickles?" Dot asked, anxiously retying the sash on her pumpkin-print apron. "Pickled eggs?" Dot believed that problems must never be faced on an empty stomach.

Cleo assured her cousin that they would have more than enough.

"You can't forget to eat," Dot said.

Forgetting to eat was rarely Cleo's problem. A library

cordoned by a crime scene and undone repairs were her problem. Threatening notes were too, and a bully chasing her best friend off the road. And a killer roving free? Cleo wished she believed the chief's theory of Belle Beauchamp, double murderer. She couldn't. Not with the notes and what had happened to Mary-Rose last night.

"So," Dot said with sudden subject-changing briskness, "when's the library reopening again?"

Instead of cheering Cleo, the words sent an anxious jolt up her core. "Next Saturday," she said. "The invitations went out ages ago, and Leanna and I took an ad out in the paper that ran last week. It's too late to issue a retraction, but how can we still hold a party? Who will come?"

"I will," Dot said firmly. She handed over the bulging lunch sack. "Now be careful out there. I'll be looking out once in a while to check on you."

"I'm in a public park in the middle of town," Cleo said. "With a bodyguard and a guard dog. Nothing bad has happened in the middle of the day."

"So far," Dot said darkly. She walked Cleo to the door and was still there when Cleo reached the park and looked back.

* * *

A fine mist fuzzed the air and clung to Cleo's hair. It wasn't the best day for a picnic, but Henry was set on seeing the positive.

"No bugs out today," he said. "No need for sunglasses or sunblock." He and his pug wore matching tartan scarfs. Rhett refused to leave Words on Wheels and the warmth of his peach crate. Other than the fine picnic and company, Cleo could see her cat's point. It wasn't worth coming out today. Only two visitors had stopped by the bookmobile, neither with borrowing privileges.

The vacationing sisters first wanted photos of the "super-cute" bookmobile. They returned soon after for a different angle, selfies with the "cursed" bookmobile that they planned to splash all over social media. Cleo hoped she'd convinced them that the library, bookmobile, library cat, and head librarian were all innocent bystanders to the Catalpa Springs crime spree.

"Do you still smell smoke inside?" Cleo asked Henry after the sisters left, giggling about getting the shivers and smelling evil.

"'Ill vapors,' I think you mean?" Henry said, quoting the sisters. He and Cleo sat in canvas folding chairs, finishing off their picnic feast. Henry brushed potato-chip shards off his knees. "No, I didn't smell any vapors," he said, "but there is a little whiff of smoke. It's this damp weather. Some heat will bake it right out."

"Or bake it in," Cleo said grimly. She reached for her cookie. She was unwrapping the chocolate-chip masterpiece when bickering voices floated their way.

"Jefferson and Jacquelyn," she whispered to Henry.

They were arguing loudly for a couple dressed as mimes. White leggings and puffy pantaloons peeked out from their matching beige raincoats.

"The mime school *will* pay off," Jefferson was saying. "It will if we get the house for free."

Jacquelyn replied with unhappy oaths about Amy-Ray stealing the house out from under them. "Best case, you two both inherit. Then we all sell the place and split the proceeds."

Cleo put away her cookie and got up from her chair. "Good afternoon," she called out, waving brightly at the unhappy couple.

Jacquelyn stopped and scowled. Jefferson waved and bounded up to her. "Miss Cleo! I meant to stop by and thank you. I asked you to help me, and you did! You caught the killer. Red-handed. Right, Jacquelyn? She saved us."

Jacquelyn looked down her nose at Cleo. "Did she? Then why did we feel like someone was outside watching us last night?"

"There are some unanswered questions for the police to wrap up," Cleo said. She wasn't about to reveal Gabby's surveillance. Had they spotted Gabby? Is that why they hadn't left? Cleo had checked in with Gabby this morning. Gabby reported having a pleasant time with her "friend," but no luck in surveilling. No new coffin threats had been reported, to Cleo's knowledge. Did that mean Jefferson and Jacquelyn were responsible? But what about Mary-Rose's crash? Jacquelyn and Jefferson had a dark-blue sedan. However, if they were home, they couldn't have run her off the road. Tension tapped out a beat in Cleo's temple that continued after the couple left, Jefferson with more hearty thanks and Jacquelyn with grumbles.

Cleo and Henry sat for another hour, Cleo quiet in her thoughts, Henry engrossed in a book. A few patrons passed by but didn't stop. Fifteen minutes before the appointed hour, Cleo decided it was time to pack up. She tried to sort out her thoughts too, but that wasn't as easy.

"I can't piece it all together," she said, summing up the troubles of who had alibis, motive, and means.

"I've been trying to work something out too," Henry said as he folded up their chairs and packed up the picnic. "Why haven't *you* gotten any threats?"

Cleo stopped short. Why hadn't she? "I don't mind being left out of that," she said, aiming to make light. But it was a good point. "Maybe the perpetrator hasn't noticed me," she said.

"You're hardly covert. You're all over the newspaper," Henry said. "If anything, I'd guess it's your reputation. Maybe they don't dare mess with you." He hefted the folding chairs, ready to walk them back to his shop. Cleo began to invite him over later, but her phone interrupted.

"Pat," she said, reading the caller ID. "I owe her a call and an update. I missed her last night."

Cleo barely got out a hello before Pat interrupted, speaking in excited bursts. She'd seen the coffin-note leaver. Maybe. Possibly. At her office door. A man in a hoodie, lurking at the door and running off when she yelled at him. Could Cleo come?

"I'll be right there," Cleo promised. "I'm already in Words on Wheels."

Henry loaded the chairs and his dog in behind her. "We're coming too."

Chapter Thirty

Words on Wheels bumped over the railroad tracks and crunched onto the gravel parking lot of Holmes Homes Cleaning Company. Pat hovered behind the glass door, a blur of nervous shifting and shuffling. As soon as Cleo parked, Pat hustled outside.

Cleo opened the door and Mr. Chaucer woofed.

Pat jumped. "Oh!" she said, running a palm across her forehead, dislodging her bangs. "I'm sorry! You didn't say you had company, Cleo. You were probably hard at work too. Here I am, interrupting again! I shouldn't have bugged you. I just . . . I got so nervous and didn't know who else to call."

"Did you call the police?" Cleo asked, unbuckling and stepping down from the bus. Henry and Mr. Chaucer followed, the little dog woofing again when he reached ground level. Rhett remained stubbornly napping.

Pat mussed her hair some more, tucking and retucking the sides behind her ears. "No, I didn't call the police. I couldn't be sure of what I saw. I knew what they'd say: a neurotic woman, a chronic complainer, just like my doctor says."

Pat sniffled. The sniffle turned into a nose twitch aimed up the steps of Words on Wheels. "Your bookmobile still smells of smoke." Pat edged by Cleo and climbed the steps, nose first like a pointer hound on the hunt. "I have an air-freshener and a detergent that would work wonders in here," she declared, sounding confident again. "My best cleaner, Ida, just came back to the office. Her job got cancelled. She'd have time. I'm sure she wouldn't mind. If you leave the vents and engine running, Ida can give everything a spray and air it out."

Cleo gratefully agreed. "But only if I can pay Ida the going rate and a big tip too," she added. She knew Ida, a hardworking mom of five kids. The kids were all voracious readers, and Ida did her cleaning to audiobooks.

Pat waved Ida over from the office. Ida was happy for the job, and Pat looked eager for company. "You and I can have some tea, Cleo," she said. "All of us can, I mean. Mr. Lafayette and his dog and Rhett Butler, if he wants to wake up.

Henry nodded to the pug, sitting next to his shoe, tongue lolling to one side. "Chaucy here is *demanding* more outdoors time. How about I coordinate with Ida and keep the four-legged crew out of the way? I'll feel more useful, and you ladies can chat."

Pat didn't argue. She was already excitedly telling Cleo about the hooded man. "I wish I could sketch. I should have taken a photo! Why didn't I? If he comes back, I'll be ready. I'll have my camera and my phone. Albert has a gun over at the house, but I don't dare use it. Oh, but I hope he doesn't come back. Come inside and we can have some coffee—decaf only, sorry!"

Cleo shot Henry an apologetic look that got her a wink and a twinkling smile in return. She left the keys in the ignition for Ida. "I'll try not to be too long," she whispered.

"Take as long as you like," he said. "I have a book to keep me company, and I'll keep Rhett and Chaucy on their leads so they don't wander off."

Cleo raised an eyebrow at that. Rhett Butler detested his harness. Whenever she put it on, the silly Persian flopped on his side, legs stiff out, tail twitching. To her amusement and slight vexation, Rhett didn't put up a fuss when Henry snapped on the harness and leash. Henry explained it as unfamiliarity. Rhett didn't see him coming, Henry claimed. Cleo had read about "bromances" in magazines and thought her cat might have a crush.

Inside, Pat was bustling around, making decaf. Cleo took a seat at the enamel table, with its view of the lawn and lot beyond. Rhett pranced proudly on his long lead. *The furry traitor,* Cleo thought with a smile. An ominous aerosol cloud filled the bus, masking the form of Ida. Cleo tried not to worry about what industrial air freshener might do to books, not to mention the ozone layer.

Pat ripped open a package of gingersnaps and poured them into a bowl. Coffee burbled, and Pat shut her eyes, trying to recall the possible prowler's features. "Youngish," she said. "Thirties? Dark gloves. I didn't see his face or skin color or eyes. Maybe he had a big nose? Oh, I'm no good at this. I'm the world's worst witness!"

"It's a good start," Cleo said encouragingly. "It shows he doesn't only go out at night. That's good to know. And it was definitely a man? That narrows down the suspects."

"I think so," Pat said. "At first I thought it was the mailman. He'd already been here, but sometimes the mail gets mixed up and he comes back." Her eyes drifted to an envelope, marked with the return address of a local medical lab.

"Didn't you say you had some blood work done?" Cleo asked. "Did you get your results?"

Pat's whole body sagged, from face to shoulders, with her back melting down her seat.

Cleo's heart clenched. *Oh no, more bad news. Poor Pat.* She reached across the table, preparing to console.

"There's nothing abnormal," Pat mumbled.

"Well, that's wonderful!" Cleo exclaimed. "Nothing bad is fine news."

"They missed something, surely." Pat reached for the envelope and turned it in her hands, as if waiting for something unsavory to fall out.

Cleo reached across for a happy squeeze this time. "No, it's good news when we need some the most. In fact, you should add it to your jar of good things." She nodded toward the jar of happy thoughts, stuffed with folded papers. Perhaps Pat was cheerier than she let on, although she certainly didn't seem like it today—or any day that Cleo had seen.

"I know what I know," Pat mumbled. "No one in my family had anything wrong with them, and then boom—gone by seventy. Well, except my aunt who had that tumor, and my granny with her lungs . . ."

"There!" Cleo said, feeling off-kilter for cheering deadly diseases. "See, this is good news, a happy thing."

"Oh, all right," Pat said grudgingly. She got up and scribbled something down on a little notepad. When the paper was torn off and folded, she stuffed it in the ceramic jar labeled "Grandma's Cookies."

Two jars of goodness? Pat had more cheer than Cleo had imagined. "I need to work on some good thoughts myself," Cleo admitted. "I could hardly sleep last night, and not only because of poor Mercer Whitty. I have a bad feeling. I was sure someone was following me recently, and then my friend Mary-Rose got run off the road last night, and now you saw prowler."

Pat drew a sharp breath. "Mary-Rose? Is she okay?"

Cleo gave the full report, assuring Pat that Mary-Rose was fine.

"She didn't see the person either?" Pat asked. She got up to pour their coffee.

Cleo nibbled a gingersnap as hard as cement. She dipped it in her coffee for the next bite. "No, you're the best witness so far."

"A lousy one," Pat said. "This awful business is distracting me from work too. I can't concentrate."

Cleo could relate. She sympathized and added, "The library reopening is coming up soon, and we have so many uncertainties."

"But you can get back to your original renovation plan now," Pat pointed out. "My ladies are still scheduled to clean right before the big party. It'll be all nice and fresh, and you have the pretty new paint on the exterior and inside too, and your overdue book is back, and the party could be part wake for Mercer Whitty too. Everyone loves a wake! Well, not *loves* them, but you know what I mean. Everyone will attend. You'll get a huge crowd, and it'll be respectful and festive all in one."

Cleo marveled. Pat had come up with a whole list of good ideas. It would be nice to honor Mercer. Only fitting too, given his service as library president, not to mention his place of demise. Her mind filled with concrete, doable tasks. She'd acquire a photo of Mercer, some black cloth for the table, a massive batch of Henry's funeral potatoes . . .

"Belle Beauchamp is locked up," Pat continued, on a good-points roll. "I read what she said in the newspaper about charging for library use and getting rid of books. I was shocked, and of course I'm stunned about what she did. A killer! You never know how people will turn out. Do you know, I found a photo of her from that camp in one of my scrapbooks? I went to that camp one summer. Only once because my parents couldn't afford it every year, like Dixie's. Let me go get it. Belle looked nothing like she does today."

Pat bustled down the hallway. Outside, Ida descended the bookmobile steps, a cloud of freshening spray billowing in her wake. Cleo ticked off ideas for a party/wake. They'd need separate buffet tables and a more somber invitation. She sat back, staring out the window. Something nagged at her, like a sliver, so fine she couldn't see it but felt it prickling. Nice thoughts, a wake . . . *your overdue book back* . . .

Cleo jolted upright. Could Pat have meant Amy-Ray's

copy of *Luck and Lore*? But Cleo had told Pat how she didn't count that as a return. She hadn't told Pat about finding the original. She hadn't even told Mary-Rose, and Henry wouldn't have said anything. He was beyond discreet. How did Pat know?

Cleo dunked a gingersnap in her coffee until it dissolved. She let it sink to the bottom of her mug. Pat's ladies got all over town. They heard the gossip and saw things. Plus, news in a small town moved at light speed. Someone working at the police station could easily have mentioned it to someone else, and the word would have shot out from there.

Cleo heard drawers opening and shutting in the back. A dark thought grew. Dixie's killer would have known her fears . . . Her best friend would too. The killer had access to Dixie's home and medicine. Did Pat? Cleo pushed back her chair, checking to make sure Pat hadn't returned. She reached for the "Happy Thoughts" jar.

Her hand hovered over the lid. She shouldn't. She was being a bad guest, a worse friend, but the jar had seemed at odds with Pat's think-the-worst nature from the start. Now it felt downright off. If Pat didn't use the jar for good news, like her happy medical report, what did she keep in it?

Cleo rationalized her snooping as she opened the lid. She *could* be adding some nice thoughts of her own. She would, if that's all the jar turned out to contain. Cleo pulled out a tightly folded slip. She read it and then reached for more, her heart beating harder with each word of blame, bile, and misplaced vengeance. One note wished death on Doc Bliss for mocking Pat's complaints. Another blamed the mailman for delivering "false" lab results. Two others chilled Cleo's core: *"Mary-Rose must die so Cleo and I can be best friends." "Henry Lafayette was in the way again. He won't be soon."* The handwriting was jagged and pressed hard into the paper. *Like the coffin notes.*

Cleo no longer cared about looking rude. Now she was worried about how she could leave without revealing her horrible revelation to Pat. She pocketed a handful of notes and replaced the jar and its lid. When she turned, Pat stood at the threshold, a scrapbook cradled in the crook of her elbow. Had she seen?

Cleo forced a grimace that she hoped resembled a smile. "I shouldn't keep you," she said, smoothing her slacks with sweaty palms. She felt shaky, from her knees to the tips of her fingers. Her heart thumped so hard she felt sure Pat could see it.

Pat stared at her, small eyes assessing.

"I should get Henry and Mr. Chaucer home," Cleo said. Her own voice sounded far away, overshadowed by the ringing adrenaline. She wanted to run, to flee, to grab Henry and the pets and Ida too and speed off to safety in her bookmobile. The engine was running. Cleo glanced outside and then sharply turned back, not wanting to betray her escape plans.

"Wait!" Pat said. "Don't leave. I have to get something."

Cleo froze. She tried to think what she could grab in defense, something to throw or use as a shield. A pan. The coffee pot. That awful jar filled with notes of hatred and vengeance.

Pat took a step forward, her cheeks red, her eyes flashing their whites. Cleo stepped back until she bumped up against the sharp edge of the counter. She turned to reach for the cookie jar, but before she could grasp it, she heard a noise. Pat ran down the hall. Something crashed, a cabinet banged, and the front door slammed.

Cleo exhaled. She looked outside, where Henry and Ida chatted on the patio. The pug and Persian lounged on a little patch of grass nearby. Mr. Chaucer lay on his back. Rhett languidly batted at a tall blade of grass. A calm, pleasant scene, except for Pat, storming toward them, her arm out-stretched. Ida backed up, mouth gaping. Henry put himself in front of her, his palms up. Cleo's eyes locked on the gun in Pat's hands.

"No!" Cleo yelled. She pounded on the window and then ran to the back door, where she fumbled with the dead bolt. She burst outside to find Pat aiming the gun at Henry.

"*He's* coming with me," Pat said, eyes skittering right, left, and nowhere. "On the bus, Henry. Get on that bus!"

"Pat, please," Cleo begged. Beside her, Ida prayed in a whispered monotone.

"It's okay," Henry said, his voice pitched low, a forced calm. "Cleo, stay here."

"Don't follow us!" Pat snapped. "Stay back!" She poked the gun within inches of Henry's nose. "You—you're driving."

He walked to the bus, stumbling once when Pat jabbed the gun at his shoulders. Pat followed him up the steps.

Henry got in Cleo's captain's seat. The door closed, and Cleo's stomach sank as Words on Wheels took off at a jolting jerk.

"Ida!" Cleo cried, swinging toward the stunned woman. "Where's your car?"

"I . . . I walked . . ." Ida stammered.

"Watch the pets!" Cleo ordered. "Take their leads. Keep yourselves safe. I'm calling the police."

Ida blinked out of her stupor. She rushed for the cat and dog while Cleo bolted back into the house. She needed her purse, her phone. She needed a vehicle. Her purse lay where she left it, on the counter, just down from the jar of unhappy thoughts.

Cleo called 911 as she scoured the kitchen for car keys. She found a key holder behind the door, dozens and dozens of keys, all on little pegs, each marked with clients' names and addresses. She struggled to explain to the dispatcher while simultaneously reading the labels. When she thought the dispatcher understood, she hung up and pawed through the keys until she found a set marked "HH van." Holmes Homes. Cleo raced back outside and was met by pacing Ida.

"Miss Pat's been acting odd," Ida said. Rhett was on her shoulder, nuzzling her ear. Mr. Chaucer hung close to her feet, his wrinkled face quivering. "Angry and snappy at us cleaners. I thought she was upset about her husband or the holidays or her health, like always." She followed after Cleo all the way to the van.

Cleo gave Rhett a quick kiss and Mr. Chaucer a pat. "Keep them safe," Cleo pleaded, and she knew from Ida's expression she would.

"Go get 'em," Ida said as Cleo climbed into the dented white van. "Don't let her get away."

Henry. Words on Wheels . . . Cleo had no intention of letting them get away.

Chapter
Thirty-One

The van coughed and sputtered. The stick shift stuck and muddled between gears. Cleo muscled it into first, but before she stomped on the gas, she put her phone on her lap and speed-dialed Gabby. She managed to turn on the speaker function and then took off, over the railroad track, her head swiveling.

Which way had they gone? She'd lost time looking for the keys and trying to explain the unexplainable to the 911 dispatcher. But, bless his heart, Henry wasn't a speedy driver, and he was in a bright yellow school bus with opalescent flames. How hard could that be to find?

"Cleo!" Gabby's voice cut across the engine noise. "I just heard! I was out on patrol, so I'm already looking. We'll get her! Do you have any idea which way they went?"

"No," Cleo said, almost choking on the word. She'd come to a three-way stop, a prong of roads with no far view in any direction. One street led straight into downtown. Surely Pat wouldn't want to go there. That left two possibilities. Right went south, left to the north. From there, Cleo pictured a spiderweb map spreading across the entire country.

"Wait!" Gabby cried. "I'm on Old Coopers Highway. I think I see yellow in the distance. Could be the bus. It's coming this way."

Cleo heard the police radio squawking on Gabby's end and a siren scream to life. Gabby was radioing in a roadblock. "Cleo, I have to go," Gabby said to the phone. "Stay where you are. Wait somewhere safe. I'll call you as soon as I have an update."

Cleo wasn't about to wait. She turned to the right, toward Old Coopers Highway. The van shuddered and took corners at shivering wobbles. She urged it on with a mental chant of *please, please, please . . .*

The road twisted through a shaded stretch of tall pines. When the landscape opened up, Cleo's heart soared. There was an unmistakable gleam in the distance: school-bus yellow. Leaning back, Cleo pressed her foot full on the gas. She caught up quickly, giving thanks that even under duress, Henry Lafayette was the slowest poke of a driver she'd ever met.

The bookmobile lurched along at under fifty miles per hour. Cleo got within several school-bus distances and slowed. She pushed the speed dial for Gabby again. Gabby answered before the first ring finished.

"I'm behind them," Cleo said.

"I see that. Slow down! I'm in front of them."

Words on Wheels weaved, and Cleo saw flashing lights and a vehicle blocking the highway. Gabby's roadblock.

"Gabby, what if he can't stop?" Tears blurred Cleo's vision. She fought them. She had to keep her eyes and head clear.

"He will," Gabby said, her tone reassuringly crisp.

Cleo prayed he would. The brake lights winked red. The long bus swerved, forcing a car on the other side of the highway onto the berm. Ditches edged the road, clogged with reedy grasses and wet, muddy depths. Cleo fixed her eyes on the back of the bus and the flashy cartoon text spelling out *"READ!"* in the space over the back window.

The bus jerked left, letting Cleo see ahead again. Gabby stood in the highway, feet planted wide, arms extended. Aiming her gun?

"Oh no . . . no, no, no . . ." Cleo eased off the gas. All she knew of car chases, she'd seen on the TV news and police dramas. Rarely did those—real or fictional—end up well. The brake lights danced. Henry had slowed to a jerky crawl, but the bus still ploughed forward. It clipped the front bumper of Gabby's car, shoving it aside like a discarded toy. Gabby jumped clear, gun still drawn but mercifully unfired.

Cleo skidded to a stop beside Gabby, and the young deputy jumped in. Cleo sped on, and Gabby radioed the chief with an update. Curses and lectures rumbled over the airwaves. Gabby pointed.

"He's turning," Gabby said. "That's the road to the gravel mine, the adventure camp."

In Cleo's day, the gravel mine had been where the wilder teens went to do the things their parents feared. Now it was a destination for other dangerous activities. Thrill seekers and tourists paid to bungee jump toward a murky lake far below.

Cleo had never liked looking into those depths. Her stomach pitched, and she felt like she was freefalling.

The van bumped onto the dirt road, sagging and scraping over ruts. Pain jolted through Cleo's fingers, already aching from her white-knuckled grip on the wheel. Gabby was updating Tookey on their location, and Cleo thought she heard sirens. Or was she just willing it so? She thought of the quarry, and her stomach plunged again.

"This road," she said. "It ends at the quarry. A drop-off. A dead end!"

"Don't think of it like that," Gabby said firmly. "It only means they have to stop. We'll talk it out. She likes you, right?"

"I thought so," Cleo said. "I thought she wanted to be my friend. But she killed Dixie, her own best friend! I found notes in her kitchen saying awful things about people she blamed for her troubles, wishing them death and failure and the worst kinds of pain. She has a gun!"

Gabby didn't respond. She was rifling in the console between their seats. "Coffins," she said.

Cleo glanced over to see her holding a handful of paper coffins. Gabby opened the glove compartment and more fell out. Gabby cursed softly.

A happy welcome sign greeted them at the adventure center. It was closed for the season, but that hadn't stopped the school bus. The entry gate hung busted open. Cleo drove through, past a ticket booth shaped like a log-cabin phone booth and a carved wooden bear, waving. The best sight of all was a colorful school bus idling in the parking lot.

The taillights indicated the engine was still running. The bookmobile stood at the edge of the lot, facing the pit.

"Go slow," Gabby said, her tone low and tense. "We don't want to spook her. Nonthreatening. Calm, engaging . . ." She sounded like she was instructing herself, recalling a training she'd never had to put into action. "Park a little bit away. I'll get out. I'll try to connect with her. Stay here."

Cleo was grateful for Gabby's bravery and calm, but she feared what Pat might do if cornered. "Wait," she said, holding out a hand. "I think Pat will respond better to me. She'll feel threatened by you. Let me try to speak to her alone first, as a friend." She had trouble saying the last word. A friend didn't do what Pat had done, certainly not to Dixie and now to Cleo too.

Gabby looked ready to refuse.

"Please," Cleo said. "Henry is in there."

Gabby bit her lip. "Okay. I'll be right outside the van here. I can get to you in a flash. Don't get within touching distance of her. Whatever you do, don't get on the bus."

Cleo's legs felt rubbery. When she reached the back of the bookmobile, she touched it for balance and luck. She made her way to the door, doing as Gabby instructed and staying a few feet away. Henry sat gripping the wheel, his face tight. Pat stood behind him, the gun aimed at his back.

Stretching a smile across her face hurt, but Cleo did it. She summoned Jefferson's miming. She waved and gestured for the door to open. Henry tentatively touched the lever. The door cracked open a few inches. Pat jabbed the gun in his shoulder, and he froze.

"Pat, please, I want to talk," Cleo shouted, giving up on the pantomime.

Pat's eyes flashed from Cleo to the pit beyond.

"Pat, please," Cleo said. "We're friends. Let's talk."

Pat's head shook fast, her bangs flapping.

"Pat, I don't want you to get hurt." This was true. Cleo didn't want anyone getting hurt, most of all Henry. She locked eyes with him and saw him mouth words she knew in her heart and had wanted to hear and say. Not like this.

I love you.

Cleo slapped a hand to her mouth, her eyes watering and fixed on his. The door flew open.

"Oh, stop it!" Pat yelled, face flaming. "You always liked him more, didn't you? You like all of 'em more. Henry, Mary-Rose—all your friends. What about me? I'm beginning to think that you're as bad as Dixie, Cleo Watkins!" She edged the gun up Henry's back to rest against his neck.

Cleo's knees wavered. Out of the corner of her eye, she saw Gabby slip from the van and run to the side of the bus, where she hunched, gun at the ready. Cleo inched out her arm, palm toward Gabby, hoping to halt her. From where Gabby stood, she couldn't see Pat's twitching trigger finger.

"I'm sorry," Cleo said. "I never meant to hurt you, Pat. Tell me what I did, and I'll do better, I promise. We're friends. Partners. Right?"

Pat scoffed. "Right. Friends like me and Dixie? Everyone said we were the best of *best* friends. She only kept me around as her frumpy sidekick to make her look better. She had the better job, better house, better looks, better luck. She always said so."

"That was wrong," Cleo said. "Wrong as a friend and incorrect too."

"How was it incorrect?" Pat demanded.

Henry winced, likely realizing what Cleo had done. She'd just talked herself into trouble. How could she claim that Pat outshined Dixie in any manner? She decided to stick to Dixie's faults.

"Dixie wasn't truly lucky," Cleo said. "Look at all the people who disliked her, all the people she offended. On the surface, her life seemed fabulous, but she wasn't who she made herself out to be, was she?" Pat certainly wasn't either, but at least she was nodding in agreement. The gun lowered a few inches.

Cleo forged on. Outright insults went against her ingrained manners, but this was a desperate situation. "Dixie was self-centered. She didn't care about Iris's health troubles or yours." Pat loved to talk about her health. Cleo hoped she'd take the bait.

"She mocked my troubles," Pat said, letting the gun sink a bit more. "She said that if I keeled over at seventy, it would be death by hypochondria."

"Rude!" Cleo declared.

"Yeah," Pat agreed. "Rude. It's frightening to see death lurking on one's doorstep. Dixie didn't understand until I showed her. Then she realized. Ha! She sure realized!"

Cleo glanced at Henry. The dear man had slumped low in

the seat, his arm and shoulders drooping low. She willed him not to give up.

Pat gabbled on, her words quickening as she described Dixie's growing terror and how Pat had tricked her into the pantry and locked the door. "She finally acknowledged me then," Pat said, her face cracking into a satisfied smile. "'You're sick, Pat,' she said. Well, I told her it was about time she noticed." Pat laughed, and in that moment Henry jerked upright, yanking the fluffy blanket from Rhett's peach crate along with him.

He flung the blanket back, over the seat and into Pat's face. As she struggled, he leapt up and hurtled down the steps, landing in Cleo's arms. "Run!" he ordered, swinging Cleo around. They hustled down the side of the bus as Gabby raced by them and Words on Wheels revved. The doors snapped shut, gears ground, and the bus jolted forward.

Cleo and Henry pulled each other back, holding tight. Gabby jogged alongside the bookmobile, trying to tug the doors open. The young deputy hung on as Words on Wheels bumped over the end of the parking lot. The bus surged, and Gabby fell to the dirt. With a screech of metal, Words on Wheels crashed through the wire fence separating the parking lot from the quarry pit. Cleo's knees buckled. Then, with a skidding of tires and gravel, the bus stopped, front wheels at the edge.

Cleo breathed again.

Gabby raced up, pushed through the doors, and pulled Pat out. The young deputy was clicking on handcuffs when a parade of vehicles arrived. There were two police SUVs, an ambulance, a fire truck, the newspaper reporter, and a sight that made Cleo's heart complete: Ida jumping out of a police SUV with a frowny-faced Persian in her arms and a waggling pug at her heels.

Chapter
Thirty-Two

The grand reopening of the Catalpa Springs Public Library took place as scheduled, with a miniature pony grazing in the garden, a proud Persian lording over the checkout desk, and a buzzing crowd, relieved to have a killer caught and their library back in circulation.

Cleo and Leanna did their own circulating, greeting visitors and showing off the library's features, new and old. After a mingling round, Cleo looped back to Henry. Her gentleman friend stood apart from the crush around the food tables laden with goodies fit for a funeral and a fete. There were cheese straws and funeral potatoes, pies, cookies, and Belle's fondue station, serving up melted cheeses, chocolate, and caramel too. Cleo, having faced her worst fears, no longer feared fondue.

Henry gazed at a wall-mounted display case. Rhett flopped on the circulation desk beside him within ear-scratching distance. Cleo smiled at the two and the locked glass case. Their clever carpenter had fashioned a shelf on which the library's copy of *Luck and Lore* stood, along with various ephemera, including a newspaper headline declaring the book's return. The original lending card was on display too, with a due date stamped three weeks after Cleo's thirtieth birthday. Cleo had already explained the card to several members of the under-thirty-something crowd. Another slip of paper tallied up Dixie's towering late fee.

"Over eight hundred dollars," Henry read out, shaking his head. "That's a massive library fine. On the other hand, Dixie Huddleston could have afforded it."

"Maybe she would have paid," Cleo said. "She would have if she thought it would turn her luck around." She patted her hair. "Of course, I was prepared to give her a little break."

Henry chuckled. "Four hundred?"

They both knew that Cleo would have forgiven all fines. She'd have forgiven Dixie too. She wished she'd gotten a chance.

"Under lock and key, I see. Clever." Mary-Rose joined them, looking lovely in a rosy dress and sweater set. Voices rose and Cleo's best friend scowled over her shoulder. By the punch bowl, the Who-Done-It mystery readers, minus their murderous member, were arguing about whether to select a book from the main library or have the bookmobile come to them. Either way, Cleo would be happy.

"That book group," Mary-Rose said, clicking her tongue. "I'm polite, so I won't say that I told you so, Cleo, but it figures it was one of them."

Cleo smiled at her friend. "I'll admit, I brushed off your concerns about the Who-Done-Its."

Mary-Rose waved a dismissive hand. Her smile sagged. "I may have told you so, but I never thought *Pat* would be the killer among them. I still can't fathom it. We all thought Pat and Dixie were best friends. They did everything together. Pat put up with Dixie. Dixie put up with Pat."

"I don't know if Dixie did real friendship," Cleo said. "It was all a competition to her. Poor Pat always lost out. Maybe that's what Dixie liked about their arrangement. Dixie was guaranteed to win. She had someone to put down, and she loved rubbing in her good fortune to Pat."

Cleo and Henry had gone to the police station after Pat's arrest. Cleo had turned over the handful of notes she'd grabbed from Pat's terrible "Happy Thoughts" jar. She'd read them as Gabby cataloged them into evidence. They were chilling.

"Her resentments went back decades," Cleo said. "To kindergarten, when Dixie embarrassed Pat in front of the class. To that camp, where Dixie and her popular friends picked on Pat. It turned into a pattern. Dixie made fun of Pat's job, a lowly cleaner. Her dull husband, her mousy looks, her plain house . . . But then Dixie would tell Pat that she was just joking, having fun. She said that's what best buddies did."

"She was a viper!" Belle Beauchamp swooped in with a wave of lilac perfume, kisses all around. The innobrarian and accused murderer had been released following Pat's confession to not only Dixie's murder but Mercer's too.

"Dixie did the same thing to me at that awful camp," Belle said. She shot an apologetic look to Mary-Rose. "Sorry,

I know your auntie-in-law ran that place. She surely didn't know what kind of snakes she had out there. The glittery girls, is how I thought of them." She smoothed her immaculate platinum bob. "The worst of it was, I dreamed of being just like them. Bold. Beautiful. Unstoppable. I guess I went a little too far, if y'all thought I was capable of murder."

"Anyone is," Mary-Rose said generously. "I was saying so to Cleo just the other day. The police thought so too. They had Cleo on their suspect list. Right, Gabby?"

Gabby had been passing by, a plate of healthy snacks in her hand, apple slices and bananas. "*I* never thought Miss Cleo did it," she clarified.

"Thank you, Gabby," Cleo said, narrowing her eyes affectionately at Mary-Rose, who was chuckling that Cleo *could* have done it.

Gabby greeted everyone, including Belle, whom she addressed with a formal "Ms. Beauchamp."

"Ms. Deputy," Belle said in return. She held out her hand, but the initial stiff handshake quickly turned into a hug. "Y'all saved me," Belle gushed. "All of y'all. That chief of yours would have locked me up for good, and right when I figured out my life's calling too." She beamed. "Go ahead—ask me what it is!"

Cleo inwardly groaned. *Oh please,* she prayed, *let it not be redecorating libraries or innovating bookmobiles.* In the days following her release, Belle hadn't returned to the library. In the innobrarian's absence, Cleo and Leanna had gotten on with their work. Leanna's technology center was set up for research and fun, but not light shows. The bookshelves were firmly bolted in place and packed with books. The walls glowed in peachy paint.

"So, you found a calling?" Cleo ventured to ask.

Belle turned dramatically, arms outstretched, taking in the place. Cleo's pulse rate surged.

"I did!" Belle said. "I've found my true calling. Now, wait for it . . ." She fluttered her fingers toward the ceiling. "Real estate!"

"Real estate?" The chorus came from all members of Cleo's cluster of friends.

"Why that's wonderful! I'm so happy!" Cleo exclaimed. She realized her reaction might appear rudely enthusiastic. "For you, I mean," she amended.

"Yep, I've had enough of libraries," Belle said. "It's tougher than I thought. People are so darned demanding about wanting books. I'd take BOOK IT! out, and people would think it was cute and whatnot, but then they'd get grouchy, demanding quiet and books and places to *read*. When I was languishing behind bars, I had a revelation. I told you I always wanted to be like Dixie. That wasn't quite true. I want to be *better* than Dixie, and I'm going to do it at her own game." Belle twinkled at them. "I looooove looking at properties, and I betcha I can find folks their dream homes a lot better than Dixie Huddleston ever could. It's about passion and pushing boundaries. Ooh . . . there are my first clients now. Did you hear? Jefferson and Amy-Ray *both* inherited equally from their mama."

Jefferson Huddleston entered, dressed in full mime attire, flanked by his frowning wife and scowling sister. Belle leaned in and said in a conspiratorial whisper, "If I can make those three happy, I'll *know* I can work with any client. The clown there wants a warehouse setting for his miming school. His wife needs to be in throwing distance of her office. His sister . . . well, she's easy. She just wants to unload her mama's house. I already have a buyer for that."

Cleo had no doubt about that. "It's a gorgeous house," she said. "That was another bitter resentment of Pat's. She and her husband were set to buy that property years ago. Pat had an in with the former owners. Then Dixie swooped in, supposedly as Pat's agent, and took it for herself."

Belle looked delighted. "Is that so? I really am set to outdo Dixie, aren't I? Guess what? *I'm* the buyer! Fair price, I swear. Although, the place has a tad of termite damage in the trusses. Plus there was that death in the kitchen. Nothing like a murder to drop the price, is there? I'm getting it for a song!"

She departed in clouds of floral perfume and air kisses.

"Good gracious," Henry said.

"Thank goodness!" Cleo exclaimed. She reached over and petted Rhett, who sputtered purrs.

"Speaking of that house," Gabby said, "We found out how Pat managed some of the death omens. Remember the birds in Dixie's kitchen? We looked over Pat's bank account. She bought two live doves at a wedding and party supply shop over in Claymore. People release them when the happy couple comes out of the church. Pat got the smoke bomb at the same place. It wasn't really a bomb. It was a 'prop,' the party people claimed. They said it was to make photos look foggy and atmospheric." Gabby's expression suggested that birds and smoke weren't on her dream-wedding list.

Cleo glanced over at *Luck and Lore*, safe behind glass and lock. "This book has chapter after chapter of omens, good and bad," she said. "Pat spent a lot of time at Dixie's and could have read the book there. She'd know what would scare Dixie. A bird in the house is definitely bad luck."

"But why bother?" Mary-Rose asked, sounding irritated. "Why not just ditch Dixie and get herself a new friend?"

They all looked to Cleo, who politely offered Gabby the chance to reveal the twisted logic.

"You found her out," Gabby said with a smile. "You get to explain. Besides, it's still too incomprehensible to me."

To Cleo too. "Pat's absolutely certain that she doesn't have long to live. She believes in fate and patterns. Her older female relatives all passed away at seventy, if not before. She's sure she will too, even though everyone from Dixie to her doctor kept telling her she's fine. Attempts at comfort upset her more. She thought no one took her seriously, no one appreciated her fears."

Mary-Rose clicked her tongue. "She talked herself into her own story, didn't she? Sad, except for the part about killing two people."

Cleo did feel sorry for Poor Pat. Pat had wanted to be Cleo's friend, and Cleo hoped she hadn't let Pat down entirely. "Pat encouraged me to investigate the case. I think she saw it as a chance for us to bond. She wanted a real friend."

"I think she wanted to keep you close," Gabby said. "You're the town sleuth. If she saw you getting too near the truth, you could have been in trouble."

Henry edged closer to Cleo. "I wondered why you didn't get any threats. That's why. She saw you as her new best pal."

Cleo tried to sound unconcerned, but Pat's deceit rattled her. "Pat tried to be nice to me in her way. She returned *Luck and Lore* to the library. I'd told her how much I wanted the original copy. I wish I hadn't been so stubborn about that! She'd taken the book from Dixie's the day she killed her, a memento, something Dixie treasured."

Mary-Rose shuddered. "Then she went after the whole town. That's the scariest part, the escalation. It makes my skin crawl if I think too hard about it. Put-down Pat must have started feeling pretty gosh-darned powerful. Laughing at all of us. Terrifying us."

Gabby nodded grimly. "Pat started with small frights. She wanted Dixie to feel death coming for her, the fear and dread Pat herself felt. Then, like you say, it escalated. She didn't want Dixie to just be afraid—Dixie had to die. Pat admitted that she replaced Dixie's medicine with sugar syrup. She got the syringes from Dixie's purse. She even bookmarked the website she consulted that showed how to do it. She had a key to Dixie's so she could let herself in anytime. She house-sat for Dixie sometimes and cleaned for her regularly too. She really resented cleaning that beautiful house that could have been hers."

"Refilling a syringe seems easy enough to figure out," Mary-Rose said, "But bees?"

"Her parents used to keep bees," Gabby said. "They'd make her help with the hives as a kid. What a chore! I used to complain about walking the dog and taking out the trash! Anyway, from her work, Pat knew of a hive that wasn't watched over very closely, and she raided it. Bees are sluggish in chilly weather. Smoke settles them too, and she had another one of those smoke canisters for doing just that. We found a beekeeper suit stuffed under a bunch of cleaning rags in her garage."

"Always the quiet ones," Mary-Rose said. "You'd never guess until they unleash and start throwing around pancake batter. That should have tipped us off, Cleo. To think, she killed her friend and then went to book group and breakfast! Pancakes, no less!"

Cleo thought back to that day at the Pancake Mill. She'd stuck up for Pat and her unusually emotional behavior. She'd thought Pat was upset because she was defending her friend, when really she'd just killed her.

Gabby confirmed the time line. "Pat swiped the honey-comb insert early that morning, like around five a.m., and stuffed it in a cereal box. Then she let herself into Dixie's house, left the cereal box open in the pantry, and closed the door. All she had to do next was pretend to show up early for coffee, so early she woke Dixie up. Dixie was groggy. She popped some bread in the oven to warm, went into the pantry, and then . . ." Gabby hesitated and everyone shifted uncom-fortably, knowing what happened then.

"The coffin threat, agitated bees, and sugar-filled syringes were all inside," Gabby said. "Pat admitted that she locked the door and fled after Dixie started yelling. She was afraid even then that Dixie would bully her out of her plan."

Laughter rose by the fondue. Cleo looked beyond her circle of friends, to the reference room. "Poor Mercer. He was in the wrong place at the wrong time."

Gabby nodded. "Pat had a key to the library, a copy she kept on file for cleaning jobs. She let herself in to return Dixie's overdue book. Then Mercer came in, planning to meet Belle. He recognized the book, and she feared he'd figure out what she'd done. Worse for him, he insulted her. He said he wasn't here to meet a *frumpy cleaning woman.* Those oversized scissors were right there on the table . . ." Gabby trailed off again.

Cleo shook her head sadly. "What I can't understand is why she targeted Words on Wheels with that smoke bomb and coffin notes, and why she did it when she was inside the bus."

"She was being 'nice' to you again," Gabby said, rolling her eyes. "She wanted to clear your name. I mean, no one could think you'd smoke-bomb your own bookmobile."

"No one," Mary-Rose said, firm this time in Cleo's innocence.

Gabby continued. "Being inside and getting hurt in the incident earned her sympathy too, which she craved. Same with the coffin notes. She pretended that she was a victim too. She started moving on with her grievances after Dixie's death. They covered pretty much the entire town. That's why she left the random threats, to spread fear everywhere. She sent personalized notes to people she especially disliked. The only note Pat didn't send was the one Jefferson received. Amy-Ray admitted she left that one, hoping to scare her brother away from their mother's house. Plus, she liked messing with Jefferson."

"Pat was getting bolder too," Cleo said. "Driving you off the road, Mary-Rose, and vandalizing Iris's studio. Iris routinely embarrassed Pat at book club."

Gabby nodded. "The resentments and retributions would have continued to build. Thank goodness you discovered her when you did, Cleo."

Cleo reached for Henry's hand and looked at her friends. "Gabby showed me Pat's list of personal hatreds. You all were on it. My best friends, the people I love the most! She'd come to see me as her new best friend and resented time I spent with you all. In some twisted way, she thought she'd find happiness if others were miserable."

Leanna had joined their little huddle. She shuddered. "That would never have helped her. It's like we were saying before this all started. Blowing out someone else's candles won't make yours burn brighter. Speaking of which . . ." Her eyes lit up. She beamed, holding up her right hand and clicking her fingers.

The front door swung open and in came. Mary-Rose's granddaughter Zoe and her friends, wheeling a cart topped with the biggest sheet cake Cleo had ever laid eyes on.

Mary-Rose led the cheers, Gabby lit the candles, and usually shy Leanna climbed on a chair and addressed the crowd. "Here's to the grand reopening of the Catalpa Springs Public Library!" Leanna said to great applause, "And to Cleo

Watkins and her *fifty* years of service as the best and bravest librarian in Catalpa County and beyond."

"How did you all know?" Cleo whispered under the roar of cheers and clapping.

Mary-Rose hugged her tight. "You know you can't keep a secret this big in Catalpa Springs, Cleo Jane. Leanna and I have been planning this for months. Did you really think it was coincidence that the contractor insisted on this day as the for-sure library completion date? Leanna was looking into the library records and discovered your first workday right here, fifty years ago today. Shame on you for not telling us!"

Cleo's eyes welled with happy tears. Henry gripped her hand.

Before her, the cake blazed, fifty candles over fluffy waves of icing. Pink strawberry icing, Cleo noted, just like the birthday cake Dixie had swooped in and grabbed her luck from all those years ago.

"Miss Cleo gets to make a wish," Leanna said, raising her voice again. "Before she does, let's all wish Cleo many continued joys on the open road as captain of Words on Wheels!" A cheer rose, louder than before.

Cleo leaned over the cake. She closed her eyes and silently repeated the wish she'd wanted at thirty and every birthday since: health and happiness for all those she loved. Then she filled her lungs and blew a great gust. She opened her eyes to wispy smoke, a boisterous crowd, and her beautifully restored library filled with friends, family, and booklovers. Leanna handed out slices of cake, and happy patrons filed by, thanking Cleo for her service to the library and in catching criminals.

Henry put his arm around her, and Cleo's heart swelled. New roads awaited her, in Words on Wheels and in life. As she gazed around, she knew Dixie had never swiped her luck. Cleo Watkins had all she could wish for and so much more.

Mary-Rose's Honey Pie

This is a sweet variant of the classic Southern chess pie. Chess pies are custard based, often with a bit of cornmeal for thickening and a splash of vinegar or, in this case, lemon juice. Whether plain or flavored with honey, peanut butter, lemon, or coconut, a chess pie is easy to whip up and sweet to eat.

Ingredients

One 9-inch pie shell (premade, your favorite recipe, or the recipe that follows)

Buttery piecrust

1¼ c. all-purpose flour
1 T. sugar
½ tsp. table salt
½ c. (1 stick) unsalted butter, diced and chilled
3 T. (more or less as necessary) ice-cold water
1 tsp. vinegar

Blend the flour, sugar, and salt. Toss in the diced butter, and incorporate it using a food processor, pastry cutter, or your fingers. Aim for a sandy texture with a few buttery lumps. Make a well in the flour.

Blend the water and vinegar together and then add to the flour mixture. Gently mix until you have a shaggy dough. Add as little water as possible, but enough so that the dough holds together. The humidity in your kitchen will affect how much you have to add.

Turn the dough out onto a lightly floured surface. Knead—be gentle but firm. Flatten the dough into a circular disk, wrap it in plastic wrap, and let it rest in the refrigerator for at least an hour.

When you're ready to bake:
- Preheat your oven to 375°F, with a rack positioned in the middle.
- Roll out your piecrust and put it in your pie plate. Let the pie dough rest and chill in the fridge while you make the filling.

Honey filling

½ c. dark brown sugar
½ c. (1 stick) unsalted butter, melted
3 T. cornmeal
2 tsp. vanilla
¼ tsp. table salt
¾ c. honey
3 eggs
½ c. heavy whipping cream
2 tsp. lemon juice

- In a medium or large bowl, whisk the melted butter, brown sugar, cornmeal, salt, and vanilla. Whisk in the honey next and then the eggs, one at a time. Finally whisk in the cream, followed by the lemon juice.

- Pour the filling into the prepared, unbaked piecrust. Place in the middle of the oven and bake for 45 to 55 minutes.
- The top should get a lovely golden brown, the color of rich honey. Look for set sides with a jiggle in the middle. Let cool for an hour or two. Top with honey-sweetened whipped cream.

Acknowledgments

I owe more than I can ever express to my family, especially my husband, parents, in-laws, aunts, and grandmother. Thank you so much for your support and encouragement. Many thanks to friends near and far and to the wonderful writers of Sisters in Crime. I'm grateful for my beta readers, who took the time to point me in better directions, and to Cynthia, the best and kindest critique partner. Eric, most of all, thank you for the love, laughs, travels, and listening to way too much talk of murder.

To Christina Hogrebe, agent *extraordinaire*, much gratitude for your insights and support and for finding this series such a wonderful home at Crooked Lane Books. To my fabulous editor, Jenny Chen, thank you for pushing Cleo Watkins into high gear and for honing the manuscript into a book. Thanks to Jesse Reisch for the gorgeous cover illustration, Sarah Poppe and Ashley Di Dio for their publicity and marketing prowess, and Jill Pellarin for meticulous copyediting.

Most of all, heartfelt thanks to library lovers and readers for joining Cleo on her bookmobile adventures.